Praise for *The D*

"A perfect beach read! I loved it."

—Pamela Kelley, *USA Today* bestsel

"Part delectable family drama, part testament to the various ways in which love blooms, Hannah McKinnon's *The Darlings* is an absolute treasure of a novel . . . Slip this one in your beach bag and share a copy with a friend."

—Kristy Woodson Harvey, *New York Times* bestselling author of *The Wedding Veil*

"Vivid and transporting—*The Darlings* will sweep you off to Cape Cod, where an explosive secret threatens to fracture a close-knit family . . . Fans of Elin Hilderbrand will find a new favorite author in Hannah McKinnon. Compulsively readable and infused with warmth, *The Darlings* is a perfect summer read."

—Kerry Kletter, author of *East Coast Girls*

"In the vein of J. Courtney Sullivan, Erin Hilderbrand, and Jennifer Close, and contrasting picturesque coastal perfection with the messiness of real life, this multigenerational saga sets familial obligations against the freedom of new opportunities, all wrapped up in a heartwarming bow."

—*Booklist*

Praise for *Message in the Sand*

"A sweet story about a small town, and the one summer that changes everything for its inhabitants. Right now, more than ever, we need stories about resilience, strength, and how the people we see every day have the power to change our lives—the latest novel by Hannah McKinnon delivers."

—Brenda Janowitz, author of *The Grace Kelly Dress*

"A gripping, heart-wrenching novel of domestic fiction by Hannah McKinnon . . . In this gripping, emotional story, a shattering tragedy upends the lives of two young girls and those in their orbit."

—*Shelf Awareness*

Praise for *The View from Here*

"A warmhearted yet clear-eyed look into what brings people together and what tears them apart, this makes a delightful case for shaking off childhood roles."

—*Booklist*

"Warmhearted and a perfect beach read."

—9to5Toys, "Best New Summer Books"

Praise for *Sailing Lessons*

"If you are a fan of sisterhood-themed beach reads by Nancy Thayer and Elin Hilderbrand, then McKinnon's latest engaging stand-alone needs to go on your summer to-be-read list."

—*RT Book Reviews*

"McKinnon writes with such imagery that you can almost smell the salt in the air."

—*Booked*

Praise for *The Summer House*

"Sure to appeal to fans of Elin Hilderbrand and Dorothea Benton Frank, *The Summer House* is an intriguing glimpse into a complicated yet still loving family."

—*Shelf Awareness*

"Charming and warmhearted."

—*PopSugar*

Praise for *Mystic Summer*

"When two roads diverge . . . take the one that leads to the beach! Hannah McKinnon delivers a charming gem of a novel in *Mystic Summer*. I adored this book."

—Elin Hilderbrand, #1 *New York Times* bestselling author of *The Identicals*

"Hannah McKinnon's *Mystic Summer* is a heartwarming story of lost love and the against-all-odds chance of finding it again . . . *Mystic Summer* is a lovely summer beach read that will keep readers turning the page until the very end!"

—Nan Rossiter, *New York Times* bestselling author of *Summer Dance*

Praise for *The Lake Season*

"Seasons of change take us home to the places and the people who shelter us. Well told, and in turns sweet and bare, *The Lake Season* offers a compelling tale of family secrets, letting go, and the unbreakable bonds of sisterhood."

—Lisa Wingate, nationally bestselling author of *Before We Were Yours*

"Hannah McKinnon's lyrical debut tells the story of a pair of very different sisters, both at a crossroads in life. McKinnon's great strength lies in her ability to reveal the many ways the two women wound—and ultimately heal—each other as only sisters can."

—Sarah Pekkanen, *New York Times* bestselling author of *The Wife Between Us*

"Charming and heartfelt! Hannah McKinnon's *The Lake Season* proves that you can go home again; you just can't control what you find when you get there."

—Wendy Wax, *New York Times* bestselling author of the Ten Beach Road series and *The House on Mermaid Point*

The
Summer Club

Other books by
Hannah McKinnon

The Darlings

Message in the Sand

The View from Here

Sailing Lessons

The Summer House

Mystic Summer

The Lake Season

For Young Adults
(As Hannah Roberts McKinnon)

Franny Parker

The Properties of Water

The Summer Club

A Novel

Hannah McKinnon

EMILY BESTLER BOOKS

ATRIA

New York London Toronto Sydney New Delhi

EMILY BESTLER BOOKS

ATRIA

An Imprint of Simon & Schuster, LLC
1230 Avenue of the Americas
New York, NY 10020

This book is a work of fiction. Any references to historical events, real people, or real places are used fictitiously. Other names, characters, places, and events are products of the author's imagination, and any resemblance to actual events or places or persons, living or dead, is entirely coincidental.

First Emily Bestler Books/Atria Paperback edition July 2024

EMILY BESTLER BOOKS/ATRIA PAPERBACK and colophon are trademarks of Simon & Schuster, LLC

Simon & Schuster: Celebrating 100 Years of Publishing in 2024

Interior design by Erika R. Genova

Manufactured in the United States of America

1 3 5 7 9 10 8 6 4 2

Library of Congress Cataloging-in-Publication data has been applied for.

ISBN 978-1-6680-2518-5
ISBN 978-1-6680-2519-2 (ebook)

This one is for my brother Jesse,
of quiet strength and immeasurable kindness.
And who still makes me laugh so hard I have to
crawl out of the room on my hands and knees,
even though we're not kids anymore.

NED

He was not a religious man, but the quiet ritual of his morning walk through the empty clubhouse came mighty close. The early light angled toward the mirrored trophy case that ran along the hall to Ned's back office. He paused to wipe a smudge off the glass with his shirtsleeve and greeted the familiar faces on the other side. Bitsy Babcock held the women's league MVP golf trophy aloft in one framed photograph. Grumpy elder Neiman Shrive scowled back at him in another, despite the coveted men's league medallion in his grip. And always, front and center was club founder Wilson Elliot Banks, whose beatific smile and reassuring gaze graced the hallowed case. The photographs of Wilson were black and white, from what many members still hailed as the glory days of Mayhaven. Ned nodded reverently at Wilson. This summer, that job was his: to restore the days of Wilson's golden era, to recall Mayhaven's days of splendor.

Wouldn't his father be proud? Well, *proud* might be too large for a man with so small of a heart. But Mayhaven held a spot in Ned's own that went back to the summer he was six years old when his father had awakened him before dawn one morning to bring him out on a golf course for the first time. It was a club Ned's family could never have afforded to belong to, and a sport his father had shared with no other person. But that morning he'd driven Ned up the winding hill to Mayhaven and handed him his first bag of clubs. He would never be the same after.

Ned's office was still dark, but even in the shadows its spartan systemization was visible. Despite the mess of demands detailed within each manila file, they were arranged in deceptively tidy stacks on his desk. As president of the club, Ned did this each night before leaving; he tucked the day's worth of complaints and issues and repair estimates and upcoming events gently into their respective files, as if tucking his own children into bed. The files contained *challenges*, he liked to tell himself, not problems. And Ned Birch was always up to a challenge.

• • • • •

That morning's challenges were numerous, but first, he settled into his leather armchair and considered his uninterrupted view of the first fairway. This was Ned's daily meditation. The first tee box rested high above the carefully shorn course and the fairway rolled away from it like an emerald sea. Behind it the Blue Hills glimmered through the last strands of morning fog. To the right of the clubhouse were the clay courts, freshly watered that morning, and beyond them, down a grassy slope lay the small spit of beach that ran along the section of Mayhaven Lake where members could swim, sun, and kayak. It was a summer heaven, and long before his job as club president, a haven to Ned through a strained childhood. But he would not think of that now.

Ned reached for the first file on his desk: *Events*. The first golf event of the season, a member-scramble, was coming up and there was much to do. The weather so far had behaved. It was New England at its finest, before the height of summer when humidity curled the edges of the restaurant menus up on the deck and the sun tinged the fairway edges yellow. But as his father used to say, New England weather was as temperamental as a scorned woman, which meant the event could be heavenly or a total washout. He sent a reminder email to members to sign up, and made a note to confirm head counts with the club restaurant. Then he said a quick prayer the weather would cooperate. As it was, the women in his house were not.

Ned wasn't sure what was going on with Darcy, but it seemed beyond the normal teenage angst other parents railed about. Ned did not have favorites, but he and Darcy had always enjoyed an effortless bond, especially on the golf course. Since she was five years old and Ned had placed a club in her hand, golf had been their thing. At least it used to be. That year Darcy had announced that she was quitting the sport. The very same sport she'd played the whole of her childhood, the one her father had taught her and the one she'd gotten so good at he and Ingrid had splurged on private lessons with Vince at the club. Darcy had moved swiftly through the ranks, starting with the 13-Under Junior New England Tour, and aging into the 17-Under. The summer before, Darcy had won the New England PGA Junior Tour. She was that good. Scouts started showing up to watch her play. Already there were phone calls coming in from colleges seeking to recruit her. And then, with no warning or reason, she'd announced last winter that she was quitting. Ned would never forget it; she'd marched into the living room one quiet evening between Christmas and New Year's Eve and told her parents that she was done with golf.

Ingrid had looked alarmed.

Ned thought she was joking. "What do you mean you're done with golf?"

Golf was Darcy's passion. Her ticket to college scholarships. The bond they'd shared. This was not just about golfing.

"You love it more than anything," he reminded her.

But the look on Darcy's face was as serious as the pain it gave him hearing her words. "I'm sorry, Dad. But I don't anymore."

He'd spent the evening staring at the dark spot on the Christmas tree where he'd missed stringing lights, wondering what else he'd missed. Darcy's announcement had come out of nowhere. It did not make a lick of sense.

"Give her time," Ingrid had said, later that night in bed. "It's been years of practice and competition. Maybe she's burned out?"

But Ned did not believe that was the case, and time had not helped. When the snow melted on the course, and the days grew longer, Darcy's clubs remained in the hallway closet shoved behind the coats. When Ned tried to raise the subject Darcy shut him down. "I'm not changing my mind. Please, stop."

"Honey, did something happen?" Ingrid ventured. "Something we need to know about?"

Something *did* happen, Ned wanted to shout. Darcy had given up on the one thing she'd pursued her whole life! Just as she stood on the threshold of it making a difference in her life: college, travel, exposure to the best of the industry. Things they could not easily provide for her on their own, with their modest living.

But Ingrid was on alert for something dark. Depression? Anxiety? Perhaps a boy who'd broken her heart?

"God, no!" Darcy insisted, her cheeks flushing with indignation. "Why can't you two just respect my choice? Let it go."

These golf-less days Darcy kept to her room, texting and scrolling on her godforsaken phone, her lovely face illuminated only by its screen and her expression muted. Except . . . when her mother called her name; then her expression flipped like a switch to profound irritation.

Ned felt sorry for his wife. Ingrid had always been an excellent parent, and Darcy's fresh ire for her mother was undeserved. True, her attention at home, like his, was often pulled more strongly in the direction of their son, Adam. Adam was fifteen years old and was on the autism spectrum. In addition to her work as a Realtor, much of Ingrid's day revolved around managing their son's school schedule and various therapy appointments and activities. With the summer season in full bloom and clubhouse demands at their height, Ned felt guilty about leaving so much of it to her. As it was, the scruffy family dog, Fritzy, was pretty much the only one excited to see him at the end of each day.

In addition to worries at home, there was a fresh worry that had also followed Ned from his house on Maple Street to work that day. The new neighbors.

He hadn't noticed the for-sale sign had come down next door. It had been up forever—something that irked Ingrid, mostly because the neighbors had listed their house with a competing agency.

According to the ever-tangled grapevine at the Rockwood Market deli counter, the Crenshaws hadn't even bothered to walk through its front door. Reportedly, the husband had discovered it online, picked up the phone, and made a full price offer sight unseen.

Rumors swirled: Was Crenshaw a famous actor seeking solitude? A Red Sox player? A rock star? After all, when it came to celebrities seeking a rural weekend escape, Rockwood was known in that *gated-wooded-enclave* sense to attract them and private enough to keep them. Among their better-known if seldom-seen weekenders were Boston Pops composers, a handful of screenwriters, and even one of Billy Joel's drummers.

But despite the ruminations, nobody knew anything for sure about the incoming residents. The Crenshaws remained a mystery whose identity and backstory had ballooned in their absence until a few days ago—when they suddenly materialized in the driveway next door.

• • • • •

Ingrid had called him at the club. "They're here!"

Ned had been in the middle of reviewing the monthly restaurant spreadsheet, which was just not adding up. "Who?" he asked, distractedly.

"The new neighbors."

"Oh." Ned had a meeting with the board chairman, pain-in-the-butt Dick Delancey, in a few minutes. "If you see them, say hello for both of us," he had offered, hoping to get off the phone.

"I'm waiting for you."

That evening they'd walked next door armed with cookies and a bottle of wine, and knocked three times. Despite the cars in the driveway (a hulking tinted Cadillac SUV and a sleek low-slung orange Lamborghini), no one came to the door.

"Maybe they can't hear us," Ingrid had wondered aloud. "It *is* a big house."

"It's not that big." They left the cookies and wine for the new arrivals and went home debating their whereabouts.

Around ten-thirty that night, they had their answer. The sky outside their bedroom window erupted in a deep vibrato. "What on earth?" Ingrid sat up in bed, clutching her book.

Ned had gone to the window and peered down. The neighbor's back pool area was lit up in neon purple, something they must have just installed. The sub-bass boomed on: *whump, ba bump, bump, bump.* The pool lights (also purple) pulsed in a seizure-inducing show.

Adam had filled their doorway. "What's that *noise*? I'm trying to *sleep*."

Even Darcy emerged from her room to see what was going on. She stood by her father at the window and shrugged. "Cool pool lights. We should get some."

Ned looked at her. "Seriously?"

"That's Drake," she said, appreciatively.

"You've met the neighbors?"

Darcy frowned. "No. That's the artist."

The music thumped on for two more hours, the same amount of time it took Ingrid and Ned to find Adam's noise-canceling headphones and settle him down. Things were not off to a good start.

• • • • •

The next day, there was another blow. Again, Ingrid called him at work.

"Ned." Ingrid's voice had been tight. "Wait until you see what they've parked out front."

He had leaned back in his office chair. How bad could it be?

"You'll see when you get home," she said.

There was no way he could not see it. A colossal silver-and-red RV was parked *in the front yard*. The very same yard shared by the Birches, separated only by Ned's carefully tended bed of rosebushes. All forty feet of the RV glinted in its chrome glory, casting Ned's own yard in an ever-changing show of reflective glare and dark shadow. His family joined him for the viewing.

"Holy shit," Darcy said.

"Language," Ingrid hissed. Then, to Ned, "Holy shit."

"It's as big as our house. They can't keep it there," Ned had assured her.

"The sooner we talk to them the better," Ingrid said to no one in particular.

Ned turned to his wife. "We? So, you're coming with me."

She handed him a small terra-cotta pot with a lone stem of basil. "Bring this." She squinted up at him. "Honey, your eye."

It had been twitching all day. It was twitching more, now.

Ned had done as his wife asked. He'd gone to the neighbors, thinking about harmony as he left his own yard and crossed into theirs. He'd knocked on the door. That time, someone did answer. What followed had been anything but harmonious.

But Ned didn't have time to think about that today: the new neighbors were a problem for another day. Now, he was at work and he had a club to open. He heard the clubhouse doors bang shut. The sound of purposeful footsteps filled the hall. Right on time there was a knock on his door. Ned smiled as Vince poked his head in the doorway.

• • • • •

"Morning, boss!" Vince, the golf pro, was probably Ned's favorite staffer, and not just because he'd coached his daughter, Darcy, to second place in last year's Junior New England PGA tournament. Vince was full of energy and enthusiasm, and a guy who not only loved to bake but brought in tins of peanut butter cookies just because. All the members loved him.

Ned didn't want Vince to call him that, but he always did, and Ned had to admit it was endearing. "Ready for the big week?" Ned asked.

"Born ready." This was what Ned liked to hear.

Since Darcy had quit playing, Ned missed talking to Vince. Like him, Vince had seemed perplexed and confused by her announcement. "It's a real shame," he'd said when Ned had called to break the news. "But I see it sometimes. The pressure can get to these kids. Darcy is really talented, but so are the others at her level."

But just as Vince knew golf, Ned knew his daughter. There was still something that didn't make sense.

Ned went to the window. This was the beginning.

At any moment members would begin pulling into the parking lot, unpacking their golf bags and tennis rackets. Golf carts would purr to life and streak across the fairway as early birds headed out for the first round of the day. The newly hired camp counselors were starting their summer orientation program. Soon Mossimo's kitchen would hum to life and the smell of fresh baked bread would waft down the stairs as the dining room opened its doors for the first luncheon of the season. There would be lobster boils and fireworks shows, and concerts beneath starry skies. Today the beloved clubhouse, crisp white against the blue summer sky, would open its doors to all of it.

But behind the backdrop of summer skies and emerald greens, Mayhaven was in trouble. Membership was faltering. The budget was waning. A spanking new club, Fox Run, had opened up across town, luring many of their own to its greener fairways and gleaming pools. Despite the historic charm of Mayhaven, it seemed members' tastes had turned from a dip in the lake to the fish-free depths of chlorinated pools, from mountain breezes on the restaurant deck to the temperature controlled recesses of indoor dining. Outdoor showers were antiquated; pulsating showerheads were coveted. Younger members wanted convenience and comfort; they did not lament the tradeoff of doors thrown open to a glorious sunset view for the mosquito-free predictability of an air-conditioned banquet hall.

Ned was no fool: he knew his recent promotion as president of Mayhaven was contingent upon his ability to turn things around for the old clubhouse. The board wouldn't dream of renewing his contract until he did. This summer was his chance. A chance to finalize club projects on budget, to ramp up new membership, and a chance for another season of family fun. It was the ship that founder Wilson Elliot Banks had captained, and it was now Ned's craft to steer. God willing, he wouldn't run it aground.

DARCY

Darcy let out an anguished sigh. Thank God the first day of camp counselor orientation was over. Heart still pounding, she walked along the length of the clubhouse past the craft tent where she'd try not to strangle herself with lanyards, to the picnic tables where she'd have to watch kids chew with their mouths open all summer. She dumped her backpack down beside another and climbed atop one of the tables. From there she could see the tennis courts where her brother, Adam, was having a lesson. All she wanted was to go home.

Coming back to Mayhaven since quitting golf had felt almost impossible. It was funny how a place you loved so hard for so long could suddenly be a place you wanted to avoid at all costs. But her father needed help. She needed a summer job, and the pay was good. And while quitting the sport was her choice, she'd come to realize that her father's job as club president prevented her from avoiding it altogether. It was just the way it was.

Despite the fact she'd rather spend her days at the beach than entertaining a bunch of snooty eight-year-olds with monogrammed golf bags, there was the very *not-stupid* fact of Spencer Delancey.

Spencer was a senior and arguably the hottest guy at their high school; he was also the son of the board chairman, Dick Delancey, her father's archnemesis. But that wasn't Spencer's fault, and Darcy certainly wasn't going to hold it against him. Working with Spencer all summer was the biggest reason she'd agreed to take the job at all.

By eight AM, she was pulling her beater Toyota into the club parking lot alongside the other counselors' cars, all luxury hand-me-downs from their parents. At least her hair was cooperating today. And there was the fun fact that she'd convinced her best friend, Lily, to work with her. It hadn't been easy. Lily's family were not members and the job was traditionally reserved for teens whose families belonged. But that fact had actually worked in Darcy's favor: when Lily knew she wasn't allowed to do something, she only wanted to do it more.

"I don't know, there are a lot of applicants this year," Darcy had lied, hiding her pleasure when Lily's eyes flashed stubbornly. They had been sitting on her bed, lamenting the fact that their summer beach-time hours would be wasted by the jobs their parents expected them to get.

"Can't your dad help get me in?" Lily had asked. "I love kids."

Darcy had smirked. "You hate kids." Then, after a dramatic pause, "I'll ask him, but no promises."

Darcy didn't relish playing her best friend like that, but she needed Lily if she was going to survive a summer at Mayhaven. What Lily didn't know was that the job was open to anyone with a pulse; there just weren't enough teenage members to fill the openings.

From listening in on her parents' conversations, Darcy had gleaned that club membership was down. Like, by a lot. It was one of the big reasons her father was promoted as president that year. The board saw him as a family man with community ties to the schools, and that meant fresh young blood. In recent years, Mayhaven had been unsuccessful in attracting new young families. It didn't help that the majority of the membership belonged to a bunch of old people who toddled to their golf carts and saddled up at the bar for their old-fashioneds at the end of a round. But whatever the reason, saving the club would now fall to her father. No pressure, or anything.

Having pretty much grown up at the club, Darcy knew her place. It had taken her dad years to work his way up from groundskeeper to president. The way he saw it, his employment there allowed their family access to all the marvels of the club: the barbecues, the Fourth of July fireworks, the themed parties. She'd learned the game of tennis, which she didn't love, and the game of golf, which she had. Even though she'd quit, she could still outdrive any man on any hole if she felt like it. But in spite of all that, Darcy had never felt like she belonged. Because, let's face it, they never had.

In the early days, Darcy had been the daughter of the groundskeeper. As such, she got to participate in the junior golf club. She and her father would golf together before or after hours, and in the offseason when they could. When her father was promoted to assistant manager, there were more perks: her family dressed up for the Fourth of July barbecue and fireworks. They attended the occasional concert on the lawn or the lobster bake over Memorial Day weekend. But once he was promoted to president, Ned Birch wanted his family present. It was not a show, Darcy knew her father was terribly proud of his family and wanted them to share in the riches (as he saw it) that Mayhaven offered. But she never felt like she was on the inside. Even when she led the junior golf league to victory, even when she was asked to join the adults during their scrambles because they coveted her talent and needed her handicap. At the end of the day, Mayhaven belonged to its members. Membership was not something the Birches could afford.

Still, when she got out of bed that morning for camp orientation, she decided she'd try to make the most of it. It wasn't so bad. She tried not to look at the first hole, once her favorite. She took the long way through the clubhouse, avoiding the pro shop. The morning had gone by uneventfully enough, and by lunch the only interesting thing was the proximity of their picnic table to a group of college kids, home for the summer. They were the ones who got the cool positions, like lifeguarding. Among them was Spencer Delancey. Fittingly, he'd snagged one of the lifeguard jobs.

Lily sucked on her yogurt spoon as she stared at their table. "Imagine Spencer in his lifeguard shorts."

"Oh my God, Lily. *Stop*," Darcy had hissed. But who could blame Lily? Spencer was gorgeous, with his thick, sandy-blond hair and already-golden skin. His broad physique made him look more like one of the college kids, and given his seat at their picnic table, they seemed to agree. She stole a look behind them at Tommy Green, a fellow junior at their school. Tommy was a textbook bully who openly ogled the girls in their grade and made their skin crawl. So far, he'd spent lunch bragging loudly to the other assholes at his table that his father was giving him his Porsche as soon as he passed his driver's test that month. Darcy looked away as he chugged his root beer, belched, and tried unsuccessfully to crush the can on his forehead. The Porsche wasn't looking very likely.

There was one last orientation class for the afternoon: the dreaded water safety class, required for all counselors who'd be taking campers down to the lake. They gathered down on the beach and went through the basics: life jacket use, how to identify a swimmer in distress, and a basic swim test that Darcy easily passed. When they finished early Darcy was excited to go, but the camp director, Mr. Potts, had a less than brilliant idea. "There's twenty minutes left to kill. How about we end the day with a little lifeguard challenge?"

Everybody roared and clapped, as if this was the best thing they'd ever heard. "This is outside our official training," Mr. Potts admitted, blowing his whistle again. "But let's have fun with it." Darcy suspected everyone there preferred the kind of fun that was outside official training.

They were divided into two groups, blue and red, for Mayhaven colors. Of course, Darcy got called for reds, Lily for blues.

"Shit, we aren't in the same group." Lily groaned.

The worst was yet to come. Mr. Potts nodded at Spencer. "Delancey, you take the reds. Pick a victim."

What happened next was pure humiliation. Whatever the *victim* thing meant, Darcy had no desire to be involved. It was bad enough she wasn't even wearing her good swimsuit.

She feigned boredom as Spencer's eyes roamed over each member of his team.

"I hate to say it, but it's actually easier if I pick a girl." His gaze halted between her and a new girl.

Darcy flinched. "Why is that?"

Spencer shrugged. "Because I have to carry whoever it is, and you two are smaller than these idiots." He nodded to the boys, who laughed and elbowed each other like they'd won something. They sort of had.

"So which one of you wants to be my victim?" Spencer's cornflower blue eyes blazed through her.

There were a lot of things Darcy might want to be when it came to Spencer Delancey, but this was not one of them.

Apparently the new girl felt the same way. She looked at Darcy and shook her head.

Darcy shook her head back, but the new girl looked so flushed and terrified she finally relented. "Fine."

Mr. Potts spit into his whistle. "Blue team! Who'd you pick?"

The other team's lifeguard, Kate, gestured to a floppy-haired boy on her team. "I picked Rob." Of course, that lifeguard had no trouble picking a boy who, Darcy also noted, wasn't exactly smaller than she was. Darcy had to give it to her: Kate had balls.

Mr. Potts turned to Spencer. "Red team?"

Spencer opened his mouth but then shut it.

"Red! Who's your victim?" Mr. Potts barked.

Spencer looked at Darcy blankly. "I picked . . . this girl."

Darcy felt her face turn tomato. He'd *victimized* her and he didn't even know her name.

She thought about making a break for the clubhouse, claiming a headache. Or a cramp. Because let's face it, puking was totally in the realm of probability.

But then she thought of her father and how stressed he looked lately. And . . . the fact that Spencer had picked her, even if he didn't know her name. She glanced over at Lily's group; lucky Lily was sitting on the sand, completely unvictimized.

"Okay," Spencer said. "Let's go."

Darcy's heart pounded harder. "What exactly do I have to do?"

"Just wade out into the water. Then pretend to drown. It's just for fun."

"Drowning is fun?" She heard Tommy Green guffaw behind her.

"Relax," Spencer said, peeling his shirt off. "It's just a little competition."

"Right." Darcy averted her gaze from Spencer's bronze chest, void of hair and flush with definition. She wasn't going to drown in the lake. She was going to die right there on the sand.

"Or you could really drown," Tommy chortled.

Darcy threw him a murderous look. No, she would not hightail it back up the hill to the safety of the clubhouse. She would not give these morons the satisfaction. It took everything she had, but she turned her back to them and tugged her T-shirt over her head.

Adding insult to injury, was her bathing suit situation. She'd meant to wear her favorite, a pale blue bikini dotted with daisies that enhanced her figure in a way God hadn't—at least not yet. But despite tearing her room apart earlier that morning, she could only find the bottoms.

So there she was, with her daisy bottoms and an old white top that did absolutely nothing for her. Or, apparently, for Spencer, whose gaze swept right past her pale body as he headed for the rescue board.

Lily caught her eye as she trailed after him in her death march to the water. The water was freezing cold in mid-June. Rob, the other team's victim, blew past, splashing like a Labrador retriever. Darcy bit her lip to keep from screaming.

"Keep going, Birch," Mr. Potts shouted.

Darcy Birch. Daughter of Ned Birch, president, but *not* a member at Mayhaven. A position that placed her in the never-land of belonging, but not really.

Gritting her teeth, she stalked through the icy brown water to where Rob was treading like a cheerful idiot.

"Ready?" Mr. Potts shouted.

No, Darcy was not ready. She had not been ready to strip down on the sand in front of the whole summer camp staff. She was not ready to flail like a fool; surely there was no other way to do it. And she would never, ever be ready for Spencer Delancey to charge into the water to "rescue" her. She would *seriously rather die.*

The whistle blew. There was the splash and surge of lake water as both guards raced in. Kate paddled toward them in the lead. Beside her, Rob splashed about, giving it his all. Darcy threw her hands overhead and pretended to be sinking. She would not do more.

And then everything happened fast. Kate reached Rob first, but only a second before Spencer swam up to Darcy. He thrust the red buoy toward her, and she reached for it. Before she knew what happened, he flipped her on her back and Darcy found herself staring skyward. One muscled arm pulled her up against him. Even in the freezing water, his bare side radiated heat against her skin. "Okay," he puffed in her ear. "I'm going to bring you in. Just relax."

Darcy froze, blinking up at the cloudless sky as he tugged her toward shore. Water splashed into her mouth, his elbow brushed her breast. Oh my God, oh my God, oh my God. And then she was being whisked up out of the water, onto the cold, hard board, the warmth of his skin gone.

When Spencer dragged the board up onto the sand, Darcy lay there stunned. Everyone was cheering and clapping. Lily's face appeared over her own. "You won! You guys won!"

Darcy sat up, swiping her wet hair from her face, tugging her bikini back in place. The sun was in her eyes as she squinted up at all the faces staring down at her. There, in the center, was Spencer Delancey's. He held his hand out to her and she took it. He tugged her to her feet, and let go too soon.

"Nice work," he said. And then he was gone, dragging the board back up the sand as others crowded about and congratulated him.

Lily threw a towel around her shoulders. "Oh my God, I can't believe you had to do that. You are so brave. I would've died, I mean *actually* died." She looked deeply into Darcy's eyes. "Did you want to die?"

Now, as Darcy watched Adam leave the tennis courts, she shivered at the recollection. Adam surged up to her. "Darcy. It's time. Let's go."

"How was your lesson?" Despite being nearly two years younger, Adam had shot up that year, and was now level with her gaze.

His sandy hair was tousled, his cheeks flushed by his lesson. “It’s time. Let’s go.”

Adam didn’t like to wait. Schedules were everything. His lesson ended at four o’clock. If they left on time (which was important) they’d be home by four-fifteen. There, he’d shower, change, and play video games until dinner. It was Wednesday, which meant “Red day.” Adam’s nightly dinners were organized by color, which meant the whole family’s dinners were, too. Red meant spaghetti and meatballs and red beets and, if there was dessert, red velvet cake. The color-assigned days never changed, which meant the menu never changed. It was how it went with Adam.

Darcy repeated her question patiently. “Did you have a good lesson?” It was what their mother said the whole family needed to reinforce, after his latest therapy session. Adam had a number of therapists. Sometimes Darcy wondered if her mother ever grew tired of it, if she’d like to skip a speech session and just drive to the town beach on a nice day, or whip up tacos for dinner, on a Wednesday. Her mother was pretty as mothers go; they shared the same curly dark hair and wide green eyes. But lately those eyes looked tired.

Adam grunted, shifting impatiently from one foot to the other.

Gently, Darcy touched his arm. Adam didn’t like to be touched, but with her, he never recoiled. “Tell me one thing about your lesson, Adam. Then we can go.”

Adam’s gaze swerved impatiently to the sky, and he chewed his bottom lip. “One thing.” He blinked as he thought. “Molly said my backswing was good.”

"That's great," Darcy told him. "Now we can go home." She was proud of Adam.

"Oh no!" Adam's face clouded. He looked around frantically.

"What? What is it?"

"My water bottle." Adam began to jig from one foot to another. "It's gone!"

Adam used the same green stainless steel bottle each day. "It's okay, we'll find it. Let's check inside your bag."

As she rummaged through it, Adam winced as if in pain.

"When was the last time you had it?"

He shook his head irritably. "I don't know. I don't remember."

"Did you use it during your lesson?" If she didn't help him locate it ASAP, she was going to have a full meltdown on her hands. It was late in the day, and Adam's patience waned with the sun.

"Wait." Adam squinted toward the courts. "I see it!"

Darcy exhaled with relief. "Run and get it, I'll wait here." She sank back down onto the picnic table. *Thank God*, she thought, closing her eyes. When she heard the return of footsteps moments later she opened her eyes. Only, it wasn't Adam. It was Spencer Delancey heading her way.

Darcy jerked upright.

"Sleeping on the job?" Spencer slowed just long enough to scoop up his backpack from the picnic table. As he swung it over his shoulder, he locked eyes with her. And smiled. "See ya tomorrow, Birch."

"See ya," Darcy managed to squeak back.

She kept her eyes trained straight ahead and counted to

thirty before she dared a glance over her shoulder. Spencer was climbing into a BMW, a car as blue as his eyes. Darcy spun around before he caught her.

Adam returned in a flurry, gripping his green water bottle. “Why are you smiling like that? You look weird. Let’s go.”

But Darcy didn’t mind. *Spencer Delancey remembered her name.*

FLICK

Why his mother moved them away from civilization to the middle of the sticks he would never know. Josie was cautious about everything when it came to him, but for the first time in his seventeen years she'd thrown caution out the window.

Flick missed Queens. He missed the noise and bustle of his old Latino community in Flushing. He missed the smell of peppers and garlic wafting up from the restaurant below their apartment, and even gruff Mr. Perez who looked at him like he was a shoplifter but made the best egg-and-cheese sandwiches at the corner bodega. Flick understood Flushing; he was used to looking over his shoulder on the subway platform. He knew the best places for dim sum. He knew which section of fence had a missing bar he could slip through into the Botanical Garden after hours. Ever since he could ride the train alone, he'd never missed a Mets opening day.

Now, in the blinding greenery and noiselessness of Massachusetts, Flick didn't know how to be. The neighbors, who lived not on the other side of his apartment wall but a whole acre away (he'd never used that word in his life) had names and waved whenever he passed them walking their dogs on the road. Flick hadn't known the names of whoever lived next door back in Flushing. Tenants changed so often, he never bothered.

It hadn't been easy, but he and his mother had done just fine on their own back there. Josie had worked in housekeeping at one of the hotels, cleaning rooms. It was honest work, she said, if hard. That all changed when she met Stan the Dry Cleaning King.

"You're kidding, right?" Flick had said with a half-smile when Josie told him. Josie went out with a lot of men; Flick had long ago stopped asking. "A king?"

"Don't judge," she'd huffed, looking offended. Josie never looked offended. "He's a successful businessman. Makes a good living."

Flick had heard this before. The successful mechanic, the deli owner, the limo driver. It was like Josie was lending them some kind of credibility if she inserted the word *successful* in front.

"You know who he is," she said. "The guy on all the billboards."

Flick knew him, alright. He also knew the tacky homemade cable TV ads. Stan was a big guy, and a big guy stuffed into a velvet purple suit left an impression. What Flick remembered more than the King's shiny head or thick finger he jabbed at the screen was his booming voice, slick with innuendo. *"Bring me your dirty laundry,"* he sneered. *"I'll take care of it."*

Flick squinted at his mother. He could tell there was more.

Josie stared at her feet. "Stan wants to meet you."

That's when Flick knew his life was about to change. Josie

may have gone on a lot of dates, but she didn't bring men home and she had never introduced any of them to Flick. They never lasted long enough.

"Stan." Flick didn't like the way it sat on his tongue, like soggy bread.

"Stan," Josie repeated. "He wants to take us to dinner." She looked up at him hopefully. Flick was used to looking down at his mom, he was almost a foot taller; but that day she looked especially small. "Do me a favor. Give him a chance?"

Flick's mom had always taken care of him, even if it wasn't the kind of care some of his friends got. Josie didn't cook, but there was always takeout on the table. His mother didn't go to school assemblies, not when he won an award for math or the one for art—maybe she was too tired. She'd never imposed any real boundaries for him; luckily he was a kid who made his own. But she'd also never asked anything of him, either.

Flick sighed. "So when is dinner with the Dry Cleaning King?"

Josie smiled gratefully. "Tomorrow. At the Italian Club."

They met for dinner. Stan did not wear his velvet purple suit from the TV ads, but Flick noted the way the lighting reacted with the fabric of his jacket, nonetheless. He tried not to wince when Stan barked his drink order at the waitress. When it was time to eat and Stan ordered for Josie without asking her, Flick stole a wary glance at his mother. But she was smiling, looking relieved not to have to choose between steak Florentine and chicken picatta—as if she were being pulled from a life raft. What Flick came to realize over his plate of gummy linguine was that *Stan* was the life raft. He'd thrust his meaty finger at Josie just like he did in his commercials, and she'd reached out and grabbed it.

Flick couldn't understand why, and he didn't much like the guy. But as long as that smile stayed on his mother's tired face Flick decided right then that he would not question it. He was seventeen and would be going off to college in another year. So if Josie chose the Dry Cleaning King, he would stomach it.

When they got engaged a month later, Flick went along with it. On the walk to school, his best friend, Mateo, ribbed him. "So does this make your mother the Dry Cleaning Queen?"

Flick shoved him.

"Relax, man." Mateo laughed. "The guy's got dough! Look at that Caddy. You're rich now."

Flick didn't care. The Cadillac was a tinted-windowed beast that Stan drove too fast, just like he talked. It was embarrassing the way Stan carried a thick wallet of one hundreds, shoving the bills under cashiers' noses for a two-dollar coffee with the same faux apology each time: "All's I've got, doll." But Josie had a giant sparkler on her finger, and expensive new clothes in her closet. She was happy. So Flick tried to be, too.

The afternoon she showed up in his doorway with an armload of cardboard boxes, however, Flick had to sit down on his bed. Instead of his racing heart, he tried to focus on the light in his mother's eyes as she explained that Stan had a new plan. He'd sold the dry cleaning business. He was buying them all a country house.

"You can't move to the country. What about your job?" Flick managed. He felt like a fool the moment the words came out.

Josie touched his cheek. "We're both retiring, kiddo. See the incredible life Stan is giving us?"

Flick could not see it. "Exactly *where* in the country are we going?"

"Rockwood, Massachusetts."

"We're moving to Massachusetts?" Flick sputtered. He'd pictured something outside of the city, in New York; at worst, Connecticut. Then, "Is it at least near Boston?"

"It's rural. You'll like it."

Rural. Flick pictured expanses of deep lakes and dark woods. It did not sound like a place that had dim sum up the street or the 7 train to Citi Field. What did people in *rural* Massachusetts even do?

Any outrage was lost on his mother, who glanced dreamily out the window. "Stan's little brothers already live up there. They say it's real nice."

Flick's belongings only took three boxes to fill. He wondered how he'd fill the big new bedroom in the big new country house Stan was dragging them to. *Just one year*, he tried to tell himself. He could always come back to the city for college.

Now, the first week of summer, they were moved in. The house was very nice and very big. There was a saltwater pool and a deck out back. Inside, there were vaulted ceilings and three different living rooms and five bedrooms and a gleaming marble kitchen bigger than their whole apartment back home. *Back home*. Flick winced.

"You have to stop saying that," Josie chided. "It hurts Stan's feelings."

Flick was not convinced Stan had feelings, at least not when it came to what others thought of him. Evidence A was parked in the driveway: a towering, blinding chrome-finished RV parked right up along the neighbor's front yard. Evidence B was the conversation with the new neighbor about Evidence A.

Just the other night, the new neighbor had left his yard,

walked around the colossal RV, and up their driveway. He had carried a small clay pot of something green and a smile, despite the consternation in his eyes. When Flick answered the door, the neighbor grinned and introduced himself in a friendly voice as Ned Birch, father of Darcy and Adam, from next door. Flick did not know who Darcy or Adam was, but he had a foreboding sense he soon would.

"Welcome to the neighborhood!" Ned proclaimed, thrusting the potted plant in his direction. "This is basil. Fresh from my garden."

Flick smiled back at Ned Birch and accepted the plant. "Thank you." But he didn't have a chance to say anything more because Stan had filled the doorway behind him like a dark cloud. A pretzel rod hung from one corner of his mouth like a cigar. Flick gave way.

"Oh, hello there!" Ned said, gazing up at Stan. "Ned Birch, from next door." He extended his hand.

Stan shook it half-heartedly, crunching on his pretzel.

Niceties were shared, mostly by Ned. There was brief small talk about the town, also by Ned. And then there was silence. But given the way Ned kept glancing over his shoulder toward the driveway, Flick could tell there was more. Unable to tear himself away, he waited for Ned Birch to get to it. Finally, he did.

"There is one thing I had hoped to ask you about," Ned said, his voice clear and hopeful. Flick felt sorry for the guy already.

Stan crossed his arms. The remains of the pretzel rod flicked between his lips. "What's that?"

"The RV?"

"Yeah?"

"We were wondering how long you plan to park it there."

Stan's eyes gleamed. "She's a beauty, ain't she?"

"Yes, for sure." Ned shifted in his penny loafers. "Though I think large vehicles are supposed to be stored in the rear of the property. At least not on top of the neighbor's line. As it is, almost on top of my rose garden."

"Rose garden."

"Yes." Ned smiled. "Heirloom variety, from my mother's actually."

When Stan said nothing, Ned Birch looked him calmly in the eye. The man was small and soft-spoken, but Flick admired his directness. "The thing is, this is a quiet residential street. Though it's been a bit less quiet lately, especially late at night. We were really hoping you might turn the music down a little?"

Stan crossed his arms and considered Ned Birch like one does a small fly on a hot day. "Let me get this straight: you don't like my RV and you don't appreciate my taste in music."

Before Ned could reply Stan forged ahead. "I thought people in the country minded their business. You know, I moved up here for some privacy. And peace and quiet."

Ned nodded. "Which is exactly what I'm asking for, too."

Stan licked a stray crumb of pretzel off his bottom lip. "Tell you what—you worry about you, and I'll worry about me. Nice to meet you, Ted."

"It's Ned."

But Stan didn't hear. He'd already reversed back inside his country house and slammed the door.

NED

Ned was not a man who believed in signs, but as a newly minted president on opening day at the club, he found himself looking all over for one.

When he turned in to the clubhouse driveway, Ned smiled at the pilgrim logo etched into the sign. The Mayhaven Pilgrim was an homage to the colonial history of their home state. Wooden gaze fixed, the pilgrim stared out beneath his wide-brim hat to the distant hills. Ned pointed his car in the same direction.

The sun was already swinging up over the Blue Hills and the fairways sparkled with dew. Ned decided this was a good sign. His walk to the front door was serenaded by birdsong, the air filled with the scent of fresh-cut grass. Along the upper decks American flags snapped smartly from their poles along the railings. The new kayaks were lined up along the beach and the sand raked so carefully it looked like it had been combed by hand. More good signs. The setting was pure New England in all its summer glory. He thought of the old members who'd left Mayhaven that year for the new club, Fox Run. With its sterile pool and faux siding and noisy roadside frontage, it had about as much character as a strip mall. You couldn't place a value on old-school elegance and history. Wouldn't they be sorry on a day like this, Ned thought to himself.

Just before nine AM the campers started rolling in with their tiny golf bags and elated-looking parents anticipating their childless day ahead. Ned watched from his post on the upper deck as the counselors lined up to greet their charges. Among the camper crowd was Darcy, sporting her new navy-and-red Mayhaven polo shirt. Ned loved that she was there off her phone, and out of her room, and out in the sunshine. It had taken some convincing, but with the salary and the promise he did not expect her to set foot on the golf course, she'd relented. He watched as she bent down to help a little girl tie her shoe. This job would be good for her.

Soon came the echo from the tennis courts, the energizing *thwack, thwack, thwack*. Vince ferried two carts of beginner golfers out to the driving range, and the lifeguards were stationed in their high white chairs ready to oversee camper swim tests. Everything was running like clockwork.

On his way inside, Ned retrieved a small cardboard box from the entryway table. Recently, Ned had set up an anonymous comment box he'd dubbed the Pilgrim Box. Reviving Mayhaven was his job, and he was counting on his membership to help guide him in that endeavor. The Pilgrim Box had been his idea to give membership a voice, and so far the members had had a lot to say. He was curious to see what this week's comments would be.

Neiman Shrive ambled through the front doors, golf bag slung over his shoulder. Neiman was always first on the course.

"Morning!" Ned said brightly.

Neiman grunted back.

Ned did not take this personally. Neiman was as seasoned a golfer as he was a long-standing member. Three days a week he played with the same foursome. To members like Neiman Shrive, Mayhaven was a second home that was just fine the way it was. He liked his old-fashioned with a twist of orange and his prime rib rare. He didn't care for out-of-state license plates in the parking lot and wasn't shy about asking unfamiliar faces on the course if they were actual members. Neiman paid his dues early, in full, always followed dress code (though Ned was pretty sure Neiman slept in a collared shirt), and did not care one lick for the new "Pilgrim Box" and its whiny contents. What a load of new age mumbo jumbo that was. Neiman was there to golf and all those handwritten *feelings* were unnecessary. That damn box was the last straw that drove him to join the board of directors that summer; as far as Neiman was concerned his sole role was to make sure nothing else changed at Mayhaven.

Neiman grimaced at the sight of Ned holding the box from the hallway table and giving it a good shake. "Wow. Seems like we've got a lot of comments this week!" Ned reported.

Neiman winced. "Oh goody."

Box in hand Ned hurried back to his office, tickled by the sound and weight within. Excitedly, he tipped the contents onto his desk. Rather than select one from the top of the heap, he reached inside the center like a child might for a lottery drawing. Ned unfolded it and put on his readers.

> Why are people wearing jeans in the dining room? Don't they know we have a dress code? And not for nothing, it's always the young members..

> The club's pilgrim logo feels dated. We're in Massachusetts, but why a pilgrim? And why a man? Where is our female representation?
>
> Has anyone noticed the growing stack of Cartier Love bracelets on Coral Delancey's arm? Rumor has it cheating-Dick may have taken more than his new Porsche for a spin after the Memorial Day dinner dance. Good for Coral for commanding fling-bling, but at this rate the poor girl won't be able to lift her arms.

Well, well. Ned made it a practice to ignore club rumors, but this one wouldn't go away. And he *had* noticed Dick sneaking cocktails to the leggy lead singer, after Coral left early. Not club business, he decided, slipping it into his pocket. (Not something he should keep from Ingrid that night at dinner, either.) He moved on to the next.

> Why are our tennis courts being used by the local boarding school? Whose grand idea was this?

Ned sat back in his chair and rubbed his head, the same head that had come up with the grand idea. One thing he'd learned since becoming president: Mayhaven had a cash flow problem quickly careening into the red. Ned suspected the board had not exactly been transparent with him for fear he might not take the job. In the same vein, he didn't share that problem with membership, for fear it might send them scurrying to the new club, Fox Run.

There was no quick fix for a cash flow problem, but there

were ways to plug the holes. A paying partnership with the local boarding school was one. Another was their decision to open the summer camp to the public, something that had never been considered before.

"Just how public?" Dick Delancey had asked when Ned proposed this to the board. He said the word *public* like it was an STD.

"Residents of Rockwood, where many of us are from, I believe," he'd reminded Dick.

Dick wrinkled his nose. "Still."

Neiman Shrive had shrugged. "This side of the gates has always been for those who are paying members. I'm all for letting folks over, but they should pay."

"That's the point," Ned explained. "We are getting paid for camp and court use. It will help our revenue." He held up the most recent spreadsheet of operating costs. "If we want to continue all of our planned projects, this is the only way."

The vote had been unanimous.

There was a knock on his door. "Mr. Birch?" It was Alta Bennington, a member so new Ned had just cashed her check that week. Alta was not only new, but young. Probably one of the jeans-wearing offenders in the restaurant. Her adorable daughter, Paisley, peeked around her. Another woman stood behind them.

Ned stood and smiled at all three. "Please, come in!"

Alta sent Paisley to sit on the hallway bench with the other woman, and marched in. Ned could not help but notice her tanned bare midriff as she sat down across from him; another reason he should send that dress code email. She did not look happy. "How are you settling in at Mayhaven?" he ventured.

"That's why I'm here." Alta cocked her head as if waiting for him to read her mind. "You don't offer daycare."

Ned was sure he'd said as much when he'd given the Beningtons a tour. "We have a summer camp for children age five and up. And, of course, our littlest members are welcome at the beach and the restaurant with their parents, anytime. But I'm afraid you're right, we do not offer childcare services *per se*." And he was pretty sure it would stay that way. Toddlers on the tennis court just did not make sense.

Alta didn't blink. "Someone needs to watch my Paisley. I can't very well play tennis with a two-year-old."

"No, I don't imagine you can," Ned said, trying to sound empathetic.

"So, you need childcare."

Ned would not tell Alta that it appeared *she* needed childcare. Instead, he said, "Have you asked any of the other members about babysitting recommendations? Many of them have teenagers who babysit. My own daughter, in fact . . ."

Alta nodded toward the woman in the hallway with Paisley. "I have a nanny. I don't need a babysitter."

"Ah! Then you do have childcare." This was becoming confusing.

"My nanny needs a break."

"Oh. I see." Actually, Ned did not see what any of this had to do with him or the club. But Alta was a member he'd personally signed, and he felt he needed to try and offer her something. "So, back to a babysitter. Would you like me to make some inquiries?"

"We can't leave Paisley with just anyone. Which is why I think Mayhaven should offer services for its members." She paused. "A certified professional with an education degree, of course."

"Of course." On it went until Paisley noisily joined them with a wet diaper, minus the nanny.

"See what I mean?" Alta cried, whisking her daughter up and away.

"Always nice to see you!" Ned called after them.

A moment later there was another knock on his door. Ned looked up, afraid to see Alta Bennington's bare midriff again. Thankfully, it was his head chef, Mossimo. But he also did not look happy.

"Sorry to interrupt, Mr. Birch, but there's a problem with the cutlery," he said, coming to stand over Ned's desk. Mossimo never sat.

Ned looked up at him. "What's wrong with the cutlery?"

"Silverware has gone missing. It started with a fork here and a knife there, so at first I didn't think much of it. But when I took inventory yesterday, I noticed that we appear to be missing complete sets of our silver."

"The good silver?" Back in the club's founding days, there had been a gift by one of its earliest and wealthiest members, Regina Blackstone, in the form of cutlery for the newly constructed dining room. According to club history, the silver had only been used twice yearly during those early years, once for the opening season dinner party and once for the closing. As the club grew and modernized, the restaurant turned to more economical and practical flatware. Since then, the good cutlery was only brought out for special club occasions, or for the odd member wedding when it was specially requested by those in the know.

"Yes, sir," Mossimo confirmed. "The Blackstone silver."

Ned sat back in his chair. The Blackstone silverware was part of the club's heritage and legacy. It had been used a few times in the last year, but to have exact sets missing was definitely odd. "Do you have any suspicions?"

Mossimo reared back slightly. "No one on my staff, I assure you." The chef was deeply sensitive about his kitchen, employees and all. Ned appreciated that.

"We'll have to keep our eyes open, I guess. When are we planning to use it next?"

"The first scramble of the season."

"Alright. Let's count it once more before the scramble dinner, and again after. Alert the staff to keep watch during service." Ned hated to ask staff to spy on members—that was in direct opposition to the spirit he hoped to cultivate at Mayhaven. But what choice did he have?

Ned glanced at the clock. He was five minutes late for the grounds meeting. As he was gathering his folders, his phone rang. It was Ingrid. He really did not have time, but he took the call.

"He's shooting, Ned. Shooting!"

Ned almost dropped his folders. "What? Who? Are you *okay*?"

"I'm sorry, honey—we're fine. I meant the neighbor. Stan is in the backyard shooting some kind of giant bow and arrow. I just saw him through the living room window."

"What is he shooting?"

"You're not going to like this. It appears to be our old scarecrow."

They had just cleaned out their garage over the weekend, and the old scarecrow was part of a large pile of tired yard decorations Ingrid had deemed garbage. Just that morning, Ned had carried it down to the curb for trash pickup, alongside a broken Halloween sign and some dead Christmas tree lights. Ned was sentimental to a fault, and he knew he could be a packrat, but he'd felt especially bad about the scarecrow, even though it was missing an arm. He and Adam had made it a few years ago in Scouts. It still wore Ned's old Red Sox T-shirt, a favorite that he'd spilled spaghetti sauce on and Ingrid had also made him give up.

"Stan went through our trash?" Ned asked. If Ingrid wouldn't let him have the scarecrow, the neighbor couldn't, either.

"Well, I wouldn't go that far. It was left on the curb, after all. But did you hear what I said about the crossbow? He's shooting that thing alongside our backyard. I'm afraid to let Fritzy out. Is that even legal?"

"It's definitely not safe."

Ingrid sighed. "Wait until you hear the sound it makes when it hits your scarecrow."

"He's actually hitting the scarecrow?" This made it even worse.

"Right through the heart of your Red Sox shirt." Ingrid brightened. "At least his aim is good!"

Ned did not like the sound of any of this: not about the bow or his scarecrow or his favorite old T-shirt. He put a hand to his own chest and glared at the clock. "Honey, I have to go."

If opening day wasn't stressful enough, now going home would be, too. Agitated and now (very) late, Ned took the stairs two at a time wondering if he'd be murdered beside his pool later, and who in their right mind shot at the Red Sox.

DARCY

Elly Watson was only six years old, but she was already primed to be one mean middle-schooler.

"Time for your tennis lesson," Darcy said in her most encouraging voice.

Elly glared up at her from where she slumped by the court fence. "Can't make me."

Darcy opened her mouth but nothing came out. It hadn't occurred to her that this was something a six-year-old would think she had the option to turn down. "But, Elly, you're signed up for tennis. And it's your turn."

Elly positioned herself away from her counselor and fixed her gaze on a dandelion which she grabbed and snapped the head off of. "Are you deaf?"

Lily, who was helping another camper tie her shoes, sputtered with laughter. All of their campers were already on the courts with Molly, the tennis instructor. Except Elly, who was refusing, and her little friend Savannah, who looked like she might cry if Elly didn't go with her.

"Elly," Darcy tried again, determined to ignore the insult, "your mother dropped you off with this beautiful new racket this morning." Darcy lifted the racket from the grass and held it up. "Look. It's even got your name engraved on it." The amount of money and time spent on superfluous details by these parents was completely wasted on their kids, Darcy thought. How many crust-less sandwiches or tiny containers of hand-rolled sushi had she seen tossed in the trash in favor of another camper's crumpled bag of Doritos? The personalized brand-name sportswear thrown on the ground, dropped on the trail, left sopping wet in the sand? These kids had so much and seemed to appreciate so little.

Elly turned to Darcy. "You can have it. I hate that racket and I hate tennis."

Darcy was at least happy she hadn't added, *And I hate you*, though from the ire in her stare it was likely.

Time for some reverse psychology. Darcy examined the racket adoringly. "Thanks! I think I will." Then, before Elly could object, she hopped up onto her feet and headed for the courts. "You coming, Lily? Savannah?"

Savannah looked unsure, but followed Lily who followed Darcy. "Let's play *together*."

Darcy wasn't any good at tennis; golf had been her thing. But it didn't matter, as long as she got Savannah out there and showed Elly what a good time she was missing.

I suck at tennis, Lily mouthed to her.

Just do it, Darcy mouthed back.

They practiced their serves, as Molly instructed the group. Tennis balls went everywhere and campers scrambled after them, but everyone was laughing. At one point Darcy caught Elly watching.

After fifteen minutes, Darcy was sweating. "This is harder than it looks," Lily said, as she dashed after a stray ball.

"So is she." Darcy nodded toward Elly, still planted in the same spot in the grass.

When the lesson ended, Darcy marched over to where she sat. "Thanks for letting me borrow your racket. It's really good."

Elly shrugged. "Too bad you aren't."

Darcy forced herself to smile. One thing she knew from being Adam's sister was that his mood often depended on worries or anxieties he had. She'd have to try to figure out what it was with Elly.

The day was hot, so she directed the campers to a shaded picnic table by the trees for lunchtime. "Cool, golf carts!" one of the little boys said, pointing.

"When can we drive those?" another asked.

Darcy followed their gaze to the row of parked carts. "We're focusing on tennis this session," she told them. "The carts are for the kids who take golf lessons." She'd chosen this group of campers only because it let her avoid the course and the game and her old instructor. At that moment, Vince pulled up. He high-fived a camper just as he used to with her. Darcy felt a pang watching them.

"Is it weird, seeing him up here?"

"What?" Darcy spun around to find Lily standing beside her.

"Your old golf coach. Since you quit, it must be weird being back and bumping into him." Lily was looking at her sympathetically. "I know your parents are still upset about it."

"Oh. No, I don't even think about it," Darcy lied. She took a seat on the bench and rifled through her lunch bag, even though she'd pretty much lost her appetite.

Lily had never really questioned Darcy about quitting. To her it was a bonus: now her best friend had the whole summer free to hang out together. Which was fine with Darcy; her parents bugged her about it enough. But still—it was different being able to open up to a friend.

She stared at the chicken sandwich her mother had made and forced herself to take a bite, but only a small one. The scale that morning had shown that she'd lost another pound, and Darcy wanted to keep it going. It felt good to finally have something moving in the direction it was supposed to. She figured if she looked good, she'd feel good, something she hadn't in longer than Darcy could remember. And especially since she was working summer camp at the club beach with the likes of Spencer Delancey. Never mind the bronzed blonde who'd shown up at camp that morning as the newest senior counselor.

"Ashley Riley," Lily had whispered as they both watched her roll in. "Even her name is a 'pick me.'"

Ashley had not been at orientation last week with the rest of them, but the girl was a country club poster child. Not that Darcy was allowed to call Mayhaven a country club. "It's an association," her father always corrected her. "Call it a club, even. But please not *country* club."

Darcy had snorted. "Like there's a difference?"

Her father looked hurt. "Country club has a negative connotation for a lot of people. They're exclusive. They don't have the best histories when it comes to inclusion or diversity. Mayhaven is so much more."

Whatever *that* meant. She'd have to ask her dad how Ashley landed a camp job at their *association* without doing the required time like she had. Rumor was she'd been vacationing in Santorini with her family, who were Mayhaven legacy members. Just like Spencer's family.

"She seems tight with everyone here," Lily observed, sounding equal parts annoyed and intrigued by Ashley Riley. "But I don't recognize her from school."

"Because she goes to boarding school," Molly, the tennis instructor had chimed in from behind them. Darcy had blushed deeply. She hadn't realized how loud they were.

"Surely you've met Ashley up here before?"

Darcy shook her head. "Don't remember if I did." Then she added, "I don't come up here as much as I used to." She was relieved when Molly didn't ask her why.

Now, Darcy and Lily stared as Ashley sauntered up to Spencer's table. He actually looked up from his lunch and flashed his killer smile. "Hey, Ash."

"He calls her Ash!" Lily hissed.

"I have ears," Darcy hissed back. "Forget her, we need to focus on our kids."

It seemed their campers needed help with everything: putting straws in juice boxes, opening thermoses, cleaning up spills. That was just lunchtime. By the time they headed to the locker rooms to change into swimsuits, there was an endless chorus of campers calling her name. *Help me with sunscreen! Where's my towel? Who took my goggles?* Darcy didn't mind. She was getting to know them and finding favorites, even though she knew she shouldn't.

For little kids they had big personalities. One camper, a wiry ginger-haired boy named Evan, was apparently a budding ornithologist. He'd spent the morning identifying birds and telling Darcy all about them. Then there was Savannah, who was tall and shy and hovered near Darcy with saucer-shaped eyes. Darcy would have to help her make friends, she could tell. And then there was Elly. Who seemed to hate everything camp had to offer, and maybe Darcy, too?

"Are you excited to swim?" Darcy asked her, as they headed down the shady trail to the lake after lunch.

Elly shrugged. Stupid question—Elly wasn't excited about anything.

"I am! I can do the crawl," Evan piped up. Then, "Hear that? That's a woodpecker. Wonder if it's the pileated kind." He squinted up into the branches.

Darcy laughed. "How about you?" she asked Savannah, who was glued to her side.

Savannah lifted one shoulder uncertainly. "I'm not very good."

"How about we swim together?" Darcy suggested. She knew the others would join; they were like little lemmings. She'd help Savannah make small talk with them when they did.

Down on the beach she was dismayed not to see Spencer up in the guard chair. Kate, the other lifeguard, sat in his place. *Damn*. She'd even worn her cute daisy bikini top.

At least the day was hot and the water felt nice. Elly refused to go in, but Savannah did eventually. Darcy became so busy playing Marco Polo while the kids took turns with Kate for swim tests that the session flew by. Suddenly it was time to bring the campers back up to the clubhouse for pickup.

Darcy was exhausted but happy; she'd made it through the first day of camp! She closed her eyes and leaned against the wall as she waited outside the locker room for her campers to change. Suddenly the front door at the end of the hall banged closed. Darcy stood at attention, expecting to see a parent. Instead, it was a boy about her age. He wasn't dressed like a member. He looked kind of cute, if lost.

He glanced up at the sparkling chandelier and flipped his dark hair out of his big brown eyes. Yep, very cute. It wasn't dress code, but she liked his Tyler the Creator shirt and red Converse. When he saw her standing there he hesitated, then headed her way.

Darcy straightened. "Hey."

The boy cleared his throat, looking nervous. "Hi, I'm looking for the main office."

Her dad's office. "You have a delivery?"

He held up his empty hands. "Seriously?"

"You looked lost. And I didn't recognize you, so I just thought . . ."

The kid shook his head. "Yeah, I got you."

"What?" Darcy grimaced. "I'm sorry, it's just that people who come looking for the office are usually here for a delivery." God, she sounded pathetic. "I didn't mean . . ."

"Mean *what*?" Darcy felt like his big brown eyes could see right through her, thoughts and all.

He had her there. What had she meant? That he was wearing street clothes instead of a collared shirt and boat shoes? That he was not a member? That his skin was darker than hers? *God, she had not meant that.* "No, I just . . . I don't know. Look, I'm sorry!" Oh God, oh God, oh God.

And then he smiled at her. A big fat playful smile that rescued them both. "Nah, I'm just messing with you. It's cool."

Darcy exhaled. She still felt like an asshole, and she knew

she deserved to. But she was grateful. "The office is right over there," she said, finding her voice again. She pointed to her father's door. "Who're you looking for?"

"Mr. Birch. I have an interview."

Darcy nodded at her father's name but gave away nothing. "Well, good luck." Then, "I'm Darcy, by the way." She extended her hand.

"Flick." Flick took her hand and she glanced down at their clasped fingers. "Thanks, Darcy."

Darcy watched him walk down the hall and through her father's office door. *Flick.* Who named their kid that?

She wondered if she'd see him again. She suddenly hoped she would.

FLICK

Mayhaven was everything his mother had hoped it would be and everything he'd feared. The clubhouse was one of those nondescript clapboard buildings that might be a church, a prep school, or a country club—all of which housed pasty people in preppy clothes. So, really, what was the difference?

The moment he walked through the front doors Flick looked down and realized his first mistake—his concert T-shirt and sneakers. When he looked up he realized his second: a place with a chandelier that sparkly probably demanded an equally glittering résumé, which he did not have. Honestly, Flick didn't want this job to begin with, and he'd known it before he even stepped foot inside Mayhaven. The idea of a summer job wasn't the problem; Flick was bored stiff in their dead-dull town and having something to do and money of his own seemed like a good idea. Despite what Stan had said to him when they moved in, Flick didn't feel comfortable asking him for pocket money. Or anything else, for that matter. The house, the pool, the sports cars—it was all as foreign to him as the empty green expanse of their new rural life and the eternal thrum outside his window each night, from what his mother informed him were peepers, whatever they were. Flick missed the sound of street noise, the bustle of city sidewalks, the throngs of people. Rockwood was too quiet, the new house so isolated. And he knew nobody. School would be the only way to meet people his age, but that wouldn't start for another two months, so a job would be a way to kill time until then. Which is why Flick had suggested he go to the local grocery market and ask if they were hiring. He'd been a cashier before, back in Queens; it wasn't rocket science. But Josie said no—that they didn't need the money, so any job he got should be about more than that. They were in a new place making a fresh start. Josie wanted him to network. To rub elbows, as she put it.

"Why?" Flick wanted to know.

"You need to meet people, so they might as well be people with connections. Kids around here come from good families and go to good colleges. Who you know can help."

Flick was mildly offended. First, just because folks had money didn't make them good. She of all people, having cleaned up after them in her housekeeping work, should know that. Second, as for good families, hadn't they already been a good family back in New York? Adding Stan the Dry Cleaning King and a forest of trees full of stinging bugs didn't count for any improvement, as far as Flick was concerned. Third, he'd always done well in school, and Josie hadn't put much emphasis on that before, beyond the fact that he went.

Now that they were living in Rockwood Josie was online every night perusing Rockwood attractions and associations, the local playhouse and the yoga classes down at the lake. Stan had his own take on it. To him moving to the country meant he had to tame it or hunt it, a novel way to assert his manhood. To his mother's horror Stan had gone out to buy eggs the other morning and come home from the sporting goods store with a giant crossbow.

"Are you crazy? You're going to kill someone with that," she'd warned him.

"That's the plan. Ever had venison?"

Josie made a face. "That's what grocery stores are for. Besides, you are not killing some poor innocent animal, Stan."

"Oh, come on, the deer are a dime a dozen up here. That's why they have hunting season."

Josie stood her ground. "You want to shoot something? Make a target in the backyard, facing away from the house. I did not move up here for you to murder Bambi."

But Josie was just as guilty with her own fantasies. "We can learn to sail!" she'd said one night at dinner, which sounded like a joke coming from the woman who got seasick on the Staten Island Ferry. It was like she'd woken up in some kind of fairy tale and she was hungry to not only get the lay of the land but to insert herself into it. Which is how she'd found out about Mayhaven.

"Look at this!" Josie was stationed at the marble waterfall counter with her laptop (another new purchase) a few nights earlier. They were having another opulent meal of oversized steaks grilled on the oversized Weber in the outdoor kitchen, which was as big as the indoor one. "There's a country club just up the road!" his mother shrieked. "I had no idea."

Stan flashed his toothy grin from his station at the grill, as though he'd had something to do with that fact. "Only the best neighborhood for my girl."

"It's called Mayhaven," Josie said. "Sounds like the *Mayflower*, doesn't it?"

Flick leaned over her shoulder to see what his mother was so excited about.

"Oh my God," Josie squealed. "Their logo is a pilgrim! I was right."

The club home page showed a white clapboard building with a towering flagpole. The whole thing looked like a mini White House with a pilgrim on a sign. Josie read the heading aloud: "*Welcome to Mayhaven, where summer is eternal.*"

Flick rolled his eyes. "Sounds stupid."

Stan joined them. "Sounds pricey." Stan did that—he commented on how expensive everything was in the same breath he insisted *only the best!*

But a dreamy look was already spreading across Josie's face. "It's just a mile from our house! Stan, this place looks nice. You always said you wanted to golf."

Stan grunted. "When did I say that?"

"We should check it out," Josie went on. "Who knows, maybe I'll take up tennis."

At that, Stan showed his teeth again. "You slip into one of those tennis skirts and I'll join today." He wrapped his big hands around her small waist and pressed his lips to hers.

Flick had to avert his eyes.

"Wait," Josie said, suddenly. "Flick, you should go, too."

"No way." He shook his head. "I don't play golf. Or tennis. Don't plan to." He made the face he reserved for *no way in hell,* something he rarely did. Josie had asked a lot of him this summer, marrying Stan and abandoning Queens. He'd been flexible and smiled until his face hurt through all of it. But Flick had his limits.

"Not for the club," Josie said, scrolling down. "For a job. Look, there's a notice for summer jobs."

Flick was still not interested. "What would I do at a country club?"

"Anything they ask you to." Stan chuckled. "Those people got money to burn. Keep 'em happy and they'll tip big."

This was another thing Stan did: spoke with authority on pretty much everything. Flick wanted to ask Stan what kind of country club experience he had. Based on Stan's wardrobe of polyester suits and gold jewelry, Flick would bet his life on zero. But he bit his tongue.

Josie kept scrolling. "Read this. Under employment opportunities, it says kitchen help wanted."

"That's what they're calling it, now? An opportunity?" Stan snorted. "Translation: dishwasher."

Josie ignored this and instead looked at Flick. "Maybe they need restaurant help. You could do that. You love to cook."

Flick *did* like to cook; before Stan and the country house, any homemade dinner that made its way onto their kitchen table in Queens was by him. But he seriously doubted a club wanted a teenage cook self-taught by watching Food Network reruns.

"Nah," Stan said. "A place like that's got professional chefs. They'll have him peeling potatoes, washing dishes, cleaning up. Grunt work."

Josie swiveled on her barstool and leveled a look at Stan. "So?" For a guy who knew everything, Stan often forgot that her line of work used to be grunt work.

Stan swallowed hard.

Flick liked that as mushy as his mother could be about her new husband, she still spoke her mind. He liked it even more that Stan had the sense to back down when she did.

"Nothing wrong with honest work," Josie added, eyes locked on her husband's.

"No," Stan agreed, excusing himself to check on the steaks. "Nothing at all."

• • • • •

Flick indulged his mother and called the club about the kitchen-help "opportunity." When he did, a man on the phone suggested he come that afternoon. They must've been desperate. Josie was thrilled. "See? You've got to hustle, Flick. You can check the place out for us while you're there."

Flick didn't get it. They weren't country club people. He would've been just as happy working at the grocery store or the ice cream shop in town, which, according to his mother, employed some cute girls she thought he should introduce himself to. He couldn't understand why Josie was so obsessed with adopting a new lifestyle just because of a new address. He and his mother were both born and raised in Queens. If, as she insisted, there was nothing wrong with their old lives, their old apartment, and her old job, why was she champing at the bit to dive into a world so different?

It didn't matter, he decided, as he stood beneath the giant chandelier in the country club foyer that afternoon. He was there. In the wrong clothes and without a résumé. He may as well get the interview over with.

The man on the phone, a Mr. Birch, had told him to report

directly to the office, but all Flick could see was a trophy case that stretched the length of the hall. The glass case was full of framed photos and engraved awards, every face white, every trophy gold. There were plenty of old men, a couple of old ladies, and a whole lot of collared shirts. Flick groaned. That's when he looked up and saw the girl.

She wore a polo shirt and khaki shorts that reminded him of a school uniform, and was standing beneath an engraved sign labeled, *Locker Rooms*. These people sure liked to engrave things.

As he walked toward her Flick recognized the Mayhaven pilgrim logo on her shirt. Man, she was in full regalia. But despite that, something about her expression told him she didn't buy into it. Flick was instantly intrigued.

In addition to her unamused expression, she was very pretty. Flick couldn't stop staring at the freckles on her nose.

And then she asked him if he was a delivery boy. And it all went sideways.

At first Flick thought she was kidding. When he realized she was not, he could feel his hackles go up. Had she said that because of his skin color? Regardless, did she not realize how insensitive she sounded? He forgot all about the freckles. "Seriously?" he challenged.

He realized then that maybe he'd been the one to read it wrong. She was instantly embarrassed. Genuinely so, by the deep flush of her cheeks and the vaporization of all the confidence he'd admired walking up to her. As she sputtered and blushed in front of him, it was his turn to feel bad.

Finally, he held up his hands. "Nah, I'm just messing with you. It's cool." And it was—sort of. She shouldn't have made those assumptions, but the thing was, she seemed like she realized it. And that was enough.

What Flick really liked was that Darcy had the guts to introduce herself, afterward. As he headed down the hall to find Mr. Birch, Flick fought the urge to look over his shoulder.

He was in for another surprise as he walked into the office.

No doubt the rich mahogany-paneled walls and gold-framed artwork would've been enough to put him on edge, like a fish out of water. Just as the pretty girl in the hallway had. But, worse, was the familiar face seated in front of him.

The man hopped up from his desk chair, mouth ajar. "I'll be darned. I believe we've met."

Perspiration was already beading on Flick's upper lip. Oh yes, they'd met. Just before Stan had slammed the door in their new neighbor's face. "Yes, sir," Flick stammered. Why was he saying *sir*?

He was fully prepared to be thrown out. Or—since they were in a country club—be *escorted* out after the way Stan had treated Ned the other night.

But instead, his neighbor extended his hand. "Nice to see you, again, Flick."

Flick felt his cheeks flood with color as he shook Ned's hand. "Nice to see you, too, sir." Again with the sir. Flick didn't even want the job, but he could already feel it being pulled off the table.

But Mr. Birch (Ned? No, not here at the club, and certainly not after what Stan had done) smiled broadly. It looked like a real smile, too, not the kind grown-ups flash you when behind their eyes they're secretly sizing you up. "I guess I didn't put it together when we talked on the phone, but this is a nice surprise. Real nice! Please, have a seat." He indicated one of two identical upholstered leather chairs opposite his desk. "Take that one. It's more comfy."

Flick sat. Was this guy for real?

Mr. Birch folded his hands. "How do you like Rockwood?"

"Oh. It's fine, I guess. I don't really know it yet."

"Yes, it's tough being new. But I bet by summer's end you'll feel more at home."

Flick nodded, unsure what to say.

"You like rap music?"

It took him a second, and then Flick understood. Stan's loud music from the other night, of course. And he was probably going to be blamed for it, because who would believe a fifty-year-old retiree listens to Drake? "That's my stepfather." He paused. "Sorry, my mom always tells him to turn it down. She was out that night."

Mr. Birch shook his head. "No need to apologize." But Flick could tell there was a need. For the loud music and also the door being slammed. And probably a host of other things Flick didn't even know about. This interview was a mistake; he could not work for a guy he lived next door to.

Before Flick could think of a way to apologize for the things Stan had done, Mr. Birch was off and running in a new direction. "So, I'm guessing you saw our job listings on the website. Which position are you interested in?"

Just like that Flick had to shift gears. Only it wasn't so much an interview as a conversation. Mr. Birch wanted to know what kitchen experience he had and didn't seem one bit concerned about the fact it wasn't formal. Could Flick be flexible and come in early some days or stay late on others? Was Flick open to prepping food before dinner service as well as bussing tables when the restaurant got busy? Flick found himself saying yes, that he was.

Before Flick knew it, he was following the guy out of the office and down the hall (Darcy was long gone). Up the carpeted steps they went, Mr. Birch talking the whole time about the club history and its founder, some guy named Wilson. Flick wondered what any of this had to do with the kitchen job, but he nodded politely. At the top of the stairs, they stopped. The second floor was one giant open space, which could either be called a large formal dining room or a small ballroom, with a bar at one end. A bank of windows ran along the wall overlooking the golf course. Outside was a wraparound deck with what Flick imagined was an even better view. Flick blinked in the sunlight.

"This is the restaurant," Mr. Birch told him. "The kitchen is in the rear, through those swinging doors. You'd be spending most of your time working there. Shall we take a look?"

Flick nodded and followed.

His Converse sneakers squeaked on the polished hardwoods and Ned looked over his shoulder.

"Sorry," Flick said, reflexively. "I didn't unpack my dress shoes yet."

"No, no," Ned insisted cheerfully. "You came dressed for the kitchen. I like it." He pushed through the swinging doors and waved hello at the cooks.

The kitchen gleamed despite the people and prep work underway. Flick eyed a stainless steel counter loaded with potatoes. Maybe Stan had been right, for once.

Alongside the mountain of peeled potatoes were boards of

chopped celery and onions. "Ooh! Did I see clam chowder on the menu?" Ned called out.

A burly man in checkered chef's pants nodded toward a deep sink. In the basin, Flick could see a pile of shellfish.

"My favorite," Ned declared. "Call me if you need a taste tester!" The chef did not smile, but he nodded, his eyes on Flick.

"Mossimo, this is Flick Creevy. He's interviewing for the kitchen prep job."

Mossimo crossed his tattooed arms and scowled. "You know how to shuck clams?"

Flick was not prepared for this. He didn't even eat clams. "I can learn."

"Good answer!" Ned said. He turned to Mossimo. "Flick tells me he has basic chopping and dicing skills."

"I'll be the judge," Mossimo said, curtly. He turned to Flick. "I can give you fifteen minutes, I am too busy to give you more."

Flick hadn't asked the chef to give him anything. He certainly didn't feel like standing in dour-faced Mossimo's kitchen. It was a sauna. Pots steamed on ranges, bread was being whisked from ovens, and two people were chopping vegetables at prep stations. The place was a zoo compared to the quiet serenity of the dining room just outside.

"Got fifteen minutes?" Ned asked.

"Sure," Flick said, not feeling sure at all.

Mossimo nodded. "Very well. Leave him to me, Mr. Ned. I'll send him back down when I'm done."

"Sounds good," Ned said, eyeing the pot on the stove. Maybe send along a little of that chowder if it's ready?" The kitchen doors swung shut behind him with a swoosh.

"Mr. Flick. You come here." Nervous, he followed the chef,

past another prep worker, about his age, and a young woman who was rolling out some kind of dough, to a small counter at the rear. Mossimo looked like he had plans for him, and Flick didn't like not knowing what they were.

Sixteen minutes later, Flick knocked on Mr. Birch's office door and poked his head in.

"How'd it go?" Ned asked, eagerly.

Under the scrutinizing stare of Mossimo, Flick had peeled and chopped one carrot, diced an onion that made his eyes run, and minced and sautéed garlic in a tiny buttered pan that he quickly realized got too hot too fast. "Sorry," he had said, holding up the smoking pan. "I've never cooked on gas before."

Mossimo chuffed like a horse and turned away.

For his final test Flick tried and failed to shuck a clam, and, before he cut off his thumb, had been swiftly relieved of the shucking knife. He'd been corrected and redirected and laughed at. He had no idea how it went, other than not great. Not great at all.

Before he could say as much to Mr. Birch, the phone rang on his desk. "Excuse me, just a moment." Ned answered and listened without a word. Then, finally, "Thank you." He hung up the phone.

Flick waited as he crossed his arms and leaned back in his armchair. "Mossimo said you did well," he said.

Flick felt his insides relax. The chef had given zero indication of that.

"How did he do?" Mr. Birch asked.

"Excuse me?" Flick was confused.

"Mossimo. Do you feel like the two of you could work well together?" As Flick struggled to reply, Mr. Birch plowed cheerfully on. "Don't get me wrong, he's a talented chef and we're very lucky to have him. Oh, you should try his Tuscan baked artichoke!" He smiled to himself before growing serious. "But Mossimo is not easy, and the work won't be, either."

Flick didn't know what to say. It had never occurred to him that anyone in Mr. Birch's position would even consider asking someone in his position how he *felt*. He was a kid. Applying for a kitchen job. In a fancy club. Mr. Birch had all the power, not him.

"One thing you should know," Ned continued, "is that we pride ourselves here at Mayhaven on our service. Our members are good people, and this is our special place. We want our staff to understand that."

"Yes, of course," Flick found himself saying. Here it was—the division of power he'd been expecting. They were at the top, he was at the bottom. Like Stan said, do what they ask.

"It's no secret that when people feel happy in a place, they will return to it."

"Sure," Flick said, sitting back in his seat. In other words, *what Stan had said.*

"So, I think the real secret is to hire good staff, and take good care of them," Mr. Birch concluded.

"The staff?" This was not at all what Flick thought was coming next.

"The staff. Because if our staff are happy, they'll provide good service. And then our members will be happy. See how that works?" He raised his index finger and twirled it gently in a circle. "What goes around . . ."

Flick was dumbfounded by how much *we* and *our* Mr. Birch used, as if they were some kind of team. Albeit a pastel-clad team, but still. In a place like this, Flick was expecting more *us* and *them*.

And then, just as quickly as the interview had begun almost an hour earlier, it ended. Mr. Birch folded his hands neatly on his desk and returned to the question at hand. "Mossimo likes to say he runs a tight ship. I like to think of it as a tight family. In that vein, do you think you'd be happy here?"

No way. Mr. Birch was asking Flick about his happiness. Despite his nerves, and despite the fact he'd never wanted this job in the first place, he considered the question. He didn't know Mossimo one lick, but the chef had been fair if firm. "I think so," he stammered.

"Good. I'm going to give us both the night to think it over and I'll call tomorrow."

• • • • •

On his way out, Flick glanced around—at the gleaming trophy case, at the empty hallway where Darcy had stood, and finally, up at the chandelier. He shook his head.

As he left the air-conditioned comfort of the clubhouse and stepped out into the heat, Flick heard the peal of kids' laughter floating up from a grove of evergreen trees, behind which he could make out the glimmer of a lake. On the tennis courts behind him, balls thwacked rhythmically back and forth, and from the upper decks of the restaurant a row of crisp American flags snapped from the railings. An old man in a golf cart putted slowly by. He lifted a gloved hand in greeting. Mayhaven was something else, that was for sure. So was Mr. Birch.

Flick had come here only to get Josie off his back. Working

in a steaming-hot kitchen all summer was the last thing he wanted to do. And these people were not his people.

Thankfully, the interview was over. His nerves had settled and so had his stomach. Flick could tell his mother he'd done it and get on with his summer. Mr. Birch had told him he'd think about it. And that Flick should, too. But who was he kidding?

After how Stan had treated him? And how Flick had shown up in Converse sneakers and a T-shirt to work in a place like this? No. Ned Birch didn't have to think, he was just being polite.

Still, as Flick headed for the safety of his car, he glanced over his shoulder once more at the white clapboard building, regal against the rich blue sky. What was it about this place? His stomach flip-flopped one last time.

Flick was halfway down the walkway to the parking lot before he realized the truth about the flutter in his stomach. It wasn't nerves. Damn. It was hope.

NED

The sound of Adam's alarm clock from across the hall rattled him wide awake at six AM. Ned groaned and covered his head with the pillow, until Adam finally turned it off.

"Why is he setting his clock for six? It's summer."

Adam's alarm tone was the sound of a fire truck siren that could wake the dead. He'd had it since he was five and fully submerged in a fire truck obsession, something he'd replaced several times since, but he could not part with the clock. At one point when the clock mysteriously broke (Ned long suspected Ingrid may have had a hand in that, on a particularly bad day), Adam's reaction was vocal and not short-lived. It had sent the family spiraling to various devices to search online for a replacement. Finally, Darcy had found a used one on eBay. Notably, it had not *broken* since.

Ned rolled over to look at his wife, snoring softly beside him. She'd learned to tune out the alarm just as she had Stan Crenshaw's loud music, which had gone on, again, until midnight. Ned was half impressed and half annoyed with his wife's ability. He didn't like lying awake, alone in his outrage at their neighbors. It was the kind that needed to be shared. It was theirs, in solidarity, to keep them awake together.

As his eyelids fluttered with fatigue, his mind wandered to yesterday's interview. He still could not believe it was Flick who'd walked through his office door. The last time he'd seen Flick Creevy's face was just before the front door had slammed shut in his own. Flick had been standing behind Stan, a mix of surprise and embarrassment clouding his expression. Well. Now, it was Ned's turn. Mayhaven had a job that desperately needed filling. And Flick seemed right for the job. Ned could open that door for him. Or not.

"What time is it?" Ingrid stretched lazily beside him and reached her arm across the growing softness of his middle. Ned had no idea when he'd last been on the course, or in the lake. The leathery depth of his office chair was the only thing he submerged himself in these days.

"It's six-ten," he said, planting a kiss on Ingrid's cheek.

"Board meeting today?"

Ned tried not to cringe. "Yep."

"You'll be okay," she said.

As a Realtor in a small town with a tough market, Ingrid understood. "We need to help Adam find a job," she reminded him. Adam had quit his last one at the local market.

It was a shame. At first, Adam liked the predictability and precision of bagging groceries, and his parents liked that it forced him to be more social. But a few weeks in there was an altercation. A customer asked Adam to put the vegetables in a separate bag. When all the groceries were bagged, he noticed that his tomatoes remained on the checkout counter. "You forgot the tomatoes," he told Adam.

Adam had replied, "You said to keep the vegetables separate."

"Yeah. So put the tomatoes in." The customer was growing impatient.

"Tomatoes are a fruit," Adam informed him.

"Just put them in."

"But they're not a vegetable."

It had ended with the customer raising his voice and Adam covering his ears and running off to the bathroom, and a phone call to Ingrid who was in the middle of an open house two towns away.

"He's not going back to the market," Ingrid later said, over a glass of wine.

"I guess the tomatoes weren't the only thing that got sacked," Ned replied, at which they'd fallen into hysterics.

But the problem remained. Adam was bright and capable, and his parents wanted him to get some work experience.

"Is there nothing at the club?" Ingrid asked. She pressed against Ned.

"Jane needs help in the front office," he said. "Data entry, invoices, that kind of stuff. It wouldn't be much fun."

Ingrid brightened. "But it's computer stuff. I bet he'd love that."

It was true. Adam loved all things tech-related. It was the people-related stuff he needed practice with. "Let me see what I can do. What about you? Any showings today?" Ned gazed at his wife. Ingrid's eyes were so green, so lovely. He wrapped his arms around her, letting his hands trail down across her equally lovely bottom. He was a lucky man. And at that moment as he held her that way, he hoped he might get even luckier.

But Ingrid wanted to talk. She propped herself up, and his hands slipped off her bottom. "Actually, I have news."

"Oh?" He reached for her, again.

"Guess what? I landed the Tree House!"

Tree House? This sounded exciting, but Ned was growing excited about something that did not involve talking. How long had it been? No matter. He needed to listen, really listen. Then, maybe, they could be excited *together*. "Is that the big cedar house overlooking the lake?" He pulled her closer.

"That's the one. Five thousand unsellable square feet, listed at an un-gettable two point five million. They signed the listing agreement yesterday."

"Wow. Why didn't you tell me last night?" He searched her eyes. This was big news.

"You've been so busy at work, and then the new neighbors . . ." Her voice trailed off.

"Honey, that's wonderful. Do you think you can sell it?"

Ingrid rolled over and away from him and stared at the ceiling.

"I have one new client from Boston. They're wealthy and quirky and they're looking for a weekend house."

"Maybe they'll be your buyer!"

Ingrid smiled. "Maybe."

"You know, I could use some new members," Ned said, rolling playfully on top of her. "Ask your buyer if they golf."

"Very funny."

"We should celebrate," Ned said.

"We should."

He pressed his hips against hers, hoping she'd feel how

celebratory he was feeling. To his delight, Ingrid pressed back.

Ned groaned with pleasure just as there was a pounding on their bedroom door.

"We're out of eggs!" It was Adam. Adam had eggs for breakfast every morning.

"There's cereal!" Ned shouted in vain, but Ingrid was already scooting out from under him.

"Sorry, honey," she said. "But we both know cereal won't satisfy him."

Ned stared at a small crack in the ceiling over their bed. The only thing he knew for sure was that *no one* would be satisfied that morning.

• • • • •

"First item on the agenda: new membership." They were the two words Ned dreaded most that summer.

Dick Delancey was looking right at him, grinning like a Cheshire cat, and for the life of him Ned could not imagine why. Dick was the board chairman. He had the same dismal numbers on the printout in front of him; the very numbers Ned had been staring at for all of June. As president, Dick should be committed to finding solutions and cheering on efforts. But all Ned got from Dick Delancey was pushback and complaints. "Fix it, Birch," he'd said, saddled up at the bar with a cold beer in front of him. "We hired you as next president to fix it."

Now, Ned rose from his chair, at the opposite head of the table. Among the eight board members were Neiman Shrive, and Bitsy Babcock, the sole female on the board, which Ned had helped facilitate. Neiman and Bitsy were elder members with a history and love of Mayhaven that rivaled Ned's. But the rest of the board were what the tennis pro had referred to in whispered tones as *good ol' boys*. "Delancey isn't a team player," she had warned Ned. "You're going to be on your own as president. And on the hook for whatever comes your way."

He'd start with the good news. "Last month we welcomed three new families to Mayhaven!"

"Did you say three?" Dick asked.

Ned nodded as Dick scribbled something in an oversized notepad. "Full membership for two of those families, and social membership for the third."

"So, if we're talking the full benefits of full membership fees, it's really more like two." Dick scribbled some more.

"I've met one of those new families: the Fullertons," Bitsy interjected. "Nice people. And the mother is an avid golfer, which will be good for us." Bitsy was right. Growing Mayhaven's female golf league was a top priority; not only were the women among some of the better golfers he'd seen, but when more than one member of a family played, it secured the chance they'd stay on. It was another reason Ned was also trying to firm up the children's program: parents invested in their kids. And Mayhaven needed to invest in the next generation of tennis players and golfers.

"How does that offset the building assessment?" Scooter Thornton asked. Scooter was a scratch golfer but just an okay kind of guy. He drank too much in the restaurant and was fond of telling jokes that became crasser with each beer. Of course, Dick loved him.

"Well, it doesn't offset it by much," Ned allowed. "We lost

the Hendersons to Fox Run." He tried not to let his posture sag along with the news.

"So no offset." More scribbling from Dick.

Ned was sorely tempted to ask Dick how he offset Coral's fling-bling. Instead he said, "Our summer camp program has its highest enrollment in club history: seventy-five kids."

Everyone around the table nodded, and Ned took heart. "My hope is that when camp is over, these kids continue with our fall and spring lesson programs. If that happens, we could be in a position to host a youth golf tournament."

"Wouldn't that be something," Bitsy said. "Maybe your girl will play again?"

Again, Ned tried not to let his posture sag.

Neiman Shrive snorted. "Sounds to me like the courts and course will get noisy."

Ned smiled. "We've got a new generation here we're trying to cultivate."

"Cultivate?" Dick screwed up his face like he'd been hit with a used diaper. "What are we, some kind of new age artsy learning center for kids?" He looked around him at the other board members. "I thought we were a country club."

Ned bit his lip. "We're an association of folks who, hopefully, become lifelong golfers and tennis players, Dick. That takes cultivation."

Dick said nothing. He leaned back in his seat, stretching lazily as if he were lounging in his own home theater. Dick was taking pleasure in watching Ned squirm.

"So, aside from kiddie camp, we've got the equivalent of one and a half new memberships."

Ned had had enough from Dick. "Which leads me to membership concerns." He lifted up the Pilgrim Box and shook it. "Since we put this out for comments, it's been filling up."

He ignored Neiman Shrive's eyeroll. "There are a few that stood out which I'd like to share with the board."

As soon as Ned read the member comment questioning the pilgrim logo, heads swiveled. "What's wrong with our pilgrim?" Art O'Connor barked. "He represents courage and strength."

Bitsy Babcock wagged a finger. "Notice you just said *he*? We also have a vibrant female membership, here. I think that's what this member is getting at."

From there the conversation careened out of Ned's control.

"So slap a woman pilgrim on the sign. Did they wear those wide-brimmed hats, too?"

"So now we're villainizing pilgrims?"

"I don't see how anyone could be offended. Do we even have any Native American members?"

"We do have membership with Mayflower lineage."

"Is that where the name Mayhaven came from?"

"Just cancel the pilgrim. That's what the young members want, isn't it? To cancel everything!"

Ned had to clap his hands over the uproar. "Clearly this member's comment raises a lot of questions. As such, I suggest we table this conversation for further review."

Dick Delancey shook his head. "Great. We're going to take down the pilgrim, a logo we've had since the club's inception, just because some woke mom got her tennis skirt in a twist. Shall we also give trophies to everyone at the next golf scramble, while we're at it?"

And just like that, everyone was shouting again.

Ned wished he had a gavel. His hands were raw from clapping by the time the table quieted down. "Alright, alright, clearly this is a matter that requires further consideration." There was a disgruntled vote to table discussion for a special session.

There was one more issue before they could adjourn.

"Where are things on the pond regeneration?" Teddy Winter asked. "Is it ready for fish?"

Ned felt the familiar tug of an oncoming eye twitch. For a water feature intended to be serene and healing, thus far the pond had imparted nothing but angst.

The pond was located on the ninth hole, once the most picturesque hole on the course. But over time the retaining wall had begun to leak, the filtration system had clogged, and due to aquatic imbalances the fishpond had eventually turned muddy and fish-less. Unlike other recent projects that raised assessment fees without providing any immediate aesthetic pleasure, the pond rejuvenation was highly visible. Members liked seeing what they were paying for, and it was by far the most visually appealing improvement of the year. But due to setbacks unforeseen and plentiful, the project had been delayed and run over budget. If there was anything Ned wanted to wrap up, it was the damn pond.

Dick Delancey brightened, for the first time, at the mention of the pond. "As you all know my darling daughter, Phoebe, is getting married here this summer. We plan to take family wedding photos at the pond. My wife, Coral, has an affinity for water features."

Unsurprisingly, Phoebe was as much a character as her parents. Since she'd been a teen, darling Phoebe had pilfered drinks from the bar and screamed at the tennis pro in front of everyone any time she missed a shot. As for Coral: last he'd heard, the front end of her Bentley was still dinged by some *errant caddy who must've hit it with a golf cart* after the Memorial Day dinner dance. There was never a mention of the one-hundred-year-old oak tree at the clubhouse entrance with a side mirror sticking out of its trunk; nor the Delancey bar tab that evening to the tune of seven whisky sours. In addition to the aforementioned water features, Coral also had an affinity for Jack Daniel's.

"Good news," Ned said. "The project is nearly done! Our aquatic specialist informs me that the plant life has taken hold and the pond is finally ready to support fish."

The announcement caused a happy ripple across the table.

"When do the fish come?"

Ned smiled. This was the best part. "We have ordered a very special variety of rare koi. The hatchery has scheduled a delivery for two weeks from tomorrow."

Bitsy clapped her hands together. "How wonderful! What kind of koi are they?"

"Hikarimono," Ned said, hoping he'd pronounced it correctly.

"Hikarimono!" the board echoed around the table. More resounding cheers!

Ned doubted that a single one of them had any clue what Hikarimono were. Until last week's conference call with the hatchery, he sure as hell had not.

He looked to Dick now. "Your daughter and wife will be

relieved to know that the koi are beautiful and on their way. We're expecting two hundred of them."

"Two hundred!" someone said.

Dick Delancey tapped his pen loudly against the table. "If only your membership numbers were so high."

DARCY

She wasn't hungry for dinner, but she was for information. Ever since he'd flashed her a smile in the hallway, she couldn't get that boy from the club out of her head. *Flick,* he'd said, when he'd introduced himself. Flick was cute. Though nothing like Spencer Delancey, let's be clear. Spencer was blond and broad and chiseled: textbook Ken doll. Flick was more . . . boyish. His dark hair was cut short, his skin the color of her favorite iced coffee. He'd looked more than a little lost standing under the chandelier in the foyer. And his clothes had been all wrong for the club. But that *smile.*

"So, how was camp today?" her mother asked too brightly, as they all sat down to eat.

Darcy blinked. She was beat from a long day with little people, and she really did not feel like regaling her mother with the exacting recap she seemed to require these days. Ever since she started working at the realty office, instead of being normal and plunking herself in front of the Bravo channel with a glass of wine like Lily's mom did (and she didn't even have a job), Ingrid Birch came home and cooked elaborate dinners and insisted on *family time.* She knew her mother wanted to spend time together, but all Darcy wanted was to be left alone. It was an exhausting dance.

"Darcy, honey? I asked how camp went?" her mother repeated.

"Fine," she replied, shoving a giant forkful of salad into her mouth before her mother could ask a follow-up.

In addition to pushing houses and aggressively parenting, Ingrid was working on communicating with her teens. The other night, Darcy had come downstairs to make popcorn and caught her mother bent over her laptop. When Darcy peered over her shoulder she caught the headline of the article she was reading: "Talking to Your Teen: Making the Most of Reluctant Conversation Partners." She'd had to bite her tongue.

Her mom had glanced up wearily, then back at her screen. "Maryanne says we need to help Adam engage in conversations." Maryanne was Adam's speech pathologist. But Darcy secretly wondered if the article had more to do with her.

She loved her mother. But sometimes Ingrid was just so . . . *Ingrid.*

As she'd waited for the popcorn to pop, Darcy couldn't help but scan the article. *Be sure to ask open-ended questions of your teen. Open-ended questions invite more detailed answers than those disappointing one-word replies, the killers of conversation.*

Why did adults feel the need to complicate everything? Maybe, like her, Adam just didn't feel like talking sometimes.

Now, Ingrid blinked expectantly at her over her untouched plate. "Just fine?"

Ingrid should probably reread that article; she hadn't learned to ask open-ended questions yet.

Darcy turned to her father, who had no excuse to look as

tired as he did: at least he'd spent his day in the air-conditioning instead of chasing kids with sunscreen and bug spray. "So, Dad—you had an interview?"

Her father nodded. "Yes. For kitchen help." He took a bite without offering anything more.

Darcy tried again. "Seems like a nice guy."

This got her father's attention. "You know him?"

"Not really. I ran into him in the hallway and showed him where your office was."

Her dad cocked his head. "Did you recognize him?"

Hadn't she just said that they'd met in the hallway? Maybe her father should read that article, too. "Should I have?"

Her father set down his fork. "So, I had a little surprise at work."

This cheered her mother right up. Darcy could read the thought bubble over Ingrid's head, *Finally, some information!*

"Turns out my interview was with our new neighbor, Flick Creevy." Her father shrugged. "He seemed like a nice kid. Decent candidate. It's too bad, really."

None of this was making any sense. Darcy knew all about the new neighbors—she'd heard the late-night music, she'd seen their obnoxious RV, she'd even smelled pot wafting from their yard one night. No one had mentioned a teenage boy. *That* she would've remembered.

"Flick is our *neighbor*?" Darcy's mind reeled. The cute boy from the hallway had not only applied for a job at Mayhaven, but also lived next door? She pushed her chair back. "I can't believe this."

"Wait, where are you going?" her mother stammered, looking in alarm at her full plate.

"Why didn't you guys tell me?" Darcy cried. Of all the meaningless things they talked about, no one had thought to mention a new teenage neighbor?

Her father was looking at her funny. "I thought we did. Besides, I only met him briefly that night I went over there to welcome them to the neighborhood."

That night. It was all her parents had talked about, in hushed tones, since. The big neighbor, Stan. His big RV. And the big slam in her father's face. All interesting intel, but not exactly relevant to Darcy. Like an opened Snap on Snapchat, fleeting and instantly replaced by the next. Still, someone *could have mentioned* a teenage son.

"Flick Creevy," Adam said, looking up from his dinner. "He moved in ten days ago. He drives a 2013 Chevy Malibu."

Yep, Adam had been listening.

"That's right," their mother said. "How did you know his car is a 2013? Have you met him, too?"

Adam shook his head.

Darcy pulled her chair back in. "So, are you giving him the job?" If Flick was going to be working at Mayhaven with her each day, she'd like to know.

This seemed to weigh on her father. "It's complicated."

"Well, I sure hope he's more polite than his stepfather," her mother said, standing up. She was the only one with a clean plate. When Adam tried to stand, too, she said, "Lemon meringue for dessert, for those who eat their dinner."

Adam plopped back down in his chair. "Chevy Malibus have been produced since 1964. The 327 V-8 had 300 horsepower." Adam took a bite of his dinner and continued with his mouth full. "It was raised to 350 in 1965."

Their father smiled. "How do you know all that?"

Adam took another bite. "I like Flick's car. I looked it up on YouTube. If he drives, he has a license. Which means he's at least sixteen." He looked at his sister. "You're sixteen, too."

Darcy rolled her eyes. Even Adam knew more about Flick than she did.

But their father was already changing the subject. "Do you know, your grandfather had a Chevy, too, Adam? It was a red Chevelle."

Adam froze in concentration. "Chevelle. What year?"

"I don't know for sure, but I was a kid when he got it. Must have been 1975 or 1976?"

Adam pushed his chair back. "I'm looking it up."

"Dessert!" their mother barked from the kitchen sink. Adam slumped back down. Darcy knew exactly how he felt.

"So, back to the interview," she prompted. Was she being too obvious?

Luckily her mother was even nosier. "Yes, you said you're desperate for kitchen help. So what makes you unsure about Flick Creevy?"

"The situation next door."

The situation: it sounded so dramatic, especially from someone as old as her father.

"The RV," Adam said decisively. "The RV is the situation."

They all gazed toward the window that looked out on the driveway, and the behemoth RV. "It's still there," her father said, gripping his napkin.

"But surely you can't hold that against Flick," her mother said.

It was one thing Darcy and her mother agreed on. "Yeah, he can't help it if his stepfather is an asshole," she added.

"Swear jar!" Adam leapt out of his seat and ran to the kitchen counter.

"Asshole is hardly a swear."

Adam plunked the jar down on the table. "Times two!"

"He's right," her mother said.

Darcy looked to her father, who rubbed his eyes wearily. "Times two."

"If he's a good candidate, it's only fair to give Flick the job." She wondered if Flick would be going to her high school. Based on the high-end cars in their driveway and the gleaming RV, they had money. Maybe he'd go to Thwarton Prep, like so many of the other kids at the club. She was glad Spencer Delancey didn't go to Thwarton.

"I'll think about it," her father said, rising slowly from the table. He looked exhausted, so Darcy let it go.

Adam leaned across the table and jingled the swear jar under her nose. "He said he's going to think about it. Now pay up."

Up in her room, Darcy opened her closet door and pushed the hangers of clothes aside so she could see better. The back of the closet floor was where she tossed things she didn't want, like old shoes or out of fashion purses. Hidden among them was an old duffel bag; it was what was in the duffel bag that she was after. As she knelt, she saw a flicker of gold. Shoved against the far side of the closet were her trophies, toppled over and half-covered by discarded clothes. Darcy sat on her haunches and regarded them.

They were only a handful of the many she'd won over the

years. The others her father stored on a shelf in his study downstairs, alongside his own, from his youth.

Hesitantly, she reached for the largest trophy, the one she hated most. It was from last October, when she'd won the Junior New England championship at Shuttle Meadow Golf Club. The last tournament she'd played, and the hardest one fought for.

Just holding the weight of the trophy in her hands brought back the memory of that day. Surrounded by hills, woods, and streams Shuttle Meadow had been challenging, but Vince had reminded her that she was used to the varied terrain of Mayhaven, and Darcy went in feeling strong. Despite that, she had not started well. On the first two holes, she double-bogeyed, and was behind the leader by five strokes. She parred the next, but the pattern went on and she finished in a lousy fourth place. Maya Lee, who led by seven strokes by the end of the first day, had run into her at the buffet under the big white tent that evening. Darcy appreciated Maya, beyond her obvious skill. She was low-key and friendly, no matter how good or bad she'd played.

"Congrats," she'd told Maya.

"It's just day one," Maya said, winking. "Tomorrow you'll be coming for me, along with the rest of them."

It was true. You wanted to start strong, for the mental edge more than anything. But Darcy had played long enough to know that on the second day leaders could have their edge swept away with just one bad drive or missed putt. Once the technical stuff crept in, so, too, did the shaking of confidence. Darcy still had a chance to catch her.

But to her chagrin, the next day she started out just as she had the first: inconsistent in her irons, and unable to secure that feeling she got when her nerves settled and her muscle memory took over.

"Shake it off and start fresh on the next hole," Vince had coached. "You play your best when you're having fun. Imagine we're back at Mayhaven, just practicing."

He was right, and she tried to follow his advice. But then she sliced the ball into the trees on the fourth hole. When she passed her parents standing in the crowd along the fairway, Darcy couldn't bring herself to make eye contact with her father. It wasn't just Vince; it was her father who she really wanted to make proud.

But then something happened when she made the turn. Her irons, which had been troubling her all morning, settled into her grip as if they were extensions of her own arms. Suddenly, the ball was flying off her clubs. She crushed her next three drives. With her nerves settling, Darcy found her rhythm. And by the final hole of the day, Darcy was one stroke behind a new leader, Ellis Quinn, with Maya now in third. On her last putt, Ellis choked. Darcy made an eagle. When she looked up and saw her father's face in the crowd, it was one of the best moments of her life.

What followed, after the awards ceremony that night, was one of the worst.

Now, hands shaking with anger, Darcy shoved the trophy back into the closet. She grabbed the black duffel bag and unzipped it. At the bottom was the green plastic jar she'd been looking for. She unscrewed the jar of weight-loss pills and tipped a handful of capsules into her hands. Their bright yellow color was hope. Summer. Sunshine. She'd discovered them on TikTok, thanks to an influencer she admired for her taut midriff and effortless style. Despite the fact she was Darcy's age, she looked eons more sophisticated. Worldly. Sexy. The influencer claimed she'd been taking those pills for just one month and was already down fifteen pounds. It was that easy. It was even easier to buy them at the link provided. No questions asked.

The bottle came three days later, and though she'd worried her parents might see it, everyone was so distracted with their own problems that summer that no one in her family noticed. She beat them to the mailbox and hid the bottle in her room. That was less than a week ago. She'd lost two pounds already. The pills made her feel jittery and she peed a lot, but it was no big deal.

The directions called for one capsule each day. Darcy paused, before popping two in her mouth and taking a long swig from her water bottle. Then she shoved the duffel bag back into her closet, beneath the clothes and shoes and purses, where her nosy mother wouldn't find it and her father wouldn't think to look.

When she went to the mirror, she imagined a new girl staring back at her with the same green eyes. A girl who didn't think about trophies or the game or the look on her father's face that day. A girl who didn't miss the weight of a four iron in her hand or the sun on her back as she surveyed the fairway from the highest point on the course. Darcy tucked a strand of stray curl behind her ear. She wondered how long it would take until it felt that way for real.

FLICK

Flick was lying in bed thinking about two things: the fact that the stupid job at the club was something he might actually want. And the girl. What was going on behind those green eyes when she smiled?

His phone dinged. It was his best friend from home, Mateo. Mateo had texted each night since Flick had moved away. The texts weren't long or particularly interesting, but they were comforting: a small lifeline back home to Queens. A link to who Flick was in this strange wooded world of Massachusetts suburbia.

What's up?

Nothing.

Get that job?

No man. Not my scene.

Why?

Rich white people scene.

Well now you've got the rich thing going for you.

Shut up.

A moment later, his phone dinged again. Flick stared at the strange number before opening the text.

Hi, Flick, Ned Birch here. It was nice meeting with you. The job is yours if you want it.

Flick stared at the screen to make sure he'd read it right. Wait until his mother heard this. Wait until Mateo did.

He barely hesitated before replying.

Thanks, Mr. Birch. I would like the job.

There was a pause followed by the line of dots as Ned texted back. Flick held his breath.

I'd hoped you'd say that. Go look on your doorstep.

Flick jogged downstairs, past the living room where his mother and Stan were watching TV, and pulled the front door open. There, folded neatly on the steps, was a blue polo shirt. Flick lifted it up: on the right breast was the Mayhaven pilgrim logo.

"Mom," he called out, holding it up. "Guess what?"

Josie stared at the shirt with a look of confusion until Flick pointed to the logo. "I got the job."

"You got it? Oh my God, you got it!" She leapt off the couch and hugged him hard. Stan managed to pull his gaze away from the screen long enough to grunt congrats.

"Wait. Where'd the shirt come from?" his mother wanted to know. "Were you saving this as a surprise?"

"No." Flick shook his head. "Mr. Birch must've just dropped it off."

"Birch?" Stan practically choked on a chip he was eating. "Are you telling me that guy works at the club?" He snorted. "Makes sense. So uptight and all."

Josie looked confused. "Our neighbor, Mr. Birch, works there, too?"

"Yeah. He's my boss."

She looked to Stan. "Why do you say he's uptight?"

Stan shrugged. "I've seen him around." So he hadn't told Josie about the night he slammed the door in Mr. Birch's face.

"You're going to have to be nicer, Stan," Josie said. "Especially since Flick works for him now."

"Nicer? I'm like the nicest guy around. Look at all the happy customers I served all those years. All those old ladies, all those suits . . ." The way he talked you'd think Stan had served his country.

Josie wasn't having it, but she did walk over and place her hands lovingly on either side of his big face. "Baby, no one here knows who the Dry Cleaning King is. You're new. We're all new. Let's play nice."

Back upstairs, Flick tugged off his T-shirt and tried on the polo. It was a perfect fit. How did Ned Birch know his size? Moreover, how did Ned Birch know he'd take the job?

He texted Mateo back.

Guess what?

What?

You're talking to the new kitchen assistant at a country club.

There was a long pause. Then his phone dinged.

Don't turn into an asshole.

Flick smiled. No chance.

His phone dinged again. And don't screw it up.

• • • • •

There were two shifts each day at Mayhaven: lunch service and dinner, and for his first day Flick would be working the lunch shift. On his way out, Josie stopped him for a good look. "Look at my little working man! So handsome."

If Mateo could've seen him, he'd have ribbed him endlessly. Ned had said navy and khaki were staff uniform, and that they'd provide the shirt. Flick figured navy blue would be good for hiding stains in the kitchen, but he was a little worried about the khaki. Luckily, he did have one nice pair of beige pants from his mother and Stan's wedding ceremony, so he'd thrown those on with a pair of dark Converse sneakers.

The whole way to the club his stomach fluttered. The first thing he noticed as he traipsed up the walkway were the clusters of kids: playing on the tennis courts, filing down the hill in swimsuits, finger painting at a picnic table under a white tent. Little kids were everywhere; and so were the teenagers who worked with them. Flick scanned their faces, trying to locate the girl from the hallway the day before—Darcy, she'd said. There were a couple of what Mateo would call *Chads* standing around instead of working, a handful of girls at the painting table, and a pretty blonde who laughed too loudly. But no sign of Darcy.

Inside the clubhouse was a stark contrast to the noise and energy outside. Flick trotted down the quiet hall, past the trophy case of serious faces, to Mr. Birch's office. Mr. Birch looked up from his computer and grinned widely. Was this guy always this happy?

"You made it!" he said, and Flick wondered if there had been doubt.

"Yes, sir." Flick paused in the doorway. "Should I go up to the kitchen?"

"Yes, Mossimo wants to start you out gently, with lunch service. Once you get your sea legs, he'll move you up to dinner."

Flick nodded.

"But, on occasion, there may be a need for you to fill in elsewhere. You may drive the drink cart out on the course or work the snack shack down at the lake. Sound good?"

The drink cart sounded good to him. And the lake sounded really good. He hoped there were some cute girls in bikinis, not just the older ladies he'd seen around so far.

Mossimo was pretty much what Flick had expected: meticulous and demanding. Not that his demands were unreasonable—there were just a lot of them. Clean workstations, timely prep, remembering *the regulars*, the recipes that were served almost nightly: seafood chowder, baby beet salad, the grilled focaccia with heirloom tomatoes. "That's kitchen life!" Mossimo would sing out (not happily) across the kitchen when swiping carrot peels off an untidy prep counter and holding them up in his fist. "Keep your stations clear." Clean workstations were just the beginning. Because the staff was small, everyone was on deck, whether you had culinary chops or not. "You will mop floors and do shelf inventory. You will chop vegetables and even prepare sauces."

"Today?"

"Today we start with beurre blanc."

Mossimo had to be crazy—the closest thing Flick had made to a beurre blanc was a package of powdered béarnaise sauce for a steak one Christmas. He was doomed.

But there was no time for self-doubt. The chef stood beside him, adding tiny cubes of chilled butter to the simmering wine in the pan. "You cannot stop whisking," he explained. "If you stop, it won't emulsify." Flick had never used that word in his life, but looking into the bowled concoction in front of him it somehow felt familiar. "Keep blending, until you achieve velvet," Mossimo directed.

Flick was not alone. Ricky, the sous chef, worked the more advanced dishes and seemed to be deputy to Mossimo's sheriff. Ricky was lean and wiry and wore a Vans snapback backward, which surprised Flick. Mossimo must really like the guy. Wendy, the head server—he guessed she was in her early twenties—didn't seem to be in charge of much in the kitchen but clearly ran the show in the dining room and snack shack. Flick watched her chew out a girl who showed up late. He'd try to steer clear of Wendy. Joe did dishes in the back, and Flick wondered what else—he rarely saw the guy.

While others darted about prepping lunch service, Flick manned his saucepan. Whisking over the gas range meant he had to wipe his forehead repeatedly: if he dripped sweat into the sauce he was DOA. Mossimo popped by twice to check in on the sauce. The first time he just looked. "No. I said velvet."

The second time he tasted. "Next one, more white wine."

But it couldn't have been terrible, because he set it aside and told Flick to move on to salad station. "Lunch is a lot of salad."

All through lunch Flick never got a chance to see who was in the dining room or how it was going. The kitchen was full steam.

"Mr. Flick, I need two chicken Caesars, one no dressing. Ricky, one halibut and two Wagyu."

For two hours, Flick's only job was to assemble salads and man the sauces. But it wasn't easy. Learning to emulsify the beurre blanc sauce for fish was tricky enough, but if your sauce wasn't ready in time for plating while the halibut was hot out of the pan, into the trash went the cold fish. And off your paycheck it came. "That's kitchen life. Get it right!"

Get it right. Flick wiped his brow, thinking that's what he'd been trying to do since he moved here. Turned out adjusting to small-town life was as complicated as a beurre blanc.

By two o'clock the orders slowed, and the kitchen went from clattering pots to a gentler hum. At two-thirty Mossimo announced lunch service was over. Everyone stopped for a beat. There was chatter and relief, followed swiftly by cleanup.

As Flick wiped down the salad station and brought his saucepans to the sink, Mossimo found him. "Mr. Flick, good work today."

"Thank you," Flick said. He was exhausted and his feet throbbed. He was pretty sure he didn't smell so great, either. But he'd made it. Almost.

“Remember, you’re on until four-thirty,” Ricky said, maneuvering around him with a giant mixing bowl crusted with some kind of dough.

There was a lull between lunch and dinner at the club, but sometimes members wandered in for a drink or bar snacks. “Apron off and hands washed,” Mossimo said, before whisking Flick’s apron unceremoniously over his head. “There is no lunch served after hours, no exceptions. There is a light snack menu until dinner.”

Flick’s head was already spinning at the idea of taking someone’s order and not dropping plates. He’d never waited tables before; what about that beach snack bar Mr. Birch had mentioned? But he was too afraid to ask.

“Here.” Mossimo handed him a printed menu. *Charcuterie. Small salads. Chips and smoked trout dip.* “I don’t want to see you behind the bar; it is the bartender’s zone, not yours. Your zone is kitchen and dining. Got it?”

Flick wasn’t sure he’d gotten any of that, really. He looked through the service doors at the mostly empty dining room. There were a couple of older men finishing up their lunch. And that was it. “Traffic is light. Pay attention and smile.”

Flick forced a smile. “Got it.”

“I will see you tomorrow.”

With Mossimo gone, the kitchen felt instantly lighter.

“So Mossimo is done for the day?”

Ricky laughed. “As if. He’s going home to rest before dinner service. He’s back on from five to close.”

“Wow.” Flick couldn’t imagine the rush of lunch service followed by cleanup, and then gearing up to do it all over again into the night.

As he scrubbed a pot, Ricky shook his head. "Lunch is for lambs, kid. Dinner is for lions. Wait until you do a Saturday night event. It's mayhem."

Flick considered this. "Are the tips at least good?"

"Yeah. But the demands are high. Don't get me wrong, some of the members are good folks, but some are real assholes."

Flick peered out the porthole window of the service door to the dining room floor. Still just the two old men. He should probably go ask.

"Check, please," one of the men said as Flick approached.

"Sure thing, sir." Flick cleared their lunch plates carefully, then remembered what Mossimo had said about member tabs. "May I have your member number, please?"

The other man looked up at him, not unkindly. "You're new here."

It wasn't a question.

"Yes, sir. First day. I'm Flick Creevy."

"Marty Robbins and Jack Gorman. I'm seven-twenty. Put it on mine today."

"Nice to meet you both." Flick smiled and took their plates to the kitchen as the two embarked on an argument about whose turn it was to pay.

As soon as the bill was paid (Marty won) the dining room was empty. Flick was about to find Ricky to ask about setting tables for dinner when he heard the thunder of footsteps coming up the stairs. A group of four guys, about his age, rounded the corner talking loudly.

Without waiting, they made their way noisily through the dining room and took the corner table by the windows overlooking the deck and the course.

Flick wiped his hands and made his way over.

The boys were still talking, ignoring him. Flick cleared his throat, awkwardly. "The kitchen is closed for lunch," he said politely, "but we're serving bar snacks."

The one who'd led the group in eyed him like he was interrupting their conversation. "We're ordering burgers."

Had he not just heard?

"I'm sorry, we just closed."

He leaned back in his chair and stared right through Flick. He had one of those preppy mops of hair that guys like him flipped out of their eyes by constantly tossing their heads. Hair-flippers, Mateo called them.

He looked ready to argue, but one of the others, who looked like he played college football, spoke up. "You said bar snacks. What've you got for those?"

Flick held his hands behind his back and recited the list from memory. "Charcuterie, pita chips and smoked trout dip, and a spring mix salad."

"Smoked trout?" One of the guys laughed. "Gross."

It was actually good, Flick had tried it; but he kept that bit to himself. "If you want chips, we could substitute guacamole for the trout dip," he said instead.

The footballer nodded. "Okay, two of those. And also a spring mix salad."

"Jesus, Trevor. What're you, watching your figure?"

Trevor shrugged good-naturedly. "Gotta keep the girls interested, man."

There was some ribbing and then the hair-flipper turned to Flick. "You said bar snacks. How about a couple beers for my friends?"

Flick felt his chest thump. No way were these guys a day older than he was. Mossimo had said card anyone who looks younger than fifty. That member kids get cheeky. But it was the last thing Flick wanted to do.

All four boys were staring at him now, waiting to see what he'd do. Flick swallowed. "Sure thing. I just need to see an ID."

The hair-flipper made a faux move to reach for his back pocket. "Damn. Left it in the car. Look, I know you're new here, but we're good."

Trevor nudged him. "Next time, Spencer."

Spencer. So that was the hair-flipper's name.

"No. We worked hard today, boys. We deserve a few brews." Spencer waited, staring at Flick.

Well, Flick could play this game, too. He stared back, willing his hands to stay still by his side. "I'm sorry, the boss insists on checking ID's."

"Oh, he does, does he? Do you know who I am?" Spencer rubbed his chin, thoughtfully. "No, you wouldn't. You're a newbie."

Flick blinked. This kid was the last person he wanted to know.

"My father is the chairman of the board, newbie. Does the name Delancey ring a bell?"

Now one of the other guys chimed in. "Let it go, man."

But Spencer wasn't that kind of guy, Flick could tell. "Look, I have to follow the rules."

"No, you look." Spencer Delancey narrowed his eyes. "Rules don't apply to everyone around here. You'll learn."

Flick didn't respond to threats. But he also had a job to do. He wished Mossimo was there.

"I'll be back with your chips," Flick muttered, turning on his heel.

He shoved through the kitchen doors so hard they swung back on their hinges. Ricky turned around. "What's up?"

"Nothing," Flick lied.

Ricky wiped his hands on a dish towel and went to look through the dining room window for himself. "Ah, Delancey. He's a little prick. Ignore him."

Flick tried. He served the table their bar snacks and refilled their waters twice, and he almost managed until he got to the bill.

"Put it on my tab," Spencer said.

"May I have your member number, please?"

Spencer snorted. "Number one."

No one said anything. Flick wasn't sure if he was serious or not. He paused, his pen hovering over the bill.

Spencer glared back at him. "I said, number one."

Flick handed over the pen, eyes averted as Spencer scribbled something in the tip line and signed the bill.

"My great-grandfather was the first member to join this club. I'm legacy here." Spencer stood, letting his napkin slip to the floor, and pressed the bill hard against Flick's chest. "Don't forget it, newbie."

As the group left, laughter following them out of the dining room, Flick stole a look at the bill.

The tip line: *$1.*

The signature line: *Number One.*

NED

For most people, a Friday night in summer meant a slow pull on a cold beer, a dip in the lake, or a stroll down Main Street for ice cream. For Ned, it meant the busiest part of his week was just beginning. Saturday afternoon was the first golf scramble of the season. Saturday night was a surf and turf dinner at the restaurant. Sunday morning the course was rented for a private party brunch. And Ned would need to be in attendance at everything. When he pulled into his driveway he parked in the ominous shadow of his neighbor's RV.

Tinged in late-day sun, it shone like a beacon of incivility. Ned chewed his bottom lip. He gazed across the way into the neighbor's backyard. Sure enough, still tied to the base of a tree was their old Halloween scarecrow Stan had plucked from their trash. It still wore Ned's Red Sox T-shirt, or at least what was left of it. Ned shaded his eyes for a better look: dead-center in the scarecrow's chest two arrows jutted out. Ned needed a beer.

He glanced up at his own cheerful front door. Inside, Ingrid and Adam would be waiting for him to join them for dinner. It was Friday, which meant green was the color of the day: there'd be salad or asparagus or chicken with pesto. Darcy was home, too, but likely not for long. Since she was no longer competing in tournaments on weekends, her surplus energies had pivoted sharply to burnishing her social life. The negotiations would begin the moment he walked in the door: *where* she wanted to go, *who* she wanted to go out with, how *unfair* her curfew was. The debate was never ending. Ingrid would already be broken down, and she'd be looking to Ned to pass the baton to. How much simpler and happier life was when Darcy was still playing golf.

Ned allowed himself one more un-assaulted moment alone in his car. He tried to focus on something cheerful. Right in front of him bloomed his prized heirloom rosebushes, looking promising this early in the season. He tried to stay there on the soothing pink-petaled meditation of his roses, but his gaze got away from him, swinging back to the RV like a dog to a bone. There would be no respite indoors or out.

Hoping to salvage a moment to himself, Ned let himself in the front door as quietly as humanly possible. Fritzy waited, wagging with his whole body. "Shhh, good boy," Ned whispered, bending to pat the dog. Maybe he'd make it out back to his new pool before anyone noticed he was home.

Adam assailed him first, hopping down the stairs in his Friday-green socks, cheeks already flushed with outrage. "The internet is down again! I was in the middle of a carburetor repair video on YouTube and it died."

Ned closed his eyes. "The carburetor or the video?"

Adam huffed. "It's not funny."

"Oh good, you're home." Ingrid appeared in the foyer. "I have to run back to the office. Those clients from Boston? They want to see the Tree House again! So I've got to put some comps together. You'll need to start dinner. Oh—and, the printer is jammed. So I need your help."

Ned slipped out of his sneakers, still sandwiched between Adam and Ingrid in the entryway. No one moved. He looked past them to the blue promise of pool water through the back windows. "I guess I'll start with the printer."

Ned was thirsting for that cold beer, but it would have to wait. He squeezed past his family into the kitchen. Adam and Fritzy trailed in tandem.

"You need to call the cable company," Adam huffed. "I cannot go on like this."

"I think they're closed now, buddy." The printer was at a small workstation in the rear, which Ingrid liked to call the command center. Indeed, the red error light was blinking angrily. Ned knew how it felt. He inspected the connections and flipped the printer switch on and off. To Adam he said, "I'll call the cable company first thing tomorrow."

"*Tomorrow?*" Adam looked ready to pass out.

"Still blinking," Ingrid said.

Ned checked the paper tray, the ink cartridges, and the connections again. The red light blinked on.

"Speaking of tomorrow," Ingrid interjected. "Stan is still shooting that poor scarecrow. Every time I go in the backyard, it's: *whump, whump, whump*. It doesn't feel safe. Maybe we talk to the neighbors. Or call town hall about regulations. We need to do something."

We meaning *Ned*. He smacked the printer hard, twice. Miraculously it hummed to life and the light stopped blinking. Ingrid clapped. "Don't forget about dinner."

He'd almost made it to the fridge when Darcy's voice rang out from the doorway.

"You're home! So, there's this party tonight, well more like a gathering, really, and Lily really wants to go, even though *I could care less*, but she's a good friend, and, actually, I haven't gone out in ages, so I figured . . ."

Ned closed his eyes. "Your father needs a minute!" There, he'd referred to himself in the third person and his voice had come out like a sharp bark. But it had the hoped-for effect.

All three faces of his loving family stared back at him, unblinking. Good! He opened the fridge, retrieved a beer, and all three started talking again, voices tumbling over each other like a burst spigot.

"I need to give Lily an answer right now!"

"How am I supposed to finish my car video? I need Wi-Fi!"

"Kids, your father just said—"

Beer secured, Ned walked wordlessly through the three of them. The dog, more clever than the rest, was already in position by the patio slider. "Hello, Fritz."

Ned slid the door ajar just enough for Fritzy to slip through with him before slamming it closed.

The beer was extra cold, and Fritzy found a fat squirrel to chase across the unmown lawn. He was not struck by an arrow sitting poolside. Ned's night was turning around.

• • • • •

Around nine-thirty, Ned padded out of the bathroom in his slippers and made a beeline for bed. They'd made it through another night. Ingrid had shown the Tree House, dinner had been served, and even better: Ned had good news to share.

"I found Adam a job," he said.

Ingrid was already in bed with a book, Fritzy curled at her feet. "You did? Doing what?"

"Jane needs part-time help in the office, and so does Mossimo in the kitchen. I figure Adam can split his day between the two."

"That's wonderful, honey! The variety will be good for him."

Ned slipped beneath the sheets, feeling hopeful. Adam was down the hall gaming with a friend—the internet had gloriously restored itself. Darcy was at Lily's. The house was quiet, the bed sumptuous. So, too, was Ingrid whose lovely long legs stretched out from under the covers. Ned had rolled over and reached for his wife when the air began to vibrate. Fritzy's head snapped up. Ingrid groaned.

"You have got to be kidding." Ned dragged himself out of bed and went to the window. Across the way the Crenshaws' pool was lit up, the lights flashing to the thumping bass.

"I'm going over there."

"Now?" Ingrid sat up. "I don't think that's a good idea."

"So we suffer another sleepless night as Stan Crenshaw holds us hostage with his obnoxious music? I've got the first scramble of the season tomorrow. I need to be up early."

"We're sure it's Stan?"

"Flick confirmed as much at his interview. Poor kid—he's got to be up early for work tomorrow, too."

Ingrid made a face. "Won't this be awkward for Flick if we complain and then he has to see you at work tomorrow?"

Ned groaned. He did not point out that *he* was the one going over to do the complaining. "Yes, Ingrid. Stan Crenshaw is making this awkward for all of us, isn't he?"

He changed back into clothes and decided to take Fritzy with him. Everyone loved Fritzy. Downstairs at the door the dog did three insane circles around Ned's feet, entangling both of them in his leash; he never went out this late. Something quite good must be about to happen.

As he crossed the dark yard, Ned could not hear the peepers or the rustle of leaves in the summer breeze; everything was swallowed by the *thump thump thump* of the clamoring bass. He strode to the front door, Fritzy trotting beside him.

Ned pressed the doorbell and stepped back. It was déjà vu standing there on the front step; and just like the last time, nobody came to the door. "Well, no wonder," he said to Fritzy. "They can't hear a damn thing, either!" He pressed the ringer again, holding it for a long time.

"They must all be out back," he said. Fritzy whined excitedly.

Ned did not want to risk trespassing on the Crenshaws' property in the dark, especially given the crossbow. But he couldn't very well go home, either. He needed to sleep. And Ingrid would be waiting to hear that he'd resolved it. And there was the principle, damn it . . . the Crenshaws needed to get with the program on Maple Street.

So he strode back across the lawn, around the RV, behind his house to his own backyard where a privacy fence separated the two properties. It was too tall to peek over, so Ned let Fritzy off his leash and found a bucket to stand on.

No sooner had Ned climbed atop the bucket when the full picture of debauchery come into view. The entire scene was cast in a purple glow from the pool water to the liquor bottles lining the outdoor bar to the smoking grill that Ned had to admit smelled enticing. People milled about in clusters, some bobbing their heads and moving their hips to the beat.

Ned narrowed his eyes. Was that Frank Miller, from up the street?

An absurd peal of laughter rippled across the pool deck and Ned recognized the high-pitched voice of Frank's wife, Eileen, at the same time he recognized her mop of curly dark hair. The Millers were a part of this insanity? It was just not possible. Frank Miller was a civil engineer who hated social gatherings and, as far as Ned could tell, most people. Frank never lasted more than ten minutes at the annual cul-de-sac Christmas party. But here they were!

His eyes traveled to a tall, willowy man bent over a table of food: Good grief, was that Jonathan Arbuckle? Jonathan was their head of neighborhood watch, always getting after people about speed limits and noise pollution. Was it possible he was here to serve a notice, but got distracted by the chips and dip? But no, there was his wife, Barbara—holding a giant margarita. The whole neighborhood knew Barbara did not drink. Not so much as a sip of eggnog for the cul-de-sac caroling. And yet—from the way she wobbled across the patio, Barbara was bombed.

In the midst of this dubious gathering stood Stan Crenshaw. His big mouth was flapping away in conversation, though Ned wondered how anyone could hear a damn thing he was saying. Apparently Eileen Miller had exceptional hearing because she threw her curly-haired head back and cackled at whatever Stan said. Astonishingly, others joined in. Loudest of all, Nathan

Clumpett, who lived alone with his cat and barely spoke. Was *everyone* from Maple Street here?

It was outrageous. Not only were the most antisocial of his neighbors here socializing, bathed in vulgar landscape lighting and déclassé company, but there was the glaring fact of the matter: Ned and Ingrid appeared to be the only ones not invited.

Awash with fresh irritation, Ned stood taller on his plastic bucket and waved his arm in the direction of the offending host. "Hello? Stan!"

Stan did not hear, but Jonathan Arbuckle did. He lifted his face from the chip bowl, looking about for the source. Ned waved again from his side of the fence.

"Ned?" Jonathan squinted and ambled over, bowl in hand. "Is that you, Ned?"

"Yes," Ned hissed. "I'm trying to get my neighbor's attention, but he can't hear me over all this noise."

Jonathan smiled. "You mean Stan? He's right over there."

"Yes, I can see him, Jonathan."

"He's great!" Jonathan stuffed another handful of chips in his mouth as if Ned were standing at the party with him instead of flailing from the other side of the fence.

"Can you get Stan's attention for me, please?"

"Why don't you just come over?"

"Because I wasn't *invited*," Ned said, stating the obvious.

"Oh. Too bad. Great party." Across the yard, his wife hooted in unwitting agreement.

"Is it?" Ned wanted to shake Jonathan Arbuckle. "What would be *great* is if you could let Stan know I'd like a quick word. But please be discreet about it."

Jonathan nodded. "You bet." Then he turned and cupped his free hand around his mouth. "Hey, Stan! Ned here wants to talk to you."

Heads snapped in their direction, eyes squinting through the barbecue haze. Barbara Arbuckle hooted again. "Ned Birch. Is that *you*?"

Ned forced himself to smile. "Sorry to interrupt. Stan, if I might have a word?"

Stan turned down the music but stayed right where he was. Was he really going to challenge Ned to shout across the yard in front of everyone? Ned was debating what to do when, finally, a small woman with long dark hair walked out of the house with a tray of food. She followed her guests' gazes to the fence. "Mr. Birch?"

Mercifully, she set the tray down and hurried over.

Josie Crenshaw was pint-sized with a gallon-sized smile. "I'm so glad to meet you! I wanted to thank you for hiring Flick." She had to stand on tiptoes to shake his hand.

"Nice to meet you, too."

"Flick is very happy to have the job. It's hard moving to a new town at his age." Her large brown eyes shone as she spoke about her son. Then, as if realizing the awkwardness of the conversation over the fence, her brow furrowed. "Is there anything I can help you with?"

Ned glanced in the direction of her husband. "Though I hate to interrupt your evening, I'm afraid the music is preventing my wife and me from sleeping. And as you may know from Flick's schedule, Saturdays are early starts at the club."

"Oh gosh, I'm so sorry." Josie turned and shouted. "Stan! Turn the music down."

But Stan was already closing the gap between them. "I already did, sweet stuff."

Ned could not imagine calling Ingrid that, in private or public.

"Something wrong?" Stan asked turning his unsmiling focus on Ned.

"I just told you." Josie poked his thick side. "The music is keeping the poor neighbors awake."

"That so?"

Ned's bucket wobbled beneath him, and he gripped the lip of the fence. "That's so." Then, because he liked Flick and Josie seemed so friendly, "We would really appreciate it if you'd turn it down."

Stan crossed his arms. "I would've thought a guy could listen to a little music in his own backyard, here in the quiet countryside." Again with the country stuff. Ned was tempted to bring up the crossbow and ask if he'd shot anything good for dinner.

Josie looked between the two men. *"Stan."*

Without taking his eyes off of Ned, Stan shrugged. "We'll try to keep it down."

Ned forced himself to say it: "Thank you. Enjoy your party." Then with as much dignity as one can muster from atop a plastic bucket fenced out of a party he was not invited to, Ned lowered himself until the Crenshaws' faces disappeared from view.

DARCY

"How about we skip stones?" Darcy tried. She was planted in the sand next to Elly Watson, who was still refusing to go anywhere near the lake.

"No." Elly didn't even look at her.

Darcy was losing patience. It was steaming hot out, and for the first time all summer she was feeling pretty hot herself, in her bikini. When she'd stepped on the scale that morning she was down three more. Her stomach cramped with hunger, or maybe it was the pills working, but whatever—it was working! If only she had the chance to actually get near the water and show off her sacrifices.

"What if I twirl you around in the shallow end? We won't go any deeper than a few inches."

"No."

To make things worse, Darcy heard Spencer Delancey coming up behind her. He must've come down to the beach to swap lifeguard shifts with Craig, who'd been in the chair all morning. "Hey, man. Sorry, I'm late," she heard Spencer say.

Darcy didn't dare turn around.

"You going to Reagan's tonight?" Craig asked.

"Yeah. You?"

There was the thud of feet landing in the sand as Craig hopped down from the chair. "I've got this stupid family dinner with my grandparents, but I should be able to get out of there by nine."

"Cool. It's supposed to be a big one. He got two kegs."

Craig laughed. "That should last an hour. Save me some."

So, Lily had been right. As soon as she'd arrived at work that morning, Lily was waiting for her. She'd overheard that Reagan Rogers, a senior, was hosting, but so far neither she nor Darcy had been able to get any details. Darcy was pretty sure Ashley Riley would know, but she wasn't about to ask her.

"What're you two thinking? It's too hot not to be swimming."

Spencer was standing with his hands on his tanned hips, looking down at them. She sucked in her stomach and nodded toward Elly.

"She says she hates the water."

Elly nodded, unmoved by either of the teenagers staring at her.

Spencer scoffed. "No one hates the water."

"I've been trying all week," she told him. From down the beach, Lily was watching them. The girl had radar for Spencer. "I've got to keep an eye on my other campers," Darcy said, not wanting to look like she was slacking at the lake, especially in front of a lifeguard.

As she went to stand, Spencer held out his hand and she let him pull her up to her feet. She was especially glad to be wearing her good bikini.

"Thanks," she said, ducking her chin and smiling like she

did for a selfie. She sure hoped he wouldn't watch her backside as she walked down to the water. But even worse, Spencer started to walk alongside her.

"Can she swim?"

"Who knows? Her parents said she can dog-paddle, but I can't get her to even take the test." She stole a glance at him and was surprised to see a look of genuine concern.

"Then I guess that's what we're going to have to do."

"What?" Before Darcy could say anything more, Spencer turned and marched back up the beach to where Elly sat.

Darcy watched as he plopped down next to her and tried to start a conversation. She almost laughed when Elly turned away as if she'd smelled something bad. Apparently Spencer Delancey's charm did not extend to the six-year-old masses. Well, give Elly time . . .

And then something unreal happened: Spencer said something and Elly nodded. When he stood up, Elly did, too. Darcy's jaw fell open as he held out his hand, and Elly Watson took it. She walked with him right past Darcy and to the water's edge, still gripping Spencer's hand. At the water's edge, Elly put on the brakes.

Darcy watched in disbelief as Spencer bent down to her level. His lips moved, but she could not make out his words. And then, after one long pause, the two of them waded into the lake up to Elly's knees. Moments later, Elly was splashing around with Spencer. Other kids came to join. They shrieked and laughed, and before the other lifeguard blew the whistle for swim time to be over, Elly Watson was soaked, head to toe. She had not yet tried to swim, but she was smiling.

Spencer strode out of the water and slicked his wet hair back like a Greek god. Then he flashed Darcy a thumbs-up.

What did you say to her? she mouthed.

Tell you later, he mouthed back.

Darcy felt herself melting into the sand. *Later.* Spencer was going to Reagan Rogers's house party. That meant she and Lily had to go, too, if it was the last thing they did.

• • • • •

"Girls, it's getting late," her mother called upstairs. "Didn't you say your movie started at nine-thirty?"

Going to the movies was a front. No way her parents would let Darcy go to a party without a million questions and rules. "Yeah," Darcy lied, hurrying downstairs with Lily on her tail. "We're leaving now. Don't want to miss the previews."

"What time does the movie end?" Her mother put the kettle on. That was Ingrid: making tea, when she could be making a martini on a weekend night. Darcy would be *so* different when she was fifty.

"Uh, around eleven-thirty? You don't have to wait up. We'll come straight home and be super quiet coming in."

She was ready for Ingrid to object, but to her surprise her mother handed her a Ziploc bag of cookies. "Sneak them into the movies in your purse." Ingrid had been on the phone all day with her client from Boston who might be making an offer on the stupid Tree House. When her mother got stressed out she baked. Darcy was not about to risk her progress by stuffing her face, but at least the cookies had distracted her mother from sticking her nose in their plans.

"So cute," Lily teased, when they were safely in the car. "Your mom made your favorite cookies!"

Darcy groaned. "First of all, those are Adam's favorite, not mine." She buckled herself in and checked her hair in the visor mirror. "Second of all, it's suffocating and needy."

Lily shrugged. "At least she gave you something nice."

Darcy turned to her best friend. "Didn't your mom recently give you a box of condoms?"

"Yeah, and in the same breath she told me not to use them. What kind of messed up message is that?"

"At least she knows you're not seven."

So far, they'd done a drive-by past Reagan's house, twice. There were only a few cars parked in the driveway, none of which they recognized.

"It's not crowded yet. If we go in there it's not like we can blend into the crowd," Darcy worried aloud.

Lily checked her lip gloss in the mirror. "I wasn't made to blend in. I say we go."

"Fine."

They were just about to get out of the car when a navy blue BMW blew past them and swung into the driveway. "For real?" Lily said, yanking her door closed just in time.

Darcy craned her neck to see who it was. Spencer Delancey slid out of the car carrying what looked to be a six-pack of beer. His friend Blaine and two others joined him.

"Looks like the party's started," Lily said. "Let's go."

The door had been left ajar, but Darcy hesitated. "We weren't exactly invited."

"No one's going to notice," Lily said, pushing past her. She was right. The foyer was packed with people from school holding Solo cups and talking in clusters. Music blared from the living room. Darcy spied Spencer and his friends by the keg. But Reagan was working the tap.

"What if he asks us to leave?" Darcy whispered.

Instead, when they got to the front of the line Reagan asked, "One or two?"

"Two," Lily said. Darcy threw her a look. They'd agreed that Lily was designated driver. "Relax," Lily whispered. "It's just one. We'll be here awhile."

Just as Reagan handed them their beers, someone cut roughly in front of them. It was Ashley Riley in a short pink dress that left nothing to the imagination.

"Uh-oh, party's just started and she's already blitzed!" Blaine shouted.

Ashley shrieked with laughter as though this was the funniest thing she'd ever heard before stumbling backward, right into Darcy.

"Look out," Lily warned, but it was too late. Darcy's beer sloshed up over the rim of her Solo cup, soaking her arm and spraying the front of her denim shorts. It looked like she'd peed her pants.

"Ashley, look what you did." It was Spencer, spinning Ashley around by her shoulders so she could see the mess.

"Oops. Sorry!" Ashley didn't look sorry, with that fake smile on her fake-tanned face. "I didn't notice you there."

Spencer stepped in. "I'm really sorry, she's had a few."

"It's not your job to apologize," Lily said. She glared past him at Ashley.

"It's okay," Darcy said, swiping at the beer stains with her hands. But it wasn't okay—on top of being told she was basically invisible, now she smelled like a keg.

"Don't move," Spencer said. He trotted off toward the kitchen and returned with a handful of napkins. "Ashley's usually a lot of fun," he said. Then, "Sometimes too much."

"She should work on that," Lily said, grabbing a napkin and dabbing at Darcy's shorts.

"Thanks," Darcy told them both. Spencer was being so nice, just like at the beach. "Hey, that was pretty impressive today with Elly Watson."

"That camper of yours who hates camp?"

"I've been trying all week to get her in the lake. What did you say to her?"

"Luckily she doesn't feel the same way about ice cream as she does about swimming. I told her that the ice cream truck was coming, but it was only for kids who went in the water."

"You lied to a little girl at summer camp?" Her voice came out much flirtier than she'd intended. The last thing she wanted was to sound like vapid Ashley.

But Spencer was grinning back at her, and she basked in the glow. (God he had so many perfect white teeth.) "Technically, the ice cream truck *is* coming," he said. "It just doesn't come until next Friday, at the end of the first session."

"Technically, there's no swimming requirement for a cone," she added.

Spencer laughed. "Personally, I think Elly looks like a kid who likes a lemon Italian ice. She's got to keep that sourpuss going."

"That's not very camp counselor–like." Spencer was funny. And maybe he was flirting just a little bit, too? Was that even possible?

"Hey, let me relieve you of that and get you a fresh one." He gestured toward her Solo cup.

"Oh, no. It's fine."

"Then let me get you the next one?"

Darcy's breath caught. "Okay. That would be great."

"Hey, Delancey!" It was Spencer's friend Eric, shouting across the room. "You've got to see this. Reagan is racing Ashley with the funnel."

Spencer winced. "Great." He lifted his cup. "Cheers. Was good talking to you, Birch."

Darcy raised her cup to his. "You, too, Delancey."

He'd barely left the room before Lily was in her face. "He likes you!"

"No he doesn't. He just felt bad."

"He rescued your shorts." Lily lifted her cup to Darcy's. "See? I told you, Darce. This is our summer. And it's just the beginning."

After that, Darcy's first beer turned into a second. Spencer did not deliver as promised, but she didn't mind. What she did mind was that Lily was also having another. "What're you doing, Driver?"

Lily shrugged. "I'm only sipping. And the party's good—we're staying awhile, right?"

Darcy didn't love the fact Lily wasn't keeping to her word, but she let it go. The night was fun. They *would* be there awhile.

They popped into the kitchen to watch the funnel races. When Lily's favorite Taylor Swift song came on, they joined a small group of girls dancing in the living room. When it got too hot, they stepped out onto the deck.

Darcy leaned against the porch railing, letting the beer settle into her limbs. Overhead the sky was dark, the stars popping. For the first time in a long time, she felt lighter. "I have the best buzz," she said proudly.

"I'm jealous. I want to join you."

"You already have!" Darcy reminded her.

"I know, but I could have more if we stayed over."

Darcy sobered just a little. Coming to the party was one thing. Crashing there was another. "My parents would freak out."

"Fine."

"And you really can't drink any more," Darcy said, studying her friend. Maybe she should have driven.

"Unless we stay." Lily raised her eyebrows. "We could tell your mom we're going back to my house."

Darcy glanced around, uncomfortably. "Where would we sleep? It's not like we're tight with Reagan. Or anyone else here, really."

"Looked like you were getting a little cozy with Spencer Delancey." Darcy knew what Lily was really doing, coaxing her along to get her way. But she also felt bad for her best friend. "I don't know, I guess maybe we could stay over."

Lily's eyes popped. "Really?"

It was so hard to say no to Lily. Darcy shrugged. "Fine."

"Oh, Darce, I love you, I love you, I love you." Lily squeezed her hard, then let go just as fast. "I'm getting a drink! Be right back."

So they were staying. Darcy took a swig of her beer and looked around, wondering if Spencer was staying, too. And just like that he appeared in the doorway. When he saw her his face fell. "Damn. I never got you that beer."

"I can get my own, thanks."

This got his attention. He joined her at the railing and their shoulders brushed. "Alright. I like an independent woman."

Woman. No one had ever called her that before. Unable to meet his eyes, Darcy looked down at her almost-empty cup, then at his. "Looks like you need a refill, too. Let me." Before he could reply she took his cup from his hand. It was bold for her, and for once she was genuinely feeling it.

She found Lily in the kitchen, waiting for Reagan to finish mixing some frothy concoction in a blender. Yellow foam was pouring out of the lid. Both Reagan and Lily found this hilariously funny. "What is that?"

"Fun juice," Reagan said, gleefully holding up the pitcher. "We tried to make piña coladas, but I didn't have any rum. Or pineapple juice." He made a face. "So we mixed gin and bananas and 7UP. Want some?"

"I'm good." She leaned in to Lily. "Maybe skip that concoction?"

"Okay, Mom."

Darcy stood in line again for the keg feeling pleased to be carrying Spencer's cup along with her own.

"Double fisting?" Lily asked, joining her. Darcy noticed she was holding a cup of Reagan's nasty concoction.

"One is for Spencer."

Lily narrowed her eyes. "You are getting cozy."

"Relax, we're just talking. Come join us."

Back outside, with two fresh beers, Darcy tried to listen as Spencer told them about his father's new boat on Mayhaven Lake. But she couldn't stop staring at his long eyelashes. She wondered if he got his blue eyes from his mother or father. She wondered if they had kids if their eyes would be green like hers or blue?

It didn't matter that she was distracted: she'd already heard the boat story. Apparently Mr. Delancey had purchased a racing boat with an engine too big and too loud for lake regulations. When her father reminded him of this, Mr. Delancey bypassed him and used his clout on the board to launch the boat from the club dock. Now there were all kinds of problems with the lake authority threatening to take the club's boat slip rights away. She decided Spencer must not know about what his father had done.

"Maybe you guys can come out on the boat sometime," Spencer said. It was a casual statement, more than an invitation. But Lily took him literally.

"When?" she asked, tipping back the last of her fun juice.

"Maybe," Darcy interjected, coolly.

Make no mistake, she would be on that boat if Spencer was serious. Even if it killed her poor father. She was just imagining herself roaring across the lake next to Spencer when Ashley Riley stumbled out onto the deck. She looked around, her drunken gaze landing hard on them.

"There you are!" She wobbled up to Spencer and threw her arms around his neck. Darcy couldn't help but notice that despite being trashed not one hair was out of place or an eyelash smudged.

"Here I am," Spencer said, catching his balance. "Whoa, looks like you're having a good night."

"Even better, now that you're here." Ashley gazed up at him like they were all alone, and Darcy's stomach sank. She could already feel the cloak of invisibility falling over her.

"I'm grabbing another," Darcy said, turning quickly to Lily. Her beer was full, but she had to get out of there. Thankfully Lily led the way.

"Wait, little girl!" It was Ashley calling after them.

"What did she just call us?" Lily halted and spun around.

Darcy knew the look on her best friend's face. "Ignore her," she implored. "She's drunk."

"Not you," Ashley called to Lily. "I'm talking to your little friend."

The deck went quiet, and Darcy could feel everyone staring. She could go inside and pretend she hadn't heard. But it was too late, everyone else had.

Ashley, one arm still slung around Spencer's neck, was staring right at her. "Sorry, I don't know your name, little girl, but grab me a beer?"

"Excuse me?" It took everything in Darcy's voice to keep it from shaking.

"I said, grab me a beer?" Ashley snorted. "Jesus, is she deaf?"

Someone laughed. Darcy's heart thudded in her ears.

Spencer took the cup from Ashley's hand. "I'll get it." He didn't correct Ashley and offer up Darcy's name. He didn't offer to get Darcy one, too. Instead, he ducked his head like he had no idea who she was and slipped by her in the doorway.

The scent of his cologne filled her nose. "Lily, I need to get out of here," she whispered.

But Lily had other ideas. "What is your problem?" Darcy could feel her friend leaning toward Ashley, ready to close the space on the deck between them. Lily was fierce.

Darcy had had enough. "Let's go." She tugged Lily's hand, whisking her back inside and through the crowd. They bumped into people in her haste.

"Ow, slow down," Lily cried.

But Darcy could not slow down. She threw open the front door and pulled them both over the threshold and outside.

"Darcy!" Lily huffed, struggling to keep pace, but Darcy was halfway down the steps and across the driveway before she let go of Lily's wrist and burst into tears.

"Hey, c'mere." Lily tried to pull her into a hug, but Darcy held out her hand.

"Why did she call me that? What the hell have I ever done to Ashley Riley?"

"I don't know, Darce. Because she's a bitch. Because she saw you talking to Spencer and she's jealous?"

Darcy hated that she was crying. She hated that they were stuck in Reagan Rogers's driveway, her clothes reeking of warm beer. Most of all she hated that she'd allowed herself to believe that someone like Spencer Delancey would be interested in someone like her.

"They're all drunk," Lily reassured her. "No one will remember."

"I will!" Darcy cried. *Little girl.* It was worse than being sworn at. Worse than being called a bitch or a whore or a slut, the usual names they all threw at each other. Because the truth was, that was exactly how Darcy felt among that crowd.

"I know you want to get out of here, but I don't think either one of us should drive yet," Lily said, softly.

It was vinegar in a bleeding cut.

"Let's get in my car. We'll listen to Taylor and wait it out."

Numb, Darcy followed Lily to the car. They rolled down the street a bit, away from Reagan's house and any view of the party, and parked in the cul-de-sac. Lily rolled down the windows and "Cruel Summer" spilled from the speakers.

"Here," Lily said. She reached into the back seat and handed Darcy the bag of cookies.

Darcy didn't know what was sadder, sitting in the car hostage to this hellish night, or the fact that the taste of her mother's chocolate chip cookies made her wish that she really was a little girl again.

FLICK

"You're at the snack shack for the morning shift," Mossimo informed him the next morning. Flick rubbed his eyes. His mother and Stan's party had gone late. "Afterward, come straight back up to the club. I need you here for the dinner party."

It was the first golf scramble of the season, and the club was abuzz. Flick had no idea what a scramble was: another silly country club word that meant nothing to him. What he did know was that the lobster boil that night was a big deal, and he was looking forward to getting some big-deal tips.

"Am I working the snack bar alone?" Flick shifted from foot to foot. He'd never worked the snack shack before.

Mossimo twisted one edge of his mustache. "Yes. But don't worry—no beurre blanc down there. Just burgers and hot dogs. It's what the people want . . ." He made a face of mild offense, then quickly recovered. "Ricky will bring you down and set you up. You can handle a grill." It wasn't a question.

Flick's small Queens apartment hadn't even had an outdoor area where they could use a grill. But he had learned to use the gigantic Weber Stan had purchased for the new house's outdoor kitchen. In fact, he'd done most of the grilling just last night at his mother and Stan's first neighborhood party. Since they'd moved in, hosting a party so they could introduce themselves to the neighborhood was all Josie had talked about.

As soon as Josie picked a date, Flick's insides had flip-flopped. So Darcy Birch would be coming over? To swim in his pool and eat steak and hang out hopefully in a bikini?

No, it turned out. She would not.

They were setting up for the party when Flick had asked. Armed with a gold candelabra centerpiece in one hand and pointing with the other, Josie was directing Flick and Stan on how to arrange the outdoor furniture.

"So, my boss and his family will be here tonight?" Flick tried to sound casual. The last thing he needed was for his mother to get in his business about a girl.

"The Birches aren't coming," Stan said quickly.

"They aren't?" Apparently this was news to Josie. "They're our closest neighbors, and I haven't even met them yet. Did they say why?"

Stan shrugged. "I didn't invite them."

"What?" Josie did not look happy.

"He's too uptight. From the first night he came over with that plant I could tell he was antisocial."

Flick opened his mouth to disagree, but from the stubborn look on Stan's face Flick knew better than to argue. Besides, he knew his mother would be all over this. Fitting into the new neighborhood had become an obsession for her.

"He came over with a plant? When?" She'd set the gold candelabra down on the table with a *thunk* and stared powerfully up from all of her four-foot-eleven-inch height to his six-foot-four frame.

Stan had actually leaned back. "Didn't I tell you about that?"

"No." Josie pressed her lips together. "What happened, Stan?"

Flick almost felt bad for the guy, shifting like he was from foot to foot. "Birch was whining about our gorgeous new RV. Said I couldn't park it in our yard, or some nonsense. Can you believe the nerve?"

She narrowed her eyes. "It is a big vehicle, Stan."

Stan threw up his hands. "So? It's on our property. Do you want me to park it in front of our garage doors? Block our driveway?"

"This is not good. They're our neighbors." She rubbed her brow. "And he's Flick's new boss."

"Don't worry, sweet thing. In a couple weeks we're taking the RV up to Maine. After that I'll see if I can figure something else out."

Josie looked relieved. "And you'll tell the Birches that?"

"As soon as I see them," Stan promised.

"Which you will, when you invite them to the party," Josie added. "Since it's too late to send one by mail, you should pop over. In person."

Ha. Stan wasn't going to do Ned any favors with the RV. Nor would he likely "pop over" and extend a last-minute invite that would only reflect badly on him.

And that was exactly what happened because the party went on and the Birches didn't show. Still hopeful, Flick had changed into a burnt orange shirt that made his eyes pop (as his mother said), and worked the grill with a smile until it was clear Darcy and her family would not be coming. He'd eyed Stan, who, as usual, was talking too loud and too much. Around ten o'clock, Flick had grown tired of the neighborhood crowd (how many times did he have to tell people how old he was and where he was going to school in the fall?) and Stan's music and had gone up to his room.

Flick didn't like that Stan had lied to his mother. And he really didn't like that an opportunity to socialize with Darcy Birch had been blown. Darcy was pretty. Darcy seemed cool. Stan was ruining his opportunity to get to know her. And maybe even pissing off his boss. Something had to be done.

Did the girl show? Mateo texted.

Nope. Thanks to Stan.

?

No invite. He doesn't like them.

What a douche cramping your style. Wait until your mother finds out.

Yeah. I'm waiting.

Waiting on the girl!

Shut up.

Maybe you'll see her at work.

Maybe.

Work your magic Creevy. Girls like you.

The girls here are different.

There was a pause before Mateo replied. Then, Don't sweat it man. You'll find your people.

Okay Mom.

FU.

Thanks man.

I know.

Now, Flick hopped in the golf cart and followed Ricky down to the snack bar.

"You'll be fine," Ricky said. "At least you get to avoid the scramble chaos."

Flick was kind of hoping to be involved in the chaos. It sounded more interesting than sitting at a snack bar all day.

It turned out the snack shack wasn't so bad. He got to be outside. There were a bunch of little kids and mothers on the beach, but there were a few hot teenage girls, too. Like Mossimo promised, the food was easy: nachos, burgers, hot dogs. There were packaged ice creams in a small freezer and bags of chips. He only ran into trouble when a college-aged girl asked him for an Arnold Palmer.

"Excuse me?" The name was so ridiculous he laughed.

Luckily, so did the girl. "It's a popular drink here. You know, half lemonade and half iced tea?"

"I did not know," Flick admitted sheepishly. "But now I do." He'd have to look up who the heck Arnold was.

The girl slid her sunglasses up on her head and grinned at Flick. She was pretty. "I'm Iris. Extra ice, please."

"I'm Flick. Nice to meet you, extra-ice Iris." When he handed Iris her Arnold Palmer she took a long sip.

"Not bad. I'll be back later for a John Daly." She winked.

"Um, okay . . ." Now he needed to look that guy up, too.

There was a burger and dog rush around noon, with a few impatient moms holding red-faced toddlers. An ice cream blitz followed. By then the mothers were feet up on lounge chairs, done with feeding, entertaining, and sunscreening their noisy charges. Instead, they doled out twenty-dollar bills to their kids and sent them Flick's way for more ice cream. He was relieved at three when Ricky drove the golf cart back down to collect him. "Survive?"

"Barely."

Ricky assessed the snack bar. "Not bad, kid."

The grill was scoured, the counter wiped down. He closed up the service window and locked the door, feeling pretty good about things. He was about to hop in the golf cart when Ricky pointed to the beach area. "Forget something?"

Flick followed his gaze. All three garbage bins were overflowing. Paper plates and cups spilled onto the grass, sticky ice cream wrappers lay stuck in the sand. Flick groaned.

By the time they'd emptied the bins and run the garbage back up to the stinking dumpster behind the clubhouse, a fleet of golf carts was already parked at the front. The exodus of players from the greens spilled onto the outdoor patio and milled about beneath the white tent. "Buckle up," Ricky said. "Snack shack has nothing on a member dinner party."

Flick eyed the crowd, who'd swapped their golf attire for linen suits and dresses and their irons for icy cocktails. A jazz band was set up on a small stage beneath the tent, and music tinkled softly across the lawn in their direction. What lay before him was exactly what Mateo had teased him about: the white-bread all-American summer dream. Flick was half tempted to snap a photo and text his friend. But he was too embarrassed—from where he stood, he wasn't in on the joke. Now he was part of it.

Upstairs the kitchen was hotter than Hades. Mossimo stood at the center island pulling cuts of meat out of marinade bags and arranging them on trays while he shouted directions. "Corn! I need the corn to go out to the grill. Where the hell is the corn? And who is on steaks? These go out in five."

Ricky was outside manning the boiling pots for the lobsters. Flick's eyes traveled to the refrigerator which someone had left open. The shelves were lined with paper seafood bags, some moving.

"Behind you!" Wendy swept up around him and grabbed two bags from the fridge. "You working or watching?" Without waiting for a reply, she began loading bags of lobsters into a plastic crate.

Mossimo clapped his hands impatiently. "Help her out, help her out!"

Apparently there would be no review of the kitchen schedule today. Flick jumped into action. When the crate was full, he ran into the pantry for another, and they filled that, too.

"C'mon, junior," Wendy said, as she hauled a crate up off the ground. "We've got to get these guys down to Ricky."

The crates were heavier than they looked, and Flick staggered down the back stairs behind Wendy.

They handed the lobsters off to Ricky, who was beet red standing over the pots.

Wendy paused, wiping her brow with the back of her hand, looking around. "Pretty different out here, huh?" She nodded toward the white tent.

Mayhaven members mingled, selecting appetizers from trays as servers buzzed about them. Ice clinked against glasses. Laughter emanated from under the tent. Somewhere a cork popped.

"Not a bad scene," Flick allowed.

Wendy squinted at the crowd. "Not my thing. They're the honey, and we're the bees."

A microphone crackled onstage; the jazz band paused and one of the golf pros stepped up to announce the winning foursome for the day. Raffle ticket numbers were called. A deliriously happy woman in a golf dress trotted off with a gift basket wrapped in gold.

"Let's just hope they get drunk enough they tip well." Wendy went back inside, leaving him to unpack lobsters.

Flick understood he was new up here, but he couldn't conjure the same ire Wendy seemed to hold. It was a country club; they knew what they were getting into. On the other hand, there were people here Flick was genuinely coming to like, from Mr. Birch who worked his tail off but was always smiling, to the older men who liked to tell him stories, and crazy old Bitsy Babcock, who always asked how he was doing and offered him a bite of whatever dish she'd ordered in the dining room. "Take a taste! No one's looking." Where before he would've made fun of these people, the more he worked there the less easy it was to dismiss them out of hand.

But, to Wendy's point, there were also the Spencer Delanceys: textbook country club cliché. Flick spotted a cluster of members around his age. The girls were in short dresses; he recognized a few as camp counselors. The guys wore polo shirts and belts with lobsters and whales, looking like their mothers had outfitted them. There, among them, was Number One: Spencer, himself.

Flick watched him throw his head back laughing. Golden boy, Mateo would say.

But then Flick's gaze landed on Ned Birch and his wife. Mr. Birch was dressed up in a sports coat, making the rounds and greeting people. Right behind him were Adam and Darcy. Darcy wore a light pink dress. She looked bored; beautiful but entirely bored. Adam fidgeted next to her, and Flick watched her lean in and whisper something in his ear. Whatever it was, Adam smiled and the fidgeting stopped.

Flick wondered why Darcy wasn't with Number One's group. Maybe her father wouldn't let her. Or—even better, maybe she didn't want to.

A hand rested on his arm, and Flick turned. Mrs. Bitsy Babcock was gazing up at him.

She put a hand to her forehead, her oversized ruby ring catching the sun. "My it's hot over here in lobster-land. Would you be a dear and get a girl a refill?"

She held out a diminutive silver flask. Flick wasn't sure why she'd brought it over to him at the lobster boil, but he took it.

"Hendrick's, please. None of that cheap stuff . . . gives me a powerful headache."

Why Bitsy was drinking from a flask at a dinner party where servers and fresh drinks were plentiful he did not understand. "Wouldn't you prefer I get you a glass with ice?"

Mrs. Babcock laughed. "I would not."

Flick glanced at the long line at the outdoor bar. Then at Ricky, who shrugged. "Be quick," was all he said.

Bitsy put her hands together. "Straight up. Lime twist, dear."

Flick wasn't sure exactly what that meant, but the bartender knew. When Flick handed him the flask, he shook his head. "Bitsy?"

Flick nodded.

She was waiting right where he'd left her, looking impossibly sober for a tiny woman who'd just polished off a flask. "How lovely." She unscrewed the cap and before taking a swig, held the bottle out to him. "You look hot."

"Oh, no thank you, ma'am."

Bitsy frowned. "Never call me that again, dear."

"Oh, I'm sorry," Flick stammered, the word *ma'am* almost popping out again. "I didn't mean . . ."

She lifted her flask between them, as if toasting. "Gin is what keeps me so young."

Neiman Shrive joined them. He surveyed the boiling pots. "Cockroaches of the ocean."

"Excuse me, sir?"

"Smelly messy endeavor, this." Mr. Shrive was wearing a pin-striped blazer that was far more festive than the look on his face. "What you need is a good steak."

Flick gestured to the large chalkboard menu. "We've got steaks on the menu."

Mr. Shrive scowled. "I can read."

Alright then. "Anything I can get you?" Flick asked. He needed to go help Wendy or he'd be dead meat himself.

"Yeah. A steak." Old people liked to eat early. Flick knew this from his grandma, back in Queens.

"They'll be right down," Flick promised. He was relieved when Wendy waved him over, despite knowing he'd get an earful.

"Hey, junior. Unless you brought your seersucker suit, I think you're wanted in the kitchen."

"Sorry."

Back upstairs the kitchen vibe had turned manic. Flick pictured all the Mr. Shrive's waiting for their steaks.

Salads were aggressively tossed, dressed, and whisked out. Trays of corn, still steaming, sailed by. Steaks were hauled to the grill where Ricky threw them onto flames. Flick found himself running up and down the stairs, between both worlds. No sooner had dinner trays gone out than appetizer trays came in. The work never slowed, nor did the directives. Flick figured he basically ran for two hours straight until the dessert course. When the jazz band picked up outside, only then did the kitchen slow. Oven mitts were exchanged for kitchen gloves. Sleeves were rolled up and dirty pots lowered into soapy sinks as burners cooled on the range. Flick's forehead was a sheen of sweat, salt, and cooking oil. He couldn't remember when he'd last eaten. Outside, tiny strawberry cheesecakes were passed on silver plates.

"Good work, good work," Mossimo chanted as dishes

were scraped and glassware loaded into the steaming mouth of the industrial washer. As the crew finished up, Mossimo disappeared to the upper deck with an old-fashioned wooden pipe. Flick had never seen the chef smoke. Maybe it was his reward. Veiled in darkness, Flick only knew he was there by the occasional flicker of orange and puff of pipe smoke.

Flick was exhausted. His Converse were filthy from spilled food, and his feet were sore. When the last of the stainless steel surfaces was wiped clean and the dishwasher empty, Wendy appeared. "Toast?"

She held up a mostly full bottle of Veuve Clicquot. "Not letting this baby go to waste."

Ricky brought out clean glasses. Mossimo came inside. After pouring for each, Wendy took a swig straight from the bottle. Flick took a swallow of his champagne, the crisp notes bubbling on his tongue. "Damn, this is good." Everyone laughed.

He was on his way home, slipping through the shadows beneath the deck when he recognized Mr. Birch's voice. "You remember my daughter, Darcy, of course?"

Flick's head snapped. He didn't notice anything about the group of people at the edge of the patio except how long Darcy's legs were in that dress of hers, and how hollow her smile. Like him, she wanted to go home.

Just then she turned his way. Flick stepped out of the shadows and raised a hand in greeting. She stared through him so long Flick wasn't sure if she recognized him. And then something unbelievable happened. Darcy excused herself, and came to stand in front of him.

"So you're my new neighbor."

She was so close Flick was sure he could smell strawberries on her breath. He would bet his life on it. "I am," he managed.

Her eyes flickered. "Let's steal a cart and get out of here."

NED

When he was six years old, his father woke him early one fall morning. At first he thought something was wrong. For starters, his father never woke him up. Not for school or church, and certainly not ever to take him somewhere on a weekend. His father paid homage to the 1950s sense of fatherhood, despite the fact it was the seventies and other dads coached baseball and cooked dinner and drove their kids to school. Providing was his father's idea of parenting, and also, as Ned would later grow to realize, marriage. Ned's father did not attend games, or rub his stomach when he was sick, or tuck him in with a story at night. So when he awoke to find his father towering over his bed in the predawn hours one autumn Saturday, Ned's first thought was that something was terribly wrong.

"Get up," his father said, his voice gruff. "I'm taking you to the course."

Ned blinked, taking in the gray light playing at the edges of his window and the man standing by his bed. Wordlessly, he slipped from his warm covers and did as he was told.

Ned dressed quickly, ignoring the rumble in his stomach, and wondered as he passed his parents' bedroom door if his mother knew anything about this. He'd been half tempted to wake Willy, who snoozed quietly with his thumb still in his mouth, but it appeared Willy was not invited. Downstairs his father was already at the door. "Come on, then." Fifteen minutes later they pulled the car into the empty parking lot at Mayhaven.

An older man named Lenny met them at the locked front door of the clubhouse and let them in. "Morning, Art."

"Thanks for this, Len."

Len was older and grayer than Ned's father, and walked with a stoop. But his gaze was warm when it landed on Ned. "No trouble at all. You two enjoy the morning."

Then, as now, Ned walked down the main hall past the glittering display case of trophies and old photos, though it seemed bigger and longer, its contents more mysterious. Len invited them into the pro shop, where he pulled a small golf bag from behind the large wooden counter. "These may be a little big for him," he said to Ned's father, sizing Ned up through milky eyes.

"He'll adjust," his father replied. Then to Ned, who was looking around the shop with large eyes, "Well? Say thank you to the man. And get your clubs."

The clubs, he would later learn, were left behind by a young member that summer, never claimed, and saved behind the counter by Len. Ned hoisted the strap over his narrow shoulders and hurried out after his father.

Ned had never heard of Len before; he would later learn that they were old school friends and as a favor on Saturday mornings before the club opened, he would let his father, Art, in to play as many holes as he could before the club opened and the staff showed up. Ned knew his father golfed on weekend mornings, but it had never occurred to him where or how. Or that you had to be a member to play, which Art Birch was not. Mayhaven was not a place his father could ever have afforded belonging to, but belong he did, striding across the fairways as the mist rose in haunting threads about them. As daylight broke over the horizon, Ned had his first lesson.

"The thing you want to remember," his father said, speaking to him for the first time like an adult, "is that you can't force your swing."

Ned did not know what his father meant then, but on other such mornings that followed he would come to. Those Saturdays would become his routine, each season, until the day his father eventually left. "The strongest man with the biggest frame can be outdriven by a wisp of a teenage boy." Here his father looked at him, his eyes twinkling. "It's never been a game of muscle. It's about grace."

Grace was a word Ned would never have ascribed to the testy man who slammed cabinet doors and stomped in and out of their home, invariably weary of what was for dinner just as he was with his wife and, Ned often felt, his children. There was no evidence of grace in their home, in his aloof nature and constant whiffs of disapproval. But that morning on the golf course it was the word he used to describe a game he was introducing his son to; the first and only real thing he'd ever shared with Ned. And Ned grasped onto it like one does hope.

On the course his father was a different animal; a less threatening animal who cracked smiles and occasionally an odd joke, especially when he played well. His instructions for Ned were spare and simple, and thankfully Ned was a natural who took direction and understood how his body moved through space. His little brother, Willy, sadly did not.

Willy, when he was older, would be brought to the course only twice, and not ever again. Over the years it became something Ned harbored deep and lasting guilt about: spending time with a father who only existed on the golf course, a man Willy would never get to know. But after a lifetime of being sized up and found lacking, Ned clutched the small sense of worth he attained on those outings; it was his only source of nourishment from a father who, until then, had starved them all.

The game of golf was not easy, nor were those early lessons enjoyable. His father was a devotee of rote practice. He began with the techniques of a swing: the art of setting up, the science of the club head striking the ball at its equator, the undeniable *ping* of good contact when the small white sphere careened through space. Ned was as determined to learn the game as he was to gain his father's praise. Weekdays, he practiced against a net in the backyard, holding his breath until Saturday when his father would take him out again. It wasn't long before he became decent, and later, excellent.

"Your father is good to you out there?" his mother once asked, warily. She was washing dishes the night Ned and his father had returned from a junior golf tournament three towns away, toting a trophy. Ned had plunked the trophy on the dinner table for Willy and his mother to admire as they ate. As usual, his father had taken his plate to his study where he dined alone, the faint notes of classical music trickling under the closed door.

"Yes," he replied. "I bogeyed the first hole but made birdie on three. I won by two strokes!" Ned was talking about his win, not his father, because that was what had come to matter. But his mother did not seem appropriately enthused.

Ned could see that he was speaking a language she was not versed in; his father had left her out, just as he had Willy, and suddenly Ned felt sorry for her.

"That's good," she said, finally, returning her attention to the sink.

They were interrupted by a sudden crash behind them, and his mother startled. When Ned spun around, he saw his trophy on the kitchen floor. It had toppled from the table. Willy stood beside it, eyes wide with fear.

"You idiot!" Ned cried, shoving Willy out of the way. It was harder than he'd intended; Willy fell backward, banging his head on the floor. A wail of crying erupted.

Before Ned could scoop up his trophy and inspect it for damage, his mother beat him to it. She snatched it up with one hand and his arm with the other, something she'd never done before.

"Don't you treat your brother like that!" she'd hissed, tears springing to her eyes. She held the trophy aloft between them. "This does not make you better."

There was a sound in the doorway, and they'd all looked up to see his father. He surveyed the scene in front of him. A bitter laugh escaped him before he walked away.

While Ned's mother turned to soothe Willy, Ned scooped up his trophy and ran upstairs to his room, righteous in his win. What followed was a surge of guilt he would spend the rest of the night pushing away from the corners of his sleep.

That memory still plagued him, more than the memory of his father leaving a few months later. By then Ned had come to realize that things were not so black-and-white, and his father's golden light he'd basked in for so brief a time was complicated.

Ned's feelings for golf, however, were not. It was a sport he loved, despite the frustration. One day you might play your best round and the very next you could blow up every hole. It was elusive and agonizing and wonderful, just as he'd found life to be. Out there, against the mountain views and sweeping breeze, Ned was reminded of his small place in the world, hopeful and humbled. There was no making sense of the unadulterated glory felt in one shot, and the despair in the next. It was, he supposed, akin to the relationship he'd had with his father.

Ned's father was an ardent golfer who never belonged to a club; a talented player who could not afford the membership dues and was not afflicted with a need to belong. As much as Ned emulated his father's game, he would never model his father's role in their sad little family. The day he married Ingrid, Ned vowed to treat his wife with compassion and respect in equal measure. Should they be blessed with children, he would hold those children; he would tend to hurt feelings and scraped knees alike. He would show up to school plays and cheer loudest at dance recitals and games. He would be the best father he'd never been shown how to be.

When Darcy was old enough to toddle behind him at the club, he bought her a child's set of clubs so small they looked cartoonish. She loved them. In good weather, they practiced in the backyard. In winter, they practiced in the garage against a net. When Darcy got older, he brought her to the course and taught her everything he could. Later, when she outgrew his expertise along with the child's clubs, he signed her up for lessons. It wasn't just the joy of the game, it was the joy of sharing something he loved with his daughter. It was the jokes between holes, the high fives after she crushed the ball, and the sympathetic looks when she shanked it. Being out on the course taught him so much about who his daughter was and what she was made of. It was a privilege to witness her sense of cool on the course, her consistency, her focus. Darcy possessed what his father had talked about: grace, in every sense of the word.

For a few years, it seemed Darcy Birch lived for the game and was destined for greatness. Which is why Ned was mystified when she up and announced she was quitting.

None of them saw it coming. That season she'd been at the top of her game. Trophies lined her bedroom shelves. Scouts began to show up. When she appeared in the living room and announced that she was done, Ned had thought she was joking.

"What do you mean you're done?" He'd laughed. The previous fall Darcy had won the qualifying round of the Massachusetts Girls Junior Amateur Championship. That spring they were headed to Braintree for the tournament. Darcy had just come home from a simulator lesson with Vince. She had to be kidding.

"I'm not kidding," she said, arms crossed.

Ingrid followed her upstairs to her room, where they remained behind the closed door for fifteen unbearable minutes talking in hushed tones. She met Ned in the hallway.

"She's quitting," Ingrid said.

"But why? Did something happen?" Sure, their daughter was just as prone to irrational teenage moments as any other kid her age; and he and Ingrid had spent their fair share of time walking on proverbial eggshells. But those moments were reserved for friendship woes or boys or failing an algebra test. Sometimes for her exasperation with her own family. But never golf. Golf was the one sacred thing that buoyed her through all of it.

"She says she's burnt out," was all Ingrid could say. "I don't understand it, either, Ned. But I have to say—I believe her."

"So, what, we give up? We let her just quit?" Ned was trying to keep his voice low and failing. He allowed his wife to pull him down the hall and into the privacy of their own room.

"No, but we do give her time. This is her decision, Ned. It's her sport." Ingrid was looking at him like she felt sorry for him. He didn't like it. "Remember, it's not about us."

He knew this, of course. And yet he could not help but feel a sense of failing that he'd been so caught off guard. How long had Darcy felt this way? Had he misread his own daughter so badly? If that was true, what else had he misread? The thought filled him with panic.

"I need to talk to her."

"Not yet," Ingrid said. "Let's wait until later tonight, okay? She's worried about upsetting you, more than anything it seems."

"Me? But why?"

Ingrid leveled him with a knowing look.

"Okay, fine. I get it—I'm wrapped up in this, no doubt. As her golf partner and in my line of work, I get all of that. But as her dad, this is different. If she says she's burnt out, how did we not see the signs?" He sank onto the bed, feeling as if all the bones in his body had just melted.

Ingrid sat beside him. She looked as confused as he felt, but notably not as hurt. "I don't know," she said. "Teens can have sweeping emotions. She's competed a lot this season—and let's be honest, the pressure at this level is high."

"She has Braintree coming up. A scout is coming to watch her."

Ingrid shrugged. "Give her time. Maybe this will all blow over."

But it did not.

Now, with a new season of golf sparkling before them, Darcy showed no signs of returning to the sport. It left Ned bereft. He missed driving up to the course, early in the mornings before work, with his daughter. He missed walking the course as the mist rose about them, just the two of them. Most of all he missed his daughter. The orbit she seemed to be on these days did not involve him, or her mother, or even very much her brother, it seemed. Darcy's young adult life seemed to be in a universe all its own, with parties and friends and high school comprising the strange new axis on which her planet spun. Ned knew this was normal; he knew that he should celebrate her independent spirit. But he could not help but feel that he had fallen from a sky they once shared, and her planet was revolving steadily into a dark season, its face turned away from the sun.

DARCY

"So you grew up with country club parties and preppy collars." Flick's tone gave no clue: it could've been awe or criticism.

In reply Darcy took a swig from the pinot noir, which she'd stolen off a table. Then she passed it across the golf cart seat to him. She liked white wine better than red, but thieves couldn't be choosers. "Pretty much."

"You golf?"

"Once upon a time. But I quit this year." It was something her father still hadn't stopped asking about, and she could tell it broke his heart. The truth was, it broke hers a little bit, too. The night air was growing cool and the party at the club was winding down. Being back out here on the course in the stolen cart felt strange; even in the dark she knew the rise and fall of the fairway.

"I saw your name on a gold plaque in the trophy case," Flick admitted. "It was on a few, actually."

"Yeah, well those days are over now."

She could feel Flick's eyes on her. "What changed?"

Darcy leaned back against the cart seat. "I guess I did." It was the truth. What happened had changed her. She didn't let herself think about the fact that her favorite hole was only twenty yards away. Or that she could make birdie on it with her eyes closed. She'd numbed herself to that part of her, the old Darcy. Now, she was just a girl sitting in a cart with a cute boy who'd snuck away from another one of her father's boring club parties. "I'm different now."

In the light of the half-moon she could just make out Flick's sharp features when she snuck a glance.

"I think I know what you mean. Moving here, I've changed, too. I don't do the things I used to. You know, the things that kind of defined me."

"What kind of things?" All she really knew was that he'd come from New York and had a stepfather with a lot of money who drove her parents crazy. But she had a sense Flick was different.

"I don't know. Little things, like how I used to ride the subway."

"The New York subway system defined you?" She'd meant it as a joke, but as the words tumbled from her mouth she heard the judgment in them. Even in the shadows she could see his expression harden.

"Never mind. It sounds stupid."

"No, it doesn't." She shifted uncomfortably on the seat. "I'm sorry. That came out kind of harsh."

Flick turned to her. "Yeah, it did." At least he didn't seem mad.

Darcy smiled inwardly. She liked that he was so direct. Direct was refreshing. All the guys she knew said one thing but meant another. "Please, tell me more about New York."

"It wasn't the subway, it was the freedom I had. I miss the

energy, the stadiums, the people, the food. There was so much to do. Here, you have to drive everywhere and, let's be honest, it's just fields and trees."

Darcy couldn't argue with any of that. "You must be so bored."

"Pretty much."

"Why'd you guys move here, if you loved the city?"

"My mom got married and then Stan, my stepfather, retired. He decided we should move up here. It was all kind of fast."

This was interesting. "Do you like your stepdad?"

When Flick shrugged, his shoulder brushed against hers. "I don't dislike him."

"So that's a no." They both laughed.

"He's okay. He's got a different outlook, let's say. Stan made a lot of money and he kind of shows it off. I think he wants us to, too."

"Yeah, I saw the Ferrari in your driveway. Hard to miss that orange."

"Don't forget about the RV. I know your father loves that."

Darcy had to laugh. Her parents were so worked up about what to do about it, and yet here she and Flick were talking openly. Adults made things so complicated. "Still, it must be nice having money. God, I would kill for a car like that."

"First of all, I don't drive the Ferrari. Though I would like to," he admitted. "But having all that stuff is weird. It's Stan's stuff, not mine."

"I get that," Darcy allowed. "So you didn't live like this before, it sounds." She hoped that didn't offend him. God knew her nosiness got her in trouble sometimes.

"No, my mom and I never lived like this. We had a small

apartment, and the Chevy I drive now. That was it." His voice grew soft. "We didn't have a lot, but we had what we needed."

His admission was so honest Darcy felt the urge to reach for his hand; it was right there, resting on the cart seat next to hers. But she didn't want to give him the wrong idea. "I know what you mean," she said instead.

When she'd seen Flick walking out of the clubhouse earlier, all she'd wanted to do was get the hell out of the party. She would've left with almost anyone. Now, she was glad to be here with him. "Thanks for helping me escape," she told him. "Club dinner parties are so lame."

Members were dressed their best but behaved their worst. The themes changed but the crowd was always the same. It all felt so fake. The sad thing was that her dad's love of this place was as real as anything. Which was another reason that she could never tell him why she'd quit golf.

"So what about you?" Flick asked. "Why'd you drag me out here?" His voice was playful, but the question was pretty bold.

Darcy turned to face him. "Do you not want to be here?" She could be bold, too.

Flick's jaw flexed as he considered this. "I don't mind it," he said. "But I'm curious. I see you around, and you're always hanging out with the camp counselors and lifeguards. So why not tonight?"

He'd pegged her. Darcy stiffened, thinking about the party the night before at Reagan Rogers's. About how well things had gone with Spencer until Ashley butted in and said what she'd said. It wasn't even Ashley's fault that Darcy was so embarrassed; Darcy shouldn't have given her the power to begin with.

But she couldn't tell Flick all that. "I see those guys all the time. Sometimes you need a break. You know?"

She'd managed to dodge his question, but she could still feel his curiosity hovering in the air between them. "You work with them, too," she said, turning the tables. "Do you know any of the guys yet?"

"I wouldn't say we work together."

Darcy wasn't sure what he meant by that. "Well, you're not a camp counselor but you work here, too. You must see them around."

"I work in the kitchen. Lifeguarding and camp counseling is summer entertainment for them. Their parents probably think it looks good on some Ivy League application. When it comes down to it, they're members, Darcy. Like you." He paused. "I'm not."

Darcy bit her lip. That part hadn't even occurred to her. He wasn't just new, he was on the outside in other ways. "I'm not a member," she admitted. "Sure, my dad is president, but it's a job. And tonight is kind of like working. Adam and I hate it. So, I'm actually not much different than you around here."

Flick put his feet up and leaned back like he had to think about that. "Maybe."

The stars overhead were popping now. The air had cooled, and Darcy could feel the warmth coming off of Flick. She wondered what it would be like to lean into.

Her father may have been president, but Flick's family clearly had a lot of money. Probably more than a lot of the ones who belonged to Mayhaven. But here he was in the kitchen, making their food and waiting on the counselors and guards. "Are those guys assholes when they come in the restaurant?"

Flick shrugged. "They are who they are."

Darcy knew exactly who they were. That was high school for you, loathing the popular kids and dying to be invited to sit at their lunch table in the same breath.

"It must suck moving your senior year, leaving your friends behind," she said. It may have been the wine or the late hour, but hearing how Flick felt like he was on the outside hit a little close to home. "Do you know Spencer Delancey? He'll be in your class at school."

"Oh, we've met." Flick snorted. "Number One."

"What?"

"His membership number. He made sure to tell me the other day in the dining room when he came in with his friends."

"Oh." She realized she'd hit a nerve. "The other guys can be jerks, but Spencer is actually pretty cool, if you get to know him."

"Is he? Because what little I do know of him is clear. He seems like an asshole."

The fresh edge to his tone was sobering. "Whoa, okay."

"Sorry if he's your friend, but he's not my people." Flick reached for the bottle from her and took a swig.

Not his people? Spencer was one of the few people who'd been nice to her that summer, despite how the party at Reagan's had ended. Ashley's behavior wasn't on him. It made her realize she still harbored hope. "You barely know Spencer."

"Yeah, I think I do. I'm wondering if you do, though."

Darcy slid away from Flick on the cart seat. He'd seemed so cool a minute ago, and here he was judging. "He's the only person who actually got through to my toughest camper this week. She refused to go near the water, and now she's practically swimming. All because of him!"

Flick laughed. "Okay. Sounds like he's got two fans."

Darcy's cheeks burned. How dare Flick say that. Her feelings about Spencer Delancey were many and complicated, but they were private. She shouldn't have brought him up. She shouldn't have been there with Flick in the first place.

"We should get back," she said, turning the key hard in the ignition. The cart rumbled to life, silencing the crickets and the peepers and all the good stuff she'd been feeling until a moment ago. She'd misread Flick Creevy.

"Already?" Did he sound disappointed? It sounded like it, but she didn't care. She dumped the rest of the wine in the grass and swung the cart around toward the clubhouse.

The party would be wrapping up, which meant her parents would be looking for her.

She didn't even try to drive quietly around to the back. Instead, Darcy blew past the white tent where members lingered over dessert, past the dance floor where she caught a glimpse of her parents dancing. Past a teenage crowd, which she scanned quickly, spying some of Spencer's friends but not him. She slowed long enough to confirm that Ashley was missing, too. Perfect.

Along the side of the clubhouse, she parked the cart roughly and tossed the key in the cupholder. "See you around," she said, trying to sound indifferent. She didn't want Flick to know how burned up she was.

"Look, I'm sorry for what I said out there. I shouldn't have dissed your friends."

"They're not my friends," she said, without thinking. Who

cared, it was none of his business, anyway. She grabbed the empty wine bottle from the basket.

"Well, you seem pretty upset, so the apology still stands." He paused, and she found herself waiting, too. "Darcy, I liked talking with you."

"Yeah, cool. My folks will be looking for me, so . . . have a good one." She dumped the wine bottle in a recycling bin and strode back out into the twinkling lights and thrum of the jazz band, leaving Flick Creevy standing in the shadows.

• • • • •

The whole ride home, Ingrid and Ned unpacked the evening in the front seat like a government debriefing. Moments earlier they'd been dancing to the band. Now, with the satiety of lobsters and jazz waning, her father was back to review and revenue.

"I'll have to get the final numbers from Mossimo on Monday, but I think it was a hit. Don't you think it was a hit?"

Ingrid nodded dreamily. "Such a lovely evening." Her mother, still flushed and fluttery, was still entrenched in that delirious state of having had too much wine. At least someone was enjoying the night.

Adam glared across the back seat at his sister. "Where were you? You took a cart. I thought you didn't golf anymore."

Immediately her father's face filled the rearview mirror. "You took a cart out?" God, her parents were nosy.

"Yeah," she said, holding his gaze in the mirror. "The party was really boring, and I was tired of it, so I took a cart."

Her father looked like he wanted to say more, but instead looked back at the road. It made her feel even worse.

"You were with Flick," Adam whispered.

Darcy threw him a look and shook her head.

"Yes, Flick," Adam said louder. "Darcy and Flick took the golf cart."

She reached across the seat and pinched his arm. Adam yelped. Her mother spun around. "Wait, you mean the new neighbor?"

Was *everyone* intent on ruining her night?

Her father's gaze flashed in the mirror again. "You were with Flick Creevy?"

"My God. For a hot minute. I showed him the course. So what?"

"What's there to see in the dark?" her father asked. But Ingrid had other questions.

"He's rather cute." She turned to her husband. "You said he's a nice kid, too, right, honey?"

"He's not that cute," Darcy said. Or very nice, she thought to herself as she stared out the window. Why was her father driving so slow? She should never have agreed to ride together to the club. This was pure, unadulterated torture.

When they pulled in the driveway she was the first to exit. "Such a lovely night," Ingrid declared again.

But her father was calling after her. "Darcy, I'm happy you went out on the course again, honey. But you need to be careful taking carts at club events. People are always watching . . ."

"Oh, believe me, I know!" She raced ahead of them through the front door.

Up in her room, Darcy slammed the door and checked her phone. There were practically a hundred texts from Lily, asking about the club party and who was there and if she talked to

Spencer. There was another from the camp director, reminding everyone about a meeting. And one last text—from a number she didn't recognize. She opened it.

> Hey. Thanks for taking me on your joyride tonight. I had fun, even if you did kidnap me.

Darcy's breath caught. How had he gotten her number?

Well, it didn't matter. Clearly Flick might not like the people they worked with at the club, but she didn't have a choice. And she wasn't about to get wrapped up in the opinions of some new kid she barely knew. High school was hard enough already, and they had a whole summer to get through. Her father was always reminding her, *Try to get along with the members. They're kind of like family.*

Oh please, she wanted to tell him. She already had a family. A messy, barely functional, insanely annoying family. If the Birches were a club, she was pretty damn sure no one would want to join.

She decided not to reply to Flick. His comment still stung. Just because she liked Spencer didn't make her some crazed fangirl. Flick Creevy had no clue.

Instead, she washed up for bed, weighed herself one last time for the day, and slid between her cool cotton sheets, eyelids already growing heavy.

When she drifted to sleep she had two people on her mind: Spencer Delancey and Flick Creevy. When she woke up around one AM, there was just one. She reached for her phone in the dark.

I had fun . . . he'd said.

Darcy paused, her thumbs hovering over the glowing keys. Then, before she could change her mind she texted back.

Same.

Saying nothing would probably have put an end to it. But there was something about Flick Creevy. And she didn't want to do that, at least not yet.

NED

The scramble proved a roaring success, and nobody, not even Dick Delancey, could deny it. Monday morning Ned strolled through the clubhouse with a spring in his step.

The event had almost sold out, with a record increase of forty percent member participation compared to the last golf scramble. Well, wait until he reported that to the board.

The success wasn't just in the numbers. The evening had been magical; the food decadent, the sky starry, and the guests had danced under the white tent right up until the jazz band bid good night.

Ned unlocked his office door. At that hour only he, the pros, and Adam were there. Adam had just started his new job assisting Jane.

"Hurry, Dad," he'd urged an hour earlier, already waiting by the front door with his lunch packed before Ned had even considered breakfast. "I have to review invoices today, and I can't concentrate when Jane gets that coffeemaker going." Apparently Adam liked coming in early, too. Like father, like son.

According to the schedule Jane had left on his desk he had a nine o'clock wedding conference with the Delanceys. Ned groaned inwardly, his good vibes from the weekend already lifting away. Next was the matter of the Koi delivery. Unfortunately, a small hurricane off the coast of North Carolina had caused several road closures, so the fish delivery for the new pond would be delayed. Which reminded him that he needed to meet with the grounds staff; there was some cart damage from a wayward driver on the fifth hole. First, Ned decided, he would review the latest comments from the Pilgrim Box. He was curious what members had to say about the scramble dinner party.

The rustle of paper within was promising, but opening the box always gave Ned pause. Statistically, people who took the time to comment were those who had something to complain about.

He took a deep breath and unfolded the first comment. The handwriting was scrawled and difficult to read. The water bottles on the course are not cold enough.

Not a crisis, Ned thought.

He opened another. Marcy Walgram is a court hog. She always shows up early and plays beyond her allotted time. Marcy needs a talking-to. Or is everyone afraid of her?

Ned grimaced. Marcy Walgram *was* a court hog. He made a note.

Next comment: The menu is too foreign. What is Thai basil? If I wanted Mojo pork I'd get on a plane. This is the United States of America. When did pork chops and mashed potatoes become offensive?

Well. This was likely penned by the same member who'd called their Australian course manager a penal colonist: a bigger issue than the aforementioned menu.

There were a couple doozies.

Is it just me, or are we being infiltrated by swingers? Someone keeps wearing his pineapple tie clip upside down and dances too close. Of course, I wouldn't know such things, but I've heard...

What is all this fuss about pineapples? I can't begin to tell you what someone suggested about my pineapple tennis top. It's Lilly Pulitzer, not sex.

Has anyone considered a Juneteenth celebration? We want everyone to feel included! What is the color theme for Juneteenth? Is that a rainbow, too??

Ned rubbed his temples. Thankfully, the next comments were less worrisome.

The new showerheads suck. If we can't have a spa on site, can we at least have a massaging showerhead?

Can we start a Lost and Found? My husband forgets his boxers in the locker room. I don't want to trespass in the men's room, but I will if I have to. Signed, Lillian Jameson.

Yikes. Either Lillian did not know the Pilgrim Box was anonymous or did not care. Either way, Ned could not risk her trolling the men's locker room. He made another note. He was about to close the box when he spied one more. It was tucked in the corner, folded so small and tight, that he'd almost missed it.

> I used to think Mayhaven was a special place. But the men need to respect the women.

Ned sat back in his chair. This was different. And concerning. Ned read the comment again. It was written in blue ink and block print. There was no telling who it was from, and there were no specifics that might give him a clue as to how to begin to tackle this, but that wasn't important. What was important was figuring out why a woman was feeling disrespected at Mayhaven. Ned tucked it in his desk drawer. This one necessitated some investigation.

Jane buzzed his office line. "Delanceys are here early. They're waiting in the meeting room."

"Fabulous," Ned said.

He heard Jane chuckle before she hung up. They'd already done rock, paper, scissors over who got to run this meeting.

Coral and the bride-to-be, Phoebe Delancey, were seated with an overstuffed pink-and-white binder labeled *Bride* in gold calligraphy resting between them. How Ned wished Mayhaven could budget for an event planner.

"Good morning!" he said as brightly as he could. But the looks on the women's faces were anything but.

"We need to make a little change," Coral said, diving right in. Her bracelets jingled as she whisked the binder open. His thoughts flashed back to the Pilgrim Box rumor from last week.

Ned tried not to stare at Coral's arm, but it was visually impossible. So much glittering gold. How much free time did Dick have?

"It's just a little change," Phoebe added brightly. Only there was not just one change, nor was it little. For the next forty-five minutes Ned listened in disbelief. He was beginning to suspect that the largest part of his job as president was to manage other people's expectations.

Phoebe kept throwing up her hands in despair. "I don't feel like the wedding captures my vibe, you know? I used to think I was Ivy style. But now I want to go for a more Boho vibe. You know?"

Ned did not know. Nor did he care about Phoebe Delancey's vibe. All he wanted was for the Delanceys to stick to a decision. His prospective members open house was looming; he needed to get out of there.

Before he managed to, Phoebe had uprooted the ceremony setup from indoors to outdoors. Timing was pushed back four hours to align the champagne toast with the sunset. The five-course white glove dinner service was abandoned for a rustic New England clambake. Ned's eyelid twitched as he made copious notes.

When Coral raised a finger to suggest releasing doves (not good for the doves or the white tent, Ned explained) he stood. "Apologies, ladies. I've got a tour to give."

Coral sniffed. "We'll have to circle back to the doves."

The problem was, Ned was certain they would.

Outside, Ned found a group of prospective members mingling on the patio. Thank God for Jane, who'd overseen setup of lemonade and scones.

"Welcome!" Ned felt a little like a pastor opening his arms to his congregation, but damned if the setting didn't call for it. The sun was high, the sky cloudless, and the distant laughter of campers rippled through the evergreens. "I'm Ned Birch, club president, and it's my pleasure to share a slice of Mayhaven with you today."

As he launched into the club's history Ned sized up the group. So far, everyone appeared interested and engaged. There was a man in a business suit, likely on break from work. A few couples, of mixed ages. And one young family with toddlers. He was about to commence the tour when he spied a familiar face in the back row. Ned's heart dropped. *No, no, no . . . what are they doing here?*

Stan Crenshaw stood at the rear with his wife, Josie, on his arm. He looked right at Ned, unsmiling. Josie waved enthusiastically.

As the group followed Ned across the lawn to the tennis courts, he couldn't take his eyes off of Stan's attire. Everyone else was outfitted per dress code. Not Stan; the guy had donned all black from his oversized bowling shirt to his wide black board shorts, a wash of monochromatic gloom until you got down to his footwear: neon green Air Jordans. Ned pressed on.

Introducing Mayhaven to new members was the best part of his job. As Ned steered them from the courts to the driving range to the lake, his gaze roamed across the group gauging their reactions. The young mother's face lit up at the sight of a doubles match, and he wondered if it brought back memories of her high school team. Down at the lake, the businessman rolled up his pants and kicked off his dress shoes to sink his toes in the sand. On the upper decks, one of the children leaned out over the railing and pointed to the mountains. "Just imagine the sunsets," the wife whispered dreamily to the husband.

Ned was used to these reactions. Prospective members came for the golf or tennis, but they left with the wonder of the great outdoors. Mayhaven had it all. There was sanctuary beneath the willows along the lake, respite in the rolling breeze, magic in the shadows. Always, it brought Ned back in time to his own introduction to the club. To the feelings, many and complicated, it unearthed.

That long ago morning his father brought him up to play before opening hours, Ned experienced awe for the first time. Walking the gilded fairways at sunrise tethered him to the splendor of nature. Often they encountered the same young buck beneath the apple tree on the third hole, the noisy geese exiting the pond on the eighth. Tromping across the dewy grass beneath the blazing sky, it was like they were the only two people on earth.

It was also the first time Ned experienced what it was like to feel inferior. His family could never have afforded to belong to Mayhaven. He understood that the bag of clubs on his shoulder were secondhand, and only because another boy his age had left them behind. Slipping through daybreak shadows, he and his father were not members or guests. They were at the mercy of an old friend's generosity, limited to a handful of hours on stolen Saturday mornings. Until the day they were caught.

They'd just finished playing the eighth hole; Ned would always remember which one it was. His father had told him to hurry, that they did not have time to play their usual nine and needed to get off the course quickly. They'd just crested the hill on their way back to the parking lot, when they saw Len standing at the edge of the fairway. Len was not alone. Another man was talking to him, arms gesturing. Ned feared it wasn't good.

When both men's heads snapped in their direction, he knew it in his gut.

"Go on," his father said gruffly. "I'll meet you at the car."

Ned worried as they parted ways. He worried his father was in trouble. Or their friend Len might lose his job. Most of all, and he felt guilty for this, he worried this would be his last round at Mayhaven. He glanced over his shoulder more than once as his father walked toward Len and the other man without him.

Though Ned couldn't hear what they were saying, the man who'd seemed angry at Len now seemed angry at his father. Ned knew anger; he'd felt it emanating off his father all his life. It was the first time he saw his father on the receiving end of it. For some reason, this frightened him even more.

He opened the trunk of the car and set his golf bag in the back. When he climbed into the front seat he tried to wait, like his father had told him. Eyes trained on the three men, he held his breath. He counted to fifty. And then, when he couldn't stand it any longer, he got out of the car.

"I could have you arrested!" The words carried over the wind and the crunch of incoming tires in the parking lot to Ned's ears. He jammed his hands in his pockets and pressed toward them. "Do you have any idea what people pay to belong here? This is criminal trespassing."

As he drew closer, Ned saw the look on his father's face. Many times in his life Ned had been afraid of his father, but for the first time he felt afraid for him.

"I'm sorry, sir," he was saying. "I'll find a way to pay you back. Len is a good man, it was not his idea."

When his father saw him, his posture sagged. All three men turned expectantly to Ned.

"This is the boy," Len said. "Honestly, Mr. Kraft. You should see his swing."

Mr. Kraft did not look like he wanted to see Ned on his course or any part of his swing. Ned was not sure what his golf swing had to do with any of this.

"I'm sorry," his father said, again. "I only wanted my boy to have a chance."

Mr. Kraft's eyes had not left Ned's face, and his gaze was so intense it made Ned wince. "Go on then, kid." It sounded like a dare.

Ned looked to his father, confused. His father nodded. "Be a good boy and get your bag."

Ned did not understand what was happening. What he did understand was how terribly naïve he'd been. It had never occurred to him that what he and his father were doing was wrong, apparently so very wrong. Len was his dad's friend. Len worked here. Until that morning, he'd felt like the lucky recipient of a generous favor.

Ned ran back to the car as fast as his skinny legs could carry him, and hands shaking, retrieved his golf bag from the trunk.

What followed on the driving range felt like a test. Ned was being asked to perform, and he understood in his heart that if he failed things would be worse. But he was so nervous, he could barely keep his fingers still on the grip.

Mr. Kraft stood impatiently to the side, arms crossed, as Ned's father handed him a tee and a ball. "Go on, Ned. Show Mr. Kraft what you can do."

To his knowledge, Ned couldn't do anything special. It had only ever been himself and his father out there. He'd not watched others play, he'd not played with others. From what his father said, Ned did alright—but that was it—it was always ever just alright.

Ned took a deep breath and tried to relax his grip. He launched into his backswing and could feel even before he made contact that he'd shanked the ball. The silence that followed was deafening. He bit his lip, afraid to meet his father's eyes.

"Try again." His father handed him another ball.

The next drive went about one hundred fifty yards, his usual.

Len whistled.

Mr. Kraft said nothing.

The third drive went about the same. The next, one hundred seventy yards.

"How old are you?"

Ned turned to look Mr. Kraft in the eye. "Eleven, sir."

Mr. Kraft looked at Len and shook his head. Then at Ned and his father. "Walk back to the office with me."

A week later, Ned was a member of the Mayhaven Junior Golf League. He was the first and only player "sponsored," by the clubhouse, allowing him to practice with the team and compete in tournaments as a club member. It had not been his last day on the course; it was a beginning.

• • • • •

When the tour wrapped up, Ned thanked the prospective members for coming, overcome as he often was by their reactions.

"We can't wait to join," a middle-aged man said, shaking his hand. "We've got three kids and this is exactly what we want for our family."

"I have to come back with my wife. When she sees that beach, she's never going to want to leave."

"We're not very good golfers, but we're empty nesters now, and we want to try something new together."

When the last prospective member left, Ned was so buoyed by the tour he found himself heading toward the campers. He wanted to see Darcy. It was a beautiful day. It had been months. He would ask her to stay after work and play with him. Just a couple of holes. No big deal. There was no reason for him to believe she would take him up on this, but believe it he did.

He passed a group of campers at the picnic tables by the craft shed. Their hands were covered in finger paint and Ned stopped to admire the leaf prints they were making. Just beautiful.

Over on the courts Molly was giving a lesson to some middle school campers; Ned was impressed to see the power of their backswings. On his way down to the lake, he glanced over at the putting green where Vince was instructing. One girl, in particular, stood out. Her confident setup reminded him of Darcy. His heart caught.

As he trotted down the dirt trail to the beach, the intoxicating smell of fresh pine and lake water rose to meet him. There, among the campers on the small spit of beach below, he found her.

Ned paused. Darcy stood at the edge of the shore, all alone. Out in the water, the lifeguards were busy giving swim lessons to a group of splashing youngsters. On the beach a handful of counselors was talking and laughing, Lily among them. Ned took in all the activity and fun and noise before his eyes traveled back to Darcy, who remained to the side, staring impassively out at the water. All the cheer he'd carried down the hill with him evaporated.

For the first couple of years, Ned's father, Art Birch, accompanied his son to all of his tournaments. He'd stand silent among the spectators, but Ned could always sense his presence. Afterward, he'd drive his son home, lauding him with praise when he did well and staring wordlessly at the road ahead when he did not. Eventually, despite the growing wins, his father's attention waned along with his attendance. After two years, his father left the family altogether. Ned never saw his father again.

He would forever wonder about that morning they were caught on the course. He wondered why his father asked him to show Mr. Kraft his swing. Despite the passage of time, Ned could never silence the burning question: Had his father done it because he saw something special in his son, or was it nothing more than a handy distraction to get him out of a jam?

In the end, the game of golf belonged to Ned, and Mayhaven remained a memory that stayed with him long after he left for college, moved to Boston, and eventually met Ingrid. For Ned it was both joy and sorrow: on some days a touchstone he carried in the palm of his hand like hope, on other days an old wound whose scab he sometimes edged the curve of his fingernail around.

"It's a superb club and a sound career opportunity," he'd told Ingrid, when he'd seen the job listing for head of groundskeeping. But it was more than that. It was the pull of a memory, the long shadow of a boy and his father cresting a hill, the echo of irons in their bags as they walked. It sometimes nourished him and often haunted him, this endless chase of a splendor he'd lost.

But years later, Ned Birch eventually found it again: out there on the course with Darcy. Finally, his heart was made full.

Now, standing behind her at the lake, a fresh sense of gloom washed over him. As he gazed upon his daughter's uncertain stance, her narrow arms like birdwings crossed against her chest, Ned found tears springing to his eyes and wondered how he'd managed to lose that, too.

FLICK

He lay in bed thinking of all the ways he'd screwed up with Darcy in the golf cart. Why couldn't he ever keep his thoughts to himself? His mom always said, *People don't like to hear the truth. It's like shoving a mirror in their face.* Flick had long suspected that had more to do with his mother's personal history with his father, whose name they did not mention, so he'd chalked it up to her own hard feelings—not a universal truth. But now he wondered if maybe she was right.

Darcy had ignored his texts after the party, but when he'd awakened the next day, there was her reply, as golden as the July sun spilling through his curtains. It wasn't the best text—in fact, it was one cryptic word—but there it was. *Same.* He'd take it.

Flick stretched lazily, wondering exactly what she'd meant, before he couldn't ignore the growling of his stomach or the smell of bacon coming from downstairs. He barely knew Darcy Birch. Why did the girl have such an effect on him?

Downstairs, his mother was waiting for him at the kitchen island with a huge spread, and a suspicious look on her face.

"What happened?" he asked. Josie didn't cook. So far Stan specialized only in grilled meats. There had not been any big breakfasts since they'd moved into the big house, so Flick knew right away that something was up.

Josie laughed. "Oh, would you relax? We have this gigantic new kitchen and it's time I started using it. Besides, if we want to entertain more, I need to practice." She elbowed Stan, who was eyeing the plate of bacon.

"Your mother has a lot of big ideas," Stan said, but he didn't look like he minded. He, too, seemed to be waiting as Flick surveyed the scrambled eggs, cut fruit, and plate of bacon. Flick reached for a piece.

"So, we have some news!" Josie announced.

With the piece of bacon halfway to his lips, Flick's stomach fell. He set the bacon down. God, he hoped they weren't having a baby. He'd given up New York and his best friend, and he'd moved here to the land of dense forests and even denser rich kids. He could handle all that if he had to. But he did not want to be a big brother. Josie had had him young, but Stan was not young. And being related to someone related to Stan was not something Flick relished. Besides, he was pretty sure Stan would not father an especially attractive child.

Flick stared at his mother, unable to speak.

"We're joining the club!" Josie shrieked. She announced this like she'd gotten into Harvard or won the lotto (though according to her she had, by marrying Stan).

Flick's stomach surged with relief as the image of a half-Stan baby vaporized, then clenched again. "Wait—what?"

"Mayhaven," Josie said, as if he didn't know which club. "Stan and I went to the open house, and it's everything I hoped for. We're joining."

Stan offered what resembled a smile, for him. "Your mother is going to learn to play tennis," he said.

"*We* are going to learn," she corrected.

"Oh no." Stan wagged a finger. "I golf. My brothers golf. We will be playing golf. Tennis can be your thing, especially if you wear one of those swishy little skirts, right?" He planted a wet kiss on her lips and Josie kissed him back. Flick had to look away.

"Anyway, we filed our application, and we'll find out soon if we're in."

"Of course, we're in," Stan said, shoving a whole piece of bacon in his mouth. "Who wouldn't take us?"

Flick could think of one person.

It had been lost on him that you had to apply to get into Mayhaven. Flick figured anyone with bags of money was a shoo-in. But if that weren't the case, and Mr. Birch was in charge, and Stan had been an asshole to him . . . "So, are you applying to any other clubs?" he asked. Maybe they should be looking at this like college applications and widen their search.

Josie made a face. "Why? Mayhaven is perfect. That's where I want to belong." She pushed the platter of eggs closer to her son. "You didn't tell me how gorgeous it is up there. The lake, the hills, the outdoor dining. Best of all, you'll be a member, too!"

Flick really did not care to be a member. Not with the likes of Spencer and his crew. He didn't play golf or tennis, and had zero interest in rubbing elbows with a bunch of elitist old folks. What he liked was his job. He liked working for Mossimo in the kitchen and learning how to cook unique things. He liked watching the campers play, and the cute college girls who strolled by in their bikinis and smiled at him when he worked the snack shack. But becoming a member?

"I don't know," he said, shoveling eggs onto his plate. "I'm not really into that scene. Maybe you guys join, and I just keep working there."

"You won't work there if we get in." Josie said this like it was already decided.

Both Stan and Flick stared at her in disbelief. "What? Why can't the kid work there?"

"Yeah, I like my job!"

It was the only thing the two had united on so far, but Flick would take it.

Josie shook her head in exasperation. "How would that look? We'll be surrounded by people who send their kids to private schools and have nannies and big jobs in Boston—but our poor kid needs to wash dishes in the back kitchen while we dine on the upper decks?"

"First of all, I don't wash dishes . . ." Flick began.

"Who cares what people think?" Stan interrupted. "The kid says he likes his job. And it's good for him to earn some pocket money."

"He doesn't need pocket money," Josie insisted. "He's got us."

This was not technically true, and it made Flick uncomfortable. Flick had Josie—*she* was his parent. Stan was not, and Flick couldn't have Stan thinking he wanted him to be. God, his mother could make such awkward proclamations when she wanted to win an argument. He pushed his plate away. "I'm going to be late for work."

"But wait," Josie said. "You don't need to work, honey. The club was a way for you to keep busy and meet new people this summer. Once we're members, you can just enjoy it."

She didn't get it. He wasn't exactly making friends at Mayhaven.

Again, Stan came to his rescue. "Listen to what he's saying, sweet stuff. I think he does enjoy it up there, right, kid?" Stan may have had his own interests in Flick being busy and out of the house more often than not, but Flick decided to give him the benefit of the doubt.

"I don't want to quit. Besides, you're not even in yet."

Josie's eyes flashed. "We will be."

Flick decided to capitalize on the one thing Josie seemed to care about. "Then you don't want me to be late, do you? It might impact what Mr. Birch thinks."

At the mention of the neighbor, Stan got fired up. "Birch? He just works there. He doesn't get to call the shots."

"Well, it's certainly not going to help our chances that you didn't invite them to our party last weekend," Josie reminded him.

Flick left them debating by the uneaten breakfast buffet.

When he pulled into Mayhaven, he couldn't help but look at it with fresh eyes. Had the lot always been so full of Porsches and Range Rovers? He locked his Chevy, which was a joke—no one here would take it—and went in. The kitchen was empty, so he checked the assignment board. Ricky wasn't scheduled until noon. Flick had been assigned to the drink cart for the afternoon. He laughed out loud.

Driving the drink cart was Wendy's gig and, man, was she territorial about it. He'd once made the mistake of asking Mossimo what it would take to get a shift on the cart. Wendy, in the midst of dicing onions, had looked up from her cutting board. "Step off, junior. If I'm cooped up indoors I get edgy." She'd rotated her knife so that the light bounced off its blade.

Flick thought she was joking, but given the look on Ricky's face and Mossimo's swift departure, he knew better. For him to get the drink cart assignment today meant Wendy was either out of state or half dead.

The cart didn't go out until noon, but there was a slew of sandwiches to prep and beverages to load. On his way to the fridge, there came a rustling sound from the back. Flick startled. In the pantry he found Adam Birch stacking cans of tomato sauce in military-precise rows. He'd heard that Adam had been hired, but this was the first time they'd crossed paths. Adam's gaze flickered his way and then back to the shelf.

"Morning," Flick said.

"Midmorning."

"What?"

"Technically, it's midmorning." He watched as Adam turned a can left then right until its label was centered.

"Right." Adam was Darcy's brother and his boss's son. Flick wanted to be friendly. "So you're working in the kitchen today?"

"No, I'm working in the pantry. Then I work in the office."

There had been whispers about Adam. Wendy had called him *special.* Ricky had said he was fine to work with as long as you didn't interrupt him, which apparently Flick was doing right now.

"I'll be at the prep island if you need anything," Flick said, trying to demonstrate camaraderie.

"Why would I need you?"

Flick smiled. It was a fair question.

When Mossimo came in a little later, Flick had assembled twenty Thai chicken salad sandwiches, twenty ham and Gruyère croissants, and fifteen vegetarian wraps for the cart.

"Good morning!" Mossimo called out in his booming voice.

Flick noticed that Adam did not correct him on the time of day.

Mossimo headed straight for Adam where Flick overheard him inquire about a delayed shipment of olive oil.

"Were you able to locate it?" Mossimo asked. "If it doesn't come in today, I'll have to source elsewhere." The chef sounded distressed.

Adam was matter-of-fact. "I called wholesale, and they said it shipped. But when I checked the tracking, it shows it never left their distributor's warehouse. So I called them next."

"And?" Mossimo asked.

"They said it should be here between three and five. I emailed you the tracking information, and I printed a hard copy. It's on your desk."

"Excellent, thank you. When you're done here, I'd like you to check inventory of dry goods. We're running low on flour and rice."

Mossimo returned to the kitchen and looked at Flick. "Something wrong?"

"No." Flick got back to work. Here he was scooping chicken salad while Adam managed shipments, delivery, and inventory.

Mossimo leaned over his shoulder and inspected his prep work. "You forgot tuna."

"Tuna?"

"The older members like their tuna salad. On white." Mossimo shuddered. "Make ten."

When Ricky came in, he helped Flick carry the sandwiches downstairs to the storage area. Two industrial refrigerators hummed against one wall. Canned and bottled beverages lined the metal shelving racks on the other. The drink cart was parked just outside. "Big day on the cart," Ricky said, sliding the door open. "Don't screw it up."

Flick couldn't tell if he were joking or not.

"Has Wendy shown you the drill before?" Ricky asked. Then he caught himself and laughed. "Of course she hasn't. Alright, sports drinks, water, and premixed beverages are stored in that fridge, and sandwiches in the other. Load half of what you made into the cart and come back to restock as needed."

He waited while Flick loaded the trays into the refrigerator. When they got to the vegetarian wraps, Flick balked. "Do you really sell many of those?"

Ricky shook his head. "This is a country club, man. You've got a lot to learn about their palates.

"Charges go on member accounts. Your job is to drive the track and offer service, same as the dining room."

"Got it. What about the cart? Is it hard to handle?" It was much bigger and wider than a golf cart.

Ricky shrugged. "It's heavy, so go easy and stick to the track. Got it?"

Flick was suddenly feeling overwhelmed. But he nodded.

"Good." Ricky slapped him on the back. "Smile for the tips, pretty boy!"

He'd just finished loading the cart with beverages when he realized he'd left his phone upstairs. Ricky had warned him to have it on the course for communication. He raced back inside.

Halfway up the stairwell, he heard men's voices at the top. "I thought we talked about this. He is to work in the kitchen, not in the office." Flick halted on the lower landing where he was out of sight.

"Yes, Mr. Delancey, he was in the kitchen all morning. He helped me solve a shipping problem, in fact."

It was Spencer's father and Mossimo.

"So why is he working in the office with Jane right now?" Mr. Delancey sounded annoyed. "When I went in there he had his hands all over billing. That kid has no business looking at members' invoices or statements; it's an invasion of privacy."

"Privacy?" Flick could tell Mossimo found this ridiculous. "I'm sorry, but Mr. Birch told me Adam could divide his time between the kitchen and the main office."

"Mr. Birch is not in charge. He works for the board," Mr. Delancey said. "And as chairman of the board, I can assure you that we are not running a daycare center here."

"Adam has a wonderful mind for numbers."

Delancey was not having it. "That boy has issues."

"His name is Adam."

"Excuse me?"

"That boy. His name is Adam."

Flick winced. He had to give it to Mossimo, the guy had balls.

Delancey leaned in, and the two men stood toe-to-toe. "He stays in the kitchen with you, is that clear?"

"Crystal," Mossimo said flatly.

"Stick to your job in the kitchen, Chef. If it's a job you value."

A heavy beat of silence was followed by swift footsteps as Delancey stalked out. Flick waited, then peered up the stairs in time to see Mossimo punch the wall. His fist landed where Delancey had been standing.

Out on the course, there was no time to reflect on what he'd just seen. Flick moved steadily along the track, stopping at each hole. Ham and Gruyère croissants flew off the cart, chicken salad coming in second place. Nobody wanted the vegetarian wraps, as predicted. The men wanted beers, the women wanted water. Tips weren't exactly life-changing. But Flick got his hopes up when he came across Mr. Upton and some clients. Upton was a big deal finance guy in the city, and his drink order ended up being a big deal, too. He eyed the premixed beverages in the cart like he'd stepped in dog poo. "James makes the best bloodies. We like them fresh." James was the club's bartender, all the way back in the clubhouse restaurant. Which is exactly where Upton sent Flick. "It'll be worth your while," he said, winking. Flick turned the cart around, knowing this would throw off his schedule, but eager to please. Driving along the bumpy cart path with a tray of four Bloody Marys proved a near disaster, but he did it. When he proudly handed them over, Upton slipped him two bills. Twenties? Fifties? Wendy bragged she once got four Benjamins from one foursome. Flick waited until Upton turned away before he looked. He was still staring in disbelief at the two singles in his palm when Upton called out.

"Better keep moving. I think you're behind schedule."

His spirits were low as he approached the next foursome, until he spied Bitsy Babcock. Bitsy introduced him around as her "delicious pal" and her partners crowded around him. Where did he go to school? Did he have a girlfriend? He made out like a bandit at that hole.

By the time he made one sweep of the course the cart needed restocking. He passed a group of campers on his way back to the clubhouse. Leading them was a girl who worked with Darcy—what was her name? Lily? Darcy had been on his mind since her one-worded text.

When he pulled the drink cart up to the clubhouse, he found a member of the Birch family, but it wasn't Darcy.

Adam was slumped against the side of the clubhouse, his hands covering his face. Not sure what to do, Flick decided to go about his business. He unloaded the bag of trash he'd collected and dumped the empties into the recycling bin. The crash of plastic made Adam cover his ears.

"Sorry," Flick said.

Adam sniffed and swiped at his nose. Flick could see he'd been crying.

"Are you okay?" he ventured.

"Please leave me alone." Adam crossed his arms tight, but his voice was soft. All of a sudden he looked much younger.

Flick remembered Mossimo and Mr. Delancey on the back stairs. He wondered if he should go find Mr. Birch.

"I have to restock this cart," Flick said. "But if you need help, I'm here." He started loading fresh sandwiches into the cooler.

"You're doing it wrong."

Flick turned to see Adam scrutinizing his work.

"The sandwiches go in flat, not sideways. You're crushing them. Nobody wants a crushed sandwich."

"No," Flick agreed. "Nobody wants that."

"Let me," Adam said, coming over. When he looked inside the cooler he gasped. "What were you thinking?" He began removing every single sandwich. "This is all wrong. Good thing I'm here."

Flick tried to hide his smile. "Yeah, good thing."

"I like your car," Adam said suddenly.

"This isn't my car."

"Duh. I meant your car. The Chevy Malibu, from 2013."

"That's right." Flick looked at Adam with surprise.

"You just missed the V-6 by one year. Too bad." Adam made a face. "But one hundred ninety-seven horsepower isn't bad."

Flick couldn't believe it. "You really do like cars."

When Adam had stored the sandwiches to his satisfaction, he turned to Flick. "All fixed now."

"Thanks," Flick said. "You're pretty good at that."

The compliment had the opposite effect. Adam's face crumpled and tears sprang to his eyes. "I'm really good at lots of things."

"Adam? What's wrong?"

They both turned to see Darcy rounding the corner. She was carrying a basket full of craft supplies, but seeing Adam's face she dumped them on the ground and rushed up to her brother. "What happened?" She turned to Flick. "What did you say to him?"

Flick hopped back. "I didn't say anything, I found him like this."

But Darcy wasn't listening.

The moment he laid eyes on his sister, Adam's defenses collapsed.

Flick ducked out of the way and finished his job as Adam cried to Darcy. It was hard to make out exactly what he was saying, but Flick froze when he heard his name.

It was a relief when Darcy finally took Adam inside. What was it with this girl? One minute she was kidnapping him to steal golf carts and wine and the next she was blaming him for upsetting her brother. He'd just started the cart when he felt a hand on his shoulder.

He turned to face Darcy's big green eyes.

"Adam told me you were nice to him. That you tried to help."

Flick felt himself soften. "He did?" Adam had given no indication he'd absorbed anything beyond the sandwich crisis.

"Adam can be . . ." She looked off in the distance at a group of campers. "Complicated. But he's very sensitive; and he knows a lot more than people give him credit for."

"Okay." He was about to share what he'd overheard on the stairs, but caught himself. Things were complicated enough with this girl. Darcy was smart. She'd figure it out.

"Thank you for being so nice to him."

Flick needed to get back out on the course. The ice was melting in the coolers and the golfers would be hungry. But he couldn't pull his gaze away just yet. "No problem," he said. "Adam is a good kid."

"So are you." Before he knew what was happening Darcy leaned in and kissed him. By the time Flick pressed his hand to where her lips had brushed his cheek, she was already jogging back to her campers.

DARCY

There was no way around it; no matter how she may have felt about Spencer, his father was a total jerk.

Normally Darcy didn't like to be seen in her father's office. She didn't want to be thought of as some goody-goody daughter of the president. But Adam needed help.

Her father's face fell the moment he looked up and saw both his kids in the doorway, Adam's cheeks stained with tears. "What on earth?"

"Adam needs a minute," Darcy said, sharing a look that the two of them had rehearsed a thousand times before.

"Come in, buddy," her father said, shutting the door behind them. "What happened?"

By then Adam's crying had slowed, but he did not want to talk. "I want to go home. It's time for me to go home."

"He was fired from the office job," Darcy explained.

"Fired?" Her father shook his head. "Adam can't have been fired. I just gave him that job."

Adam sniffed. "Mossimo says I have to stay in the kitchen. Because Mr. Delancey said so."

Darcy glared at her father. It was one thing for her to have to suffer a summer job here, but the silver lining had been that at least Adam liked his.

"There must be some kind of misunderstanding," her father said decidedly.

"So I can go back to the office?" Adam sputtered.

"Wait here, first. I'm going to go upstairs and sort this out right now."

Darcy exhaled. Their father seemed so sure, his expression as unruffled as his collared shirt. It always surprised her just how fierce she could be for Adam, a strength she could not seem to muster for herself. "You're sure?" she asked. How she wanted to believe him, standing there in his Mayhaven polo shirt, with that stupid staring pilgrim emblazoned on his chest.

"Leave Adam with me and get back to work," he assured her.

• • • • •

But after work, there was more trouble. Molly, the tennis pro, called for an emergency camp staff meeting. Darcy lined up with the others as Vince, Molly, and her father gathered everyone at the picnic tables. Their expressions were grim.

"All three new kayaks are missing," Molly announced to the group. "Does anyone know anything about this?"

There was silence, followed by a flood of murmurs, but no one offered up any information. Blaine, one of the lifeguards, was whispering something to Spencer, but Darcy couldn't hear.

Lily leaned in. "They were there yesterday because I had to drag the kayaks up on the beach after swim time."

Darcy tried to focus on what Lily was saying and not her old coach's golf hat, as Vince stood in front of them. Her father had given him that hat after her last tournament, right after she won.

She had one just like it, shoved in the back of her closet back at home. Right next to the trophy she'd won.

Ashley Riley raised her hand like she was in third grade. "Maybe someone borrowed them and they're banked somewhere up the lake?" Everyone nodded, like she'd come up with the right answer.

"We've already searched the shore on both sides," Molly informed them. "Unfortunately, before this happened a paddleboard also disappeared over the weekend. Along with paddles."

Vince cleared his throat. "What appeared to have been one missing piece of equipment is starting to look like a string of thefts." He let this settle in as his gaze roamed over the counselors. Darcy looked past him to her father. Like everything else, camp was under his jurisdiction right down to the last oar.

"If you saw anything or know anything, please come see us," he said. "These are expensive club items, and this is a serious matter."

Given the day her father was having, she was almost afraid to ask if he'd sorted things out for Adam. When she found him in his office, she had her answer: he looked like he wanted to punch something.

"Apparently Mr. Delancey decided that Adam is only cleared to work in the kitchen." Her father was fuming.

"What? I thought you were in charge." She looked around. "Where's Adam now?"

"He was so upset I took him home."

Poor Adam. "Dad, this makes no sense. Did something happen in the office?"

"No, Jane loves having Adam help out. She keeps telling me what a wonder he is with the accounts."

Adam had always been a numbers guy. Since he was little he would sit in the shopping cart at the checkout line and predict within a dollar what the cost of the groceries would be before the cashier even rang them up. When Darcy needed help on her precalc homework, Adam was the only one in the family who could give it. Someone could tell him their birthdate, and in less than thirty seconds he'd calculate their present age to the minute. Darcy would bet her life he was better in that office than anyone at this stupid club. "Why would Mr. Delancey do this?"

Her father shook his head. "He told Jane that member accounts are private business, and non-salaried employees shouldn't have access."

"Do you believe that?" Again, she already knew the answer.

It was the thing that got Darcy's hackles up the most: so many people took Adam at face value. They saw a lanky shy kid who didn't make eye contact. Who rarely spoke to people outside his family, or talked rapidly and without pause when he did. They assessed the averted gaze and the social awkwardness and did their own math to sum him up. Darcy knew better than anyone; she'd been watching people do it to him her whole life. Now Mr. Delancey was, too.

Her father stood up. "It doesn't matter what Dick Delancey thinks. I'm going to have a word with him and fix this. Don't worry."

This time Darcy didn't find solace in her father's resolve. Gone were the days she believed her father could fix things as easily as he once did her scraped knee or Adam's toppled ice cream cone. One thing she'd learned that year was that people disappointed you left and right; sometimes the ones you cared about the most.

"Dad, just because you're president doesn't mean you can fix everything."

Her father looked like she'd smacked him. "Darcy, this has nothing to do with my position. Mayhaven is about welcoming families—and what Dick did isn't in line with that."

Here he was again, toeing the club line. "How can you keep defending this place if this is how Adam is treated?"

"Hang on, honey. Dick Delancey does not represent Mayhaven."

"Doesn't he?" She snorted. God, her dad had such a blind spot. "He's the chairman! Of course he does."

"No," her father insisted. "I do. So do board members like Mrs. Babcock, who's loved both you kids since you were little. And Mossimo and his team. And the pros, who've instructed you guys and all the other kids here over the years."

Darcy flinched when he mentioned the pros, but her father was too impassioned to notice.

"This is a place where everyone belongs."

Darcy looked at her father, and almost felt sorry for him. "What if we don't *want* to belong?" Before he could say anything more she turned and stormed out. This was his fault, too. For being so naïve, for not seeing what was right under his nose.

She pushed through the back door and was about to head for the parking lot when she heard a burst of laughter. Spencer Delancey was walking up the hill from the lake with the other guards. Well, well, well. What was it her mother always said? Apples don't fall far.

Fuming, she strode up to him. "Got a minute?"

The other lifeguards halted, looks of amusement on their faces. "Uh, sure. What's up?"

Darcy ignored them. "I need to talk to you. Like, now."

Spencer followed her to a bench in the shade and sat down. He flipped his blond hair out of his blue eyes and leaned in. God, he was beautiful. "Something wrong?"

She would not be swayed. "You know my brother, Adam?"

Spencer nodded. "Sure."

"He got a job in the club office this summer, but he was just let go."

"Oh. That sucks." Spencer looked confused. "What does that have to do with me?"

"Your dad was the one who said he doesn't belong there."

"My dad?" He fidgeted on the seat next to her. "Why would he care?"

"Good question." Spencer needed to know what his father did. "Adam is really smart, and he could do that job better than anyone with an accounting degree, so I'm just trying to figure out why the board chairman thinks it's okay to stick him in the back of the kitchen. Like he's hiding him away." Her tone was high and ripe with anger, and she knew she was probably embarrassing herself, but she couldn't stop. "What your dad did—it's not fair."

Spencer didn't say anything. But to his credit he didn't get up and walk away, either. "Look, Darcy, I don't know anything about this. But I can see how angry you are." He reached over and put a hand on hers, and that was all it took.

"It's not right," she said again, staring at their intertwined hands.

"So you should talk to someone about that. But I don't think that someone is me."

"You're right." Her voice broke. "I shouldn't have bothered you with this." Spencer wasn't the guy to go after. But she was so mad: at her father, at his father, at the stupid club. She swiped at her eyes where, to her horror, tears were starting to pool. "Sometimes I get protective of my brother."

"It's okay." He shrugged. "My sister and I barely talk. Adam's lucky to have a sister who sticks up for him."

Darcy looked up at Spencer. He seemed genuine. Maybe being a jerk didn't run in the family.

"Hey, Spence!" They were being interrupted. "You coming to the beach or not?"

They both turned to see Ashley Riley striding across the grass. She was wearing a red bikini top and a short white skirt. When she saw Darcy, she glared at her. Neither girl said hello.

"I'll be down in a bit," Spencer said, his gaze returning to Darcy's. Darcy couldn't believe it.

Apparently neither could Ashley. "Well, I can't stay for long. So if you want to hang . . ."

"Got it." His tone was as cool as his expression, and he stayed right where he was, next to Darcy. Ashley did not budge, either. Darcy could feel the vibration of her impatience as she stood behind them.

"You can go if you want," Darcy began, trying to sound casual. But in her head: *Please stay, please stay, please stay!*

Spencer shook his head. To Ashley he called, "I'll catch you later."

"Whatever." Ashley stomped away from them down the hill toward the lake.

Spencer flipped his hair out of his eyes like a fly had been buzzing between them. "Sorry. You were saying?"

Darcy was so shocked by what just happened, she forgot what she'd been saying. "Nothing. We're good."

"Okay. Cool." He stood up, and she felt her heart leap up off the bench with him.

"Actually, wait. There is something." She swallowed. "I owe you an apology for lighting into you like that."

Spencer smirked.

"What?" This was not funny. Even if he'd just sent Ashley Riley on her way, Darcy had still made a complete fool of herself. She could not end on this note.

"You did light into me," he said. But his expression remained amused. "It was kind of cute, actually."

Darcy looked away, trying to hide her blush. God, why couldn't she control her emotions better? "My dad said he'll figure it out," she said, switching the subject. "Thanks for letting me vent."

Spencer waved a hand like it was nothing. "We've all got to blow off steam sometimes. Look, my dad can be tough, but he's a good guy. I'm sure there was some kind of misunderstanding." He looked back at the clubhouse. "Both of our fathers are in charge of this place. It can be cool sometimes, but it can also be a pain in the ass for us. Right?"

"So true." It had never occurred to her that she'd have something in common with Spencer, and yet here it was. "My dad acts like this place is heaven on earth," she confided.

Darcy let her gaze roam out over the course, past the first tee box illuminated in late afternoon sun; a spot she used to feel so sure of things when she stood up there, driver in hand.

"Don't stress so much, Birch. It's summer." Spencer held out his hand and she let him pull her up from the bench. "Look around. Let yourself have some fun."

Darcy forced a smile. "Right."

As she watched him walk away, Darcy had to wonder if Spencer got her. Despite this messed up club and her crazy family, it was summer. He was right. She did deserve some fun. And maybe it would be with him.

NED

Ned was not a man of violence, but he wanted to kill Dick Delancey. Who the hell did he think he was going behind Ned's back while he was away at a meeting and pulling his son from his new job?

Ingrid was working late again, and it was well after dinner when she finally came home. Ned had already cooked, cleaned the kitchen, and walked Fritzy. He'd tried Dick Delancey both at home and on his cell, to no avail. He'd asked both kids multiple times to go for a swim with him in the pool; he needed to unwind. For the first time in ages, Darcy was in a happy mood, but she'd stayed on the phone giggling with Lily all evening. Adam, who still wanted to be left alone, was watching car videos. "I need to go back to the office," he kept saying. "I only got through half of the invoices."

"I know, buddy," Ned said. "I'm trying to fix the misunderstanding."

It wasn't true. The only misunderstanding was Dick Delancey's sense of authority. Ned knew from Neiman Shrive that Dick was the only board member who opposed Adam's hiring, in favor of a friend he'd wanted the job to go to. He also knew

Dick was uncomfortable around Adam; he saw it in the way Dick addressed Darcy and Ingrid, but always looked right past Adam as if he weren't there. And in the way Dick looked at Adam, on the rare occasion he did. Well, it was time Dick was enlightened about a few things.

Ingrid found him pacing up in their room, trying Dick's cell phone. She looked as exhausted as he felt.

"Have you eaten?" he asked. Bad news on an empty stomach was a deadly combo for Ingrid.

She kicked off her shoes. "I just want to get out of these work clothes and into bed. After all those showings, the Boston couple is waffling on the Tree House. Maybe the other agents were right. This house is impossible to sell."

"I'm sorry," he said. Ingrid had been killing herself on that sale.

She tugged open her closet door and stood staring into it like she'd forgotten what she was doing there. "It's been a long day."

Ned hated that what he had to say would make it even longer. "Honey, something happened at the club today." He went and closed the bedroom door.

Ingrid was a rat terrier with a bone when she sensed anything wrong with her kids. "What happened? Was it about Adam? It was Adam." She did that, too—drew conclusions without even letting him finish a sentence—but damned if she weren't usually right.

"Dick Delancey doesn't think he should work in the office. He assigned Adam to kitchen work only."

"What?" Her outrage was predictable. "Why not? Based on what information?"

"I haven't been able to reach him. The only information I have is that he's an asshole." Ned flopped on the bed.

"Damn it, Ned. This is the first job Adam has liked. And it got him out of the house every day. You have to get it back for him." She looked at him imploringly. "For all of us."

"I will. Don't worry."

She rummaged irritably through the dresser drawer and yanked out her pajamas. "Are you sure about that?"

Ned did not like the doubt in her tone. "Of course I'm sure."

"Then how did Adam lose the job to begin with?" She shook her head. "I don't know, Ned. I know you love that place, but that board seems out of control lately. They put all these crazy expectations on you but are never supportive of changes you try to make. This is just one more example." She paused in her outrage to undress. Ned was instantly distracted. His eyes traveled up her legs to the curve of her stomach to her breasts and paused there. "This is your family they're going after."

He sensed that she was referring to some invisible line between them. Were they not on the same side of this? "No one is going after anyone, honey," he said. "And it's not us against them. Adam belongs at the club just as much as anyone else."

Ingrid snorted. Just the way Darcy had, in his office earlier. It gave him a bad feeling. "Don't you believe that?"

"Ned." She tugged her nightgown over her head and her lovely breasts disappeared.

"Mayhaven has changed. Or maybe we have. I don't know." She sighed. "I just hope you can figure this out as quickly as you seem to think you can."

He waited as she stalked down the hall to see the kids. Ingrid was a good mother. Here she was working her tail off at the realty office and still holding their household together. If Adam didn't have a job to go to and insisted on staying home, he knew it would make her feel like she had to, too. She'd worked too hard for Ned to let that happen.

When Ingrid returned, she had a suspicious look on her face. "Darcy's in a good mood. What happened?"

Ned smiled, ruefully. Damned if he knew. Darcy used to be in a good mood most of the time. "I'm worried about her."

"Her moods are all over the place this summer. I think she should talk to someone." Ingrid had been suggesting they find Darcy a therapist all summer. Ned had thought she was getting ahead of herself; teenage emotions were about as stable as an electrical storm. But lately he had to wonder if Ingrid were right.

"I think she should talk to a college recruiter. Maybe that would get her head back in the game."

"Ned."

"What? College isn't going to pay for itself. And that was her ticket—"

"Stop, please. If she's ever going to come back to golf, it has to be her idea." Ingrid pulled the covers back and climbed into bed next to him. "We may have to figure something else out for college."

Ned rolled onto his back and stared at a spot on the ceiling that probably needed to be repainted. "I never should've had the damn pool redone."

"We had to do something. It was turning into a frog pond." It was true, they'd inherited the pool with the house, and it had been a crumbling, leaking mess ever since. But the pool was a small price to pay. They'd afforded a house, albeit humble, in a good town with good schools. It was worth every sacrifice he'd made at work to make that happen.

"Ingrid, you know I'd do anything for our family."

"Yes, honey." She propped herself up on one elbow. "I also know we don't always see things the same way. You like to tell me to be more positive, and sometimes I want to tell you to be more realistic."

Ned knew what his family thought of him; that he was sentimental, head in the clouds. But the world was a dark place, too. He'd pushed away darkness since childhood and now, as a father, it was his job to keep it from his children. "I'm trying, Ingrid."

He sank back into the pillows and she rested her head on his chest. "Sometimes I wish I could be as optimistic as you are," she said. "If Adam isn't working, there's no way I can leave him sitting home alone all summer."

Ned pulled her closer against him. "It's not fair." When the kids were babies they'd struck a deal: she wanted to stay at home and he would work. When she went back into realty, they knew it would be an adjustment.

"You don't have to work," he said, carefully. "If you don't want to." Things were tight, but he didn't want her spreading herself too thin.

Ingrid sat up and looked at him. "But I do. I need to, for myself."

Her eyes were so green, just like Darcy's. And so full of determination. "Then we'll figure this out."

Not long after Ingrid turned out the light, her soft snores filled the room. Normally the cadence of them lulled Ned to sleep. But that night he tossed and turned, the weight of his whole world sitting on his shoulders.

• • • • •

First thing the next morning Ned headed straight for the pro shop. Sure enough, Dick Delancey's reserved time slot was written in. He wasn't really supposed to do that, but there it was.

"Beautiful day today, eh, boss?" Vince was all smiles and jocularity, but it didn't have its usual effect. "Been a while since I've seen you put that A-game to good use. You heading out for a round?"

"Not today," Ned said, glumly. He hadn't played yet that summer. It was the irony of being president of a golf club.

Vince shook his head. "I dunno, you've been going nonstop. If you change your mind, I'll grab you a cart and set you up with some lunch."

He wished Ingrid was there. This was one of the reasons Ned loved this place so much: people like Vince and the convivial spirit.

"Thanks, Vince. Has Dick come in yet?"

"You just missed him." Vince nodded out the window toward the first tee box.

"He's been hooking 'em lately. Real shame." Vince winked. He wasn't a huge Delancey fan, either. It was well known that Dick never tipped the pros or the caddies.

"Real shame, indeed."

Outside Ned found Dick shoving his driver into his golf bag, angrily. "Tough drive?"

"Just warming up," Dick said, fixing him with his Cheshire cat grin. "What can I help you with, Ned?"

Alrighty then, he'd skip the niceties. "You pulled Adam out of the office?"

Dick didn't hesitate. "I did." Nor did he offer apology or explanation.

"That wasn't your place," Ned said. "What was the reason?"

"Oh, come on, Ned. We both know our kids have privileges here because of us." Ned would not allow himself to be sucked into any fraternizing.

"Dick, you must know the board posted the part-time office job themselves. Adam applied and he's good at it. Is there some kind of budgetary issue I'm unaware of?" Adam would do that job for free, but Ned wasn't about to offer that just yet.

Dick scuffed the ground with his toe; Ned really wished he wouldn't do that. "Your son is a good kid, but there is no room for error with member accounts."

"Has there been an error?" Dick didn't say anything, and Ned knew then for sure: this was about something else.

"The board and I don't think it's appropriate that a kid has access to confidential member information. Accounts and charges are private. So are methods of payment."

Ned didn't say anything.

"He's just a kid," Dick said finally.

"Not just any kid," Ned said.

"Come on, Ned."

"No, you come on, Dick. That's what this is about, isn't it?"

Dick held out one hand. "I never said that."

"You didn't have to."

"Let's not take it there, Birch. This is unnecessary."

"You already did. This isn't about confidentiality or any of that nonsense. This is about Adam. Because he's on the spectrum. And you don't understand it or don't like it, I can't say for sure, but this is about *you*, Dick."

"You can take this to the board and file a complaint. But it won't change anything."

Dick was not going to budge. If Ned took this to the board it would take even more time and draw more attention to Ned's position. Maybe, Ned realized, that was what Dick had wanted all along.

"Your job is up for review this fall, Ned. Some might say that gifting your son a highly sensitive position was an overstep on your part. I'm happy to open this for further review if you insist."

Fists clenched, Ned watched Dick Delancey motor off in the cart. It was little solace to see him stop a mere fifty yards away to play his crappy drive.

Back in the office, he found a file sitting on his desk affixed with a note from Jane: *New Member Applicants*. This was the last thing he cared to deal with right now.

But he needed some good news. After his robust membership drive that summer, Ned hoped for around twenty new applications, but he'd take fifteen. Hell, he'd take ten.

"Let there be at least ten," he whispered as he flipped open the file and scanned the list. It didn't take him long: there were four measly applications. When he got to the third one, he slammed his fist on the desk: *Stan and Josephine Crenshaw, Maple Drive.*

FLICK

There was a new membership board meeting that afternoon. Normally this would mean nothing to Flick, but Mossimo got a call in the kitchen. The meeting had run so late that Mr. Birch had asked for lunch to be brought in.

"Me?" Flick asked. He really did not want to go in there. He did not want to overhear anything. Let his mother and Stan get the email or the call or whatever embossed fancy stationery was sent to the house, if they were accepted. All it boiled down to was the fact that not everyone in his house would win: good news for his mother meant bad news for him.

For days his mother had talked about nothing except their pending application. Worse, she'd gone shopping for new "outfits" to wear to the club, and they didn't look anything like what the other women at the club wore.

That morning, before work, she'd cornered him. "So? Has Mr. Birch given you any indication?"

"Mom, I'm just a kitchen and snack bar kid," he'd reminded her. "If it's not about cheeseburgers or beurre blanc sauce, it doesn't apply to me."

Josie had not been dissuaded. "Work hard this week. And if

you see Mr. Birch go out of your way to smile." She pinched his cheek. "Such a gorgeous smile!"

Flick doubted very much Mr. Birch would say anything to him, and in fact he prayed he would not. It would be awkward. Plus, he had very mixed feelings about his mother and Stan joining. Not only did he not like the other teens who belonged there, but he had to admit it—bad as he felt for saying so, it didn't seem like a place Stan and his mother would really fit in.

Josie was a whole lot younger than the other moms with kids his age. Sure, she kept herself in shape, but she favored blingy jewelry and animal prints and tight-fitting clothes. He'd bet his life she did not own any monogrammed sweaters or lobster-print skirts. And let's not get started on Stan. Stan's idea of *dining room attire* was a purple satin shirt unbuttoned down to the tangle of gold necklaces in his abundant chest hair. Flick shivered just imagining him seated next to Mrs. Babcock in the dining room, bellowing "Pass the hot sauce!"

"Knock first," Mossimo said to him now, as he helped Flick load the service cart. "The board members don't like to be interrupted."

Resigned, Flick pushed the cart down the hall and knocked. When it opened, Bitsy Babcock stared up at him through her thick glasses. "Well, well, well, look what the cat dragged in. How delicious!" She ushered him inside.

The meeting was deep in progress, and no one besides Bitsy noticed him or the food, or seemed very happy, for that matter.

"Set it where everyone can reach, dear," Bitsy whispered, pointing to the center of the table around which the board members were seated. Besides Mr. Delancey and Mr. Birch, who sat at opposite ends, Flick didn't recognize many faces. They all looked to be locked in some kind of debate.

Neiman Shrive's staid expression flickered to life at the sight of the food, and he snatched a sandwich from the platter before Flick even set it down. No one else so much as blinked. The tension in the room was thick, and Flick wanted to beat it out of there as fast as he could.

"We cannot ignore the fact that membership numbers are at a historic low, and if all we've got are four applicants then we need to consider all four," a man was saying.

Mr. Delancey threw his pencil on the table, irritably. "Forget consider. I say we just take them."

Flick's heart skipped. He could already hear his mother shrieking with glee.

"Agreed," another said. "We need the funding for operations."

A rousing discussion erupted, and Mr. Birch stood up. "That may be the case, but Mayhaven has always had a selective process in place. No need to abandon that."

Flick was just finishing filling water glasses and about to excuse himself when Mrs. Babcock piped up.

"Ned, you seem hesitant," Bitsy said. "Please tell us, is there an applicant in particular that you're concerned about?"

The water pitcher in Flick's hands slipped. For the first time since he'd entered the room, Mr. Birch's gaze swung his way.

Flick knew exactly which application Mr. Birch was concerned about. He steadied the pitcher, whispered an apology, and ducked out.

"Everything go okay?" Mossimo asked.

Despite his armpit stains, he nodded. There was no reason to be upset: Flick never wanted to join in the first place. Now he could keep his job.

But then he thought of Josie. His mother had worked hard raising him as a single parent. She wanted this badly. And whether she fit it or not, that was up to her to figure out. The more Flick thought about it, she deserved to be there as much as any of those pearl-clutching members he served each day. Even more.

A wave of fresh doubt about Mr. Birch washed over him. The guy had been so nice—even after the way Stan treated him. But was Flick wrong about Mr. Birch? Was this payback for the stuff going on between the neighbors?

Mossimo's booming voice interrupted his thoughts. "You're scheduled for the snack shack. Don't forget to replenish the condiments and paper goods, yes?"

"Yes." Flick was on his way to the pantry when he stopped. "Excuse me, Mossimo?"

The chef looked up from a pot of bisque he was stirring.

"Mr. Birch, he's a good guy, isn't he?"

Mossimo frowned. "Why do you ask?"

Instantly Flick regretted opening his mouth. Mossimo was his boss, not his friend.

But then he pictured his mother's expression if she found out that they didn't get in. Could Flick work in a place where his own family wasn't welcome?

"My parents applied for membership," he blurted out.

Mossimo flicked off the gas range and turned to Flick. "You're going to join Mayhaven?"

"That's the thing. I'm not sure they—we—are going to get in."

The chef stared thoughtfully into the pot of soup. Flick worried he'd overstepped. "Mayhaven is a lovely place," Mossimo said. He gestured to the swinging door separating the dining room from the kitchen. "Their world is on that side of the door, and our world is on this side. Today you are on this side." He shrugged. "Tomorrow, who knows? To answer your question, Mr. Birch is a good man. He has a vision for this place. This place, however, is a bubble." He held out his arms. "Yes?"

Flick nodded.

Mossimo returned to his pot. "It is a beautiful bubble though, no?"

In the pantry, Flick thought about what the chef had said. Mayhaven *was* a bubble. Just walking through the front door each day, Flick felt transported. And the beauty of the place—the insane sunsets and mountain views, the glossy stretch of lake water when the last swimmer exited for the day—well, if there was anywhere prettier, Flick had not yet been. Sure, there were the cliché haves and have-nots, the members and the staff. Just look at the cars in the lot. But up here at the club, you felt like the world was okay. Hell, it wasn't just okay—it was grand. From the clink of ice in a tawny glass of bourbon to the fairways as green as the money that played them, these people were unconcerned by the everyday. It wasn't their fault. It was the bubble.

He'd loaded a crate with paper goods for the snack shack when Mossimo poked his head in the pantry.

"Mr. Flick?"

Flick set the crate down.

Mossimo paused. "One more thing: we are in the service industry. It's not just a job. It's an honor."

Flick had heard all this before. *Us and them, servers and members.* "Yeah, I know. We need them."

"No, no." Mossimo shook his head. "They need us."

They need us. Flick repeated it silently to himself as he scooped melted ice cream and poured lemonades at the snack shack. It was a reversal from what he'd thought the chef meant, and he liked the sound of it. He liked it a lot.

When a mother with a screaming toddler asked him to recook a cheeseburger, medium not well, Flick told himself that this mother needed him. When a family left a mess of ketchup-covered napkins and spilled soda on a picnic table, he repeated the mantra while he picked up their trash and wiped the surface clean. And when Spencer Delancey and a crew of his friends lined up at the shack window, chests puffed and bare, he screamed it in his head.

"Hey, man," Blaine said. "So, we need some dogs and burgers to take out on the boat."

"And drinks," one of them added, turning to watch a girl in a bikini walk by. "Don't forget the drinks."

Flick really hoped they weren't about to ask him to serve them beer again. Instead, he wrote down their orders, keeping his face neutral.

"Okay," he said, reading the order aloud to Blaine, because he didn't want them coming back. "Three cheeseburgers, one burger no cheese, two hot dogs, four fries."

"And six Coronas." Flick looked up. It was not Spencer Delancey this time, but one of his floppy-haired wingmen, Russ.

"You know I can't do that, man," Flick said, looking him dead in the eye.

Russ leaned in. "Because you're a pussy?"

Flick swallowed. "Because you're not twenty-one. And I'll lose my job."

"So get a job at McDonald's. What's the difference?" Russ laughed along with the others, Spencer included. What did Darcy see in this guy? "Come on, do me a solid, and I'll do one for you." He pulled a folded bill from his phone case and stuck it in the plastic tip jar. Flick could see the Benjamin.

Flick didn't want to help Russ out any more than he wanted to owe him anything. He stared at the one-hundred-dollar bill. "Sorry, man."

Russ's face went dark. He was losing the argument and in front of his friends. "You kidding me? What the fuck."

"Hey, come on." To Flick's surprise it was Spencer who'd spoken up. Maybe Flick was wrong about him. But no. "He's not worth it, man." Spencer clapped Russ on the back like he'd win next time. "You're right, he's a pussy."

Spencer jammed his hand inside the tip jar, whisked the one-hundred-dollar bill out and gave it back to Russ.

The smug look on his face made Flick want to leap over the counter and pop him.

But a father with two little kids got in line, and the guys gave way. As he fried their burgers, Flick watched them head to the dock out of the corner of his eye. Only Blaine stuck around. Flick wrapped all the food neatly, even though he wanted to spit in it, repeating what Mossimo had said.

He watched Blaine carry the order to a slip where a sleek blue speedboat idled loudly. Spencer stood at the wheel. Blaine had barely boarded when Spencer threw the boat in reverse. The sound of the engine rumbled across the beach. Flick didn't know a damn thing about boats, but he knew the rules. Motorized watercraft were supposed to taxi in and out at low speed, but the second Spencer put it in gear they took off. One of the guys stumbled backward. Someone's hat blew off into the water. Their laughter carried on the wind as the boat tore out of the marina. The wake churned the water, lifted the dock, and left all the other boats rocking wildly against their moorings. *They need us,* Flick repeated. Only Mossimo's words did little to lift his spirits this time.

As he drove home, Flick's thinking had skittered back to doubt. The people at Mayhaven weren't his people. And they never would be.

It made him miss home, and Mateo, and his old neighborhood even more.

In the driveway he parked behind Stan's car—*Lambo*, as Stan in all his genius had nicknamed it. What would Spencer and Russ and those assholes think if he pulled up in that thing tomorrow? Flick allowed himself to revel in the image—he bet even that flashy attention-getter, Ashley Riley, would hustle over to check it out. Russ could take his one-hundred-dollar bill and shove it where the sun didn't shine.

The one face he couldn't conjure was Darcy's. What would she think if he rolled in in the Lamborghini? He was pretty sure she'd be less than impressed. Maybe that was a good thing. Darcy was real, even if she was the daughter of the president of the bubble.

When he finally walked through the front door, his mother was waiting for him, breathless. "It's unbelievable!"

Oh no. She'd gotten the news. He'd have to lie and tell her he'd heard there were hundreds of applicants, anything to soften the blow. It was for the best. She'd come to see that. "Look, Mom, who cares what those people think."

"What people?" She cocked her head. "Wait—you don't

know, do you?" She turned and shouted to Stan, planted in his usual spot in front of the TV. "He doesn't know, Stan!"

"So tell him."

She turned back to Flick. "We got in!" she cried, jumping up and down. "The new member dinner is this Friday." Then, "Oh, honey. We need to get you a suit!"

Flick stood in the foyer as Josie spun away and down the hall, still talking. It was official: he was a member of the bubble.

Up in his room, he texted Mateo.

Bad news. We got in.

A few minutes later, Mateo replied. Welcome to the dark side. I mean, the white side. LOL

Flick wanted to tell him, *No man, it's not like that.* But he couldn't think of a single member of color at Mayhaven. Not a one.

He texted back: Not so white anymore

I guess not. What about the girl?

What about her?

What'd she say?

Flick wondered if Darcy knew. He seemed to be on her good side again, after the other day with Adam. But he hadn't crossed paths with her since.

Didn't tell her.

Doesn't she work there?

Yeah but haven't seen her.

Beginning to wonder if this girl exists.

Flick went to his window and looked outside. There, in the backyard next door, as if summoned by his thoughts, was the entire Birch family. Mr. Birch and his wife stood by a smoking grill. Adam was floating on a yellow raft. And there, sitting at the edge of the pool, was Darcy. She wore a white bikini and she was dangling her legs in the water. For a second Flick was tempted to take a photo and send it to Mateo: *proof of life*. But it felt wrong.

At that moment, Darcy looked up. Flick hopped back behind the curtain. Surely the houses weren't close enough for her to see him standing up there? He waited, then peeked out again. Now she was talking to her brother.

Flick allowed himself to watch as she swung her legs back and forth in the water. They were strong and suntanned and lovely. As lovely as the other day when she'd kissed him on the cheek and he'd watched them carry her across the grass away from him. A longing stirred inside him. He was still staring when Darcy looked up again. This time, she waved.

He went to get his phone off the bed to text Mateo back, but it dinged before he got there.

Meet me outside later?

It was Darcy.

Flick didn't hesitate. When?

DARCY

Her parents were losing it that summer. All her mother could talk about was the Tree House property she couldn't sell. Darcy had bigger issues and so did Adam. She was beginning to think her dad did, too.

She was still upset from what happened that afternoon. After camp she'd bumped into the Junior Golf Team. All summer Darcy had been strategic about avoiding them; camp ended at three-thirty and the team's daily practice started at four.

Sometimes she saw one of them from a distance and she'd wave before ducking in the opposite direction. So far it had worked, until that afternoon when she'd run into Hallie Majors outside the locker room. Hallie was a former teammate, one division beneath her. Word was that with Darcy off the team, Hallie had moved into her spot. She was good, but she wasn't that good.

"Hey, we miss you," Hallie said, her big blue eyes searching Darcy's face. Darcy knew they all wondered why she'd quit so suddenly.

"Yeah, I miss you, too," Darcy lied. She was caught off guard by Hallie's red-and-blue team visor, just like she used to wear.

"I figured it's time to play something new, you know, for college applications and all."

Hallie regarded her curiously. Everyone who knew Darcy knew her golf ranking was enough to get her into a good school. "Oh, that's cool. So, what're you playing?"

"Playing?" Darcy stared blankly at her, instantly regretting what she'd said. "Um, I haven't decided yet. Maybe tennis." Then she'd abruptly excused herself, saying she had to go find a camper.

On her way out, she couldn't help but glance over at the driving range. Practice was starting. Three carts were lined up at the edge of the range, ready to go. There was Vince talking with Hallie, and a couple of the other girls from the team. When Vince rested his hand on Hallie's shoulder, the way he used to with her, Darcy pulled her gaze away and hurried for her car.

Now, she was stuck in her backyard pool listening to her parents argue about the club. All summer her father had complained that nobody was using the new pool. So what happened when she and Adam finally used it? Her parents burned dinner on the grill and fought. God, she could not wait for college.

The worst was they were pretending not to fight, which no parent anywhere could ever pull off. It was a joke, really. They'd already spent the last couple days arguing about Adam's office job—which her father had sworn he'd get back—and so far hadn't. Adam refused to go back to the club until he did.

Every night at dinner was the same monologue, "I have to finish the July billing with Jane. It has to be mailed out Friday!" And then, "There was a problem with the Brennans' account. They were double-charged at the restaurant. I don't know if Jane told them about it." The kid was hyper focused on a job he didn't realize he was probably never getting back. Her mother was mad at her father. The whole thing was a mess.

But today (good news!), there was something new to argue about. "So, the Crenshaws are in?" Her mother sounded amused, which seemed to bother her father even more.

"The Crenshaw-Creevys," her father corrected her morosely. "And yes, they're in."

"I thought you said over your dead body . . ."

"I say a lot of things about my job, Ingrid," her father said flatly. "In case you can't tell, things aren't exactly going as I'd planned."

"What about my job?" Adam started.

In unison, both parents replied, "Dad is working on it!" Liars.

Darcy had only been half-listening until the mention of the neighbors' new membership. It was the only interesting thing her parents had said in days.

She glanced across the fence at the neighbors'. They were kind of crazy, no doubt. From the RV to the scarecrow shooting to their loud parties and the pot smoke, they were nothing like the other families on Maple Drive. Which Darcy was beginning to think might not be such a bad thing.

Darcy had only ever seen Flick's mom at a distance, but she was memorable. Mrs. Crenshaw was tiny with wild dark hair and tight bright-colored clothes. Vivid, compared to Ingrid with her shapeless dishwater wardrobe. But whatever—if you had it, flaunt it, as Lily always said. (Except when it came to Ashley Riley, who did nothing but flaunt it.) As for the stepdad, Darcy could understand her father's angst. The guy was huge in all ways: huge vehicles, huge money (hello, orange Lamborghini), huge parties, and huge rudeness. Flick didn't seem to like Stan much, was the vibe she'd gotten. But as different as the Crenshaw-Creevys may have been, at least they weren't boring.

The same could not be said for the club. From the faded chintz curtains to the old people in their starched shirts to the tired chicken cordon bleu on the menu, Mayhaven was like a time capsule permanently frozen in the *boring* era. Nothing there ever changed. If the neighbors were going to be members then maybe, finally, things might get shaken up.

Her eyes were drawn to a flutter of movement in one of the second floor windows. Darcy looked up and saw Flick. Was he spying on her? She sucked in her stomach and waved. And then—because everything else was already going wrong—she decided to text him.

Just after midnight, Darcy slipped downstairs and out the back door. The pool surface danced as clouds drifted across the face of the moon, and she hurried barefoot through the back gate. Her heart pounded as she approached the RV. It was almost too dark to see, but every now and then the moonlight on the ground shifted with the sky.

"Flick?" she called softly.

"Over here."

Her eyes darted to the side of the RV where a person took shape in the shadows, and she exhaled. It had been her idea to meet up, but now she wondered if it was a mistake. *Too late*, she told herself as she took a deep breath and walked up to where he stood.

"Hi," she said, hoping her shaky voice didn't betray her.

"You showed."

He sounded like he'd been unsure, and it emboldened her. "So, are you giving me a tour or what?"

The RV, the source of her father's consternation, was also a source of mystery. If Stan Crenshaw wasn't going to move it, then Darcy figured she had a right to at least see what was inside.

Flick dangled the keys between them. "Okay, but we can't turn on any lights or make any noise, got it?"

"Got it."

"And you should probably take your shoes off," Flick said. "If Stan finds out we've been in there . . ."

She raised a bare foot in the moonlight and he shook his head in exasperation.

"Relax, I'll wipe them off," she said, clapping him on the back like an old friend. Already, this was fun.

Flick unlocked the door and held it open. As she climbed the steps, the synthetic smell of new leather and carpeting hit her. "Wow, have you guys even used this thing yet?"

"Stan and my mom are supposed to take it to Maine later this summer."

Darcy walked down the narrow aisle, feeling like she was in a high-end kiddie clubhouse. "I think even my dad would appreciate this," she joked, running her hands over the burnished wood tabletop in the kitchen.

Flick made a noise. "Probably not."

"No. Probably not."

Beyond the kitchen and dinette was a sitting area with a long leather sofa, two side chairs and an overhead TV. "What's in the back?" she asked.

"The master bedroom."

"Oh." Darcy sat down on the sofa. No need to give him any ideas.

Flick took a seat next to her.

It was so quiet in the dark RV, with the door closed, the peepers and all the night noises shut out. Suddenly she had no idea what to say. Her palms started to sweat on the leather sofa. "So . . ."

"So, did Adam get his job back?"

She was touched that Adam was the first thing he wanted to talk about.

"No. My parents are butting heads over it. My dad is still trying, but I guess the board has to meet about it or something."

"That's stupid."

"I know I said it already, but it was nice of you to check on Adam like that. He doesn't usually like talking to new people."

Flick laughed softly. "I don't think he did."

"No," Darcy assured him. "Believe me, that was Adam not minding."

"Well, it was no big deal. I felt bad."

"I talked to Spencer about it, after. I'm hoping he'll say something to his dad."

Even in the shadows she could see Flick tilt his head back and smile. "I'm sure that will solve everything."

She was reminded of the night in the golf cart. "Why do you hate him so much?"

Flick looked over at her. "Why did you ask me out here tonight?"

He had her. If she were completely honest, she'd admit that she didn't know herself. That she'd hoped on some level that seeing him might answer that very question, among others. Like why she thought about him. And why she felt safe enough with him to talk about Adam and her parents fighting. "I heard you guys joined the club," she said instead.

"My mom and Stan did, yeah."

"Not you?" She was surprised at his lack of enthusiasm. "I thought that would be a big deal."

"A big deal?" He snorted. "Like, I'm lucky I got in?"

That was a low blow, but she could send it back to his court. "Lucky how?"

"Come on, Darcy. I'm not some preppy rich kid."

"Neither am I."

But she'd hit a nerve and Flick was on a roll. "I'm from Queens. I wasn't born with a silver spoon in my mouth. I'm not white."

"You need to relax. I meant it would be a big deal because you seemed to like it there. And you're new in town." Why was it they seemed to argue every time they talked? She couldn't imagine a single thing she'd argue with Spencer about, besides what his dad did to Adam.

"I don't care about belonging to the club," he said, finally. "I know you think I should."

"I don't think that at all. I don't belong."

"Your dad is the president."

She laughed. "It's just his job." She let this sink in. "My dad works there, I work there. Until a few days ago, Adam worked there, too. We're the staff, you're the member. So, now who's the rich kid?"

Flick grew quiet. "Sorry, I guess I assumed it was different for you. President is a step up from kitchen help. You guys live in the same neighborhood as I do, and you're always at the club, so it seemed like . . ."

"Yeah, well, a lot of things seem other than they are."

"You don't seem to like the club," Flick said. "And you quit golf. So why do you work there?"

Where to begin? Sure, she hated Mayhaven, but not for the reasons he seemed to. "I needed a summer job."

"There are lots of places you could work." Flick studied her in the dark. "I don't think you hate it as much as you say you do."

"Oh, I do." But even as she said it, Darcy felt the effort it took. It was the hating part that took the most out of her. Because the truth was that mixed in with all that anger was so much of her history, so much of it good. And hating your history required you to hate a part of yourself. "But I didn't always," she admitted softly. "Did you ever try to forget something bad from the past?"

Flick leaned in. "Tell me more."

Darcy didn't have the words at first, but they came to her like rainfall on a summer night: a gentle pitter-patter, followed by a storm surge. She told Flick how all her childhood birthday parties were held at the club beach, and how Mossimo made her a three-layer princess cake at least five years in a row, even though he said he didn't bake cakes for anyone, ever. That when she was eight years old she'd learned to waltz at the Fourth of July dinner dance when grumpy old Neiman Shrive, who was much less grumpy then, held her hands and let her place her feet atop his and sailed her around the dance floor. She told Flick about the time she was learning to drive and her mother gave her a parking lesson in the club lot, but she accidentally hit the gas instead of the brakes and ran over an entire stand of golf bags. And how last summer she and Lily snuck a bottle of wine and got drunk for the first time and Lily dared her to jump naked off the docks. And how some of the caddies came down to get stoned and she had to run into the woods naked while Lily snuck back for her clothes. As the stories spilled from her mouth, Darcy told Flick that it was impossible to untangle the good stuff from the bad stuff, and if she couldn't do that, she feared she'd be carrying all this hate around with her for the rest of her life.

Flick listened hard to all of it. She could feel it in the way he leaned forward as she spoke. She could sense it in the weight of his gaze. And though she could only imagine what he was thinking of her now, what a relief it was to hold it out there between them, and know that he saw it. He saw all of it. Which meant he saw her.

When she was done, she collapsed back against the sofa, waiting for him to say something.

"Darcy, those are all good memories."

She shook her head. She hadn't told him all of them.

"You know what I think?"

"What?" She was almost too scared to know.

"Your family belongs to that place more than the members. You're kind of like lifers."

"Lifers," she repeated. He'd gotten that part right.

"So where's the bad?"

"Golf," she said, softly. "Golf was where it went bad." Suddenly she was so tired, and the hour so late.

"Was the pressure too much?" She could tell he was struggling to make sense of it. It wasn't his fault. She was giving him dots to connect, but not all of them.

"It was too much," she admitted. What she didn't admit was that they were talking about two very different kinds of pressure.

Flick edged closer on the sofa. It was chilly inside the RV. She could feel the warmth of Flick's skin bridging the space between their bodies. This close, he smelled faintly of soap and citrus. She had the inexplicable urge to rest her head on his shoulder. She had the feeling he wouldn't mind.

Did Flick want more? she wondered. Or had she used up his patience with all of her talking? Teenage boys were like a hot flame with a short burn time; by the time you figured out if they even liked you, they'd already lost interest. She wanted to think Flick was different.

Flick wrapped his fingers gently around hers, and a current passed through her fingertips. For a second she wished he'd pull her to him. She felt like this was just one conversation of many she wanted to have with Flick Creevy.

"Darcy, I like you."

She smiled in the darkness but didn't say anything. She was out of words.

"Last week you asked me to steal a golf cart with you, but then it seemed like I made you mad. Just the other day you accused me of upsetting Adam, but then you kissed my cheek." His voice was somewhere between whisper and song, like the state between drifting and sleep. She felt her eyelids flutter.

"I like you, too," she said.

"It doesn't always seem like it." It was a fair thing to say. She was all over the place this summer, and she knew why even if she couldn't tell him.

"I'm sorry," she said. "I'm not really myself, lately."

"So why did you ask me out here tonight?"

Darcy could not explain why she kept coming back to Flick Creevy. Despite her crush on Spencer. Despite the fact she and

Flick were so different. It was a feeling she could not put words to, but in it was a simple truth. "Because you listen to me."

Flick nodded as though this was enough. He squeezed her hand. "Alright. Then let's keep talking."

When she woke up, early light dappled them as gently as the memory of the night before. And then she realized where she was.

Stretched beside her on the RV sofa was Flick, his eyes still closed with slumber. One arm rested across her. How she wanted to close her eyes and sink into him. But she couldn't.

"Flick," she said, shaking him. "What time is it?"

Flick stretched and looked around. "Oh, man."

"I have to go!" Darcy rolled away from him and hopped up. All the things she'd said the night before came tumbling back and she felt suddenly exposed in the light of the new day.

Outside the air was cold and the grass wet when she stepped down into the yard. She glanced around warily, then back at Flick. "I'll see you later."

"Wait," he said, closing the door quietly behind them.

"What? We have to hurry." She did not want to get caught. Just as much, she did not want him looking at her like this, rumpled and exhausted.

Flick did not seem bothered. He smiled. "That was nice, last night."

Darcy stared back at him, a knot of nerves. "All we did was talk," she blurted out.

"I know. I was there." Flick placed his hands very gently on either side of her face. Darcy inhaled. His eyes were large and brown, and despite the fear of being found out and her haggard appearance and her racing head, Darcy felt her heart slow.

When Flick Creevy pressed his lips to hers, she stilled. The yard quieted. Flick's lips were full and warm and behind her closed eyes the sun burned. Darcy kissed him back. And just like that they parted.

"Was that okay?" he asked.

Unable to speak, Darcy nodded.

A bird erupted in song. Across the street a door slammed and a car started. Darcy turned. When she turned back, Flick Creevy was already sprinting across his yard.

• • • • •

All morning at work, Lily stared. "You sure you're okay? You seem out of it today."

"Just tired," Darcy lied. She didn't want to tell Lily yet. It felt like a secret made sweeter by keeping it to herself.

She'd managed to sneak back in her house, undetected, and she wondered if Flick had, too. At breakfast her parents were so distracted trying to figure out plans for Adam that no one noticed how exhausted she looked. For once her mother didn't nag her to eat more scrambled eggs or comment that she looked thin.

All day she kept her eyes peeled for Flick. When camp got out, she was wiped out but the thought of seeing him boosted her, so she ran up to the clubhouse. She was so distracted by the replay in her head from the night before, that when she entered the back door of the clubhouse, she walked straight into the pro shop without thinking.

Vince popped up from behind a clothing rack. "There she is." If he was surprised to see her, he recovered quickly. "Have you seen our new inventory? We just got a new delivery of golf attire."

Darcy froze. How was it that someone she used to spend so much time with she could now barely look at?

"I'm looking for my dad," she sputtered.

"Once upon a time, you used to rush in and pore over every new shipment." Vince held up a peach-colored golf skirt on a hanger. Its ruffled edge rippled in the air between them. "You know, the team could really use you this season . . . if you change your mind."

Darcy stared wordlessly at the ruffled edge of the skirt.

"Any chance you'll get back in the game?"

"My dad's waiting for me," she lied, turning on her heel. Darcy rushed out the door, past her dad's office and around the corner. There, she propped herself up against the wall, heart thundering.

She did not hear the sound of footfalls coming up behind her. "Hey." A hand landed on her shoulder and reflexively Darcy swatted it away.

She turned to see Flick. He held up both hands. "Whoa! Didn't mean to startle you."

"Sorry," she gasped.

"What's wrong?"

She glanced over his shoulder at the pro shop doorway. Thankfully Vince had not come after her. "Nothing. I'm fine."

Flick followed her gaze. "You don't look fine. Darcy, what just happened?"

The concern in Flick's eyes was too much. Just as what she'd told him last night was too much.

"Darcy?" he pressed.

"Just mind your business!" she snapped.

The hurt in his eyes rooted her to the ground. What was it he'd said just after she'd told him she liked him? *It doesn't always seem like it.*

Before he could say anything, Darcy pushed past him, and through the front doors. She didn't look back. She already knew the look on Flick Creevy's face, and it just made her cry harder.

NED

Things were missing at Mayhaven. It wasn't just the fish-less pond, still waiting for a delivery of two hundred koi that were delayed in North Carolina. It wasn't just the kayaks and the paddleboard from the beach. Nor was it his son missing from the office. That morning, Mossimo came down to Ned's office to inform him that liquor had disappeared from the bar. It was the second time in a matter of days.

"At first I thought our inventory was off. But this morning there are more bottles missing from behind the bar."

"How much?" Ned asked, with dismay.

"Four handles of Grey Goose, and three magnums of Hendrick's."

Ned covered his face with his hands. "They've got expensive taste." The new member dinner was the next night, and the bar needed to be stocked. "Do you have any idea who might have taken it?"

Mossimo shook his head. "Perhaps it's a member. Perhaps some of the teens?"

It was a betrayal, either way. "Is there anything else missing? Food from the pantry? Cookware?"

"More of the Blackstone silverware. A complete setting, I'm afraid. Also, I need to talk to you about the Delancey wedding." The chef looked even more pained.

Mossimo never complained about events; his elegance under pressure was something Ned cherished. For him to bring it up to Ned, it must be bad.

"Miss Delancey has changed the menu. Again."

"Again?" Ned was dumbfounded. The wedding was in less than two weeks. "But I just met with her."

Mossimo pursed his lips. "First, I designed a five-course formal dinner. Then, we switched to a New England clambake of seafood, chowders, and steaks."

Ned nodded. This was where he'd left off with the Delanceys, and everyone seemed happy.

"Now, there is a new theme. Shangri-La."

Ned repeated the word. "Shangri-La?"

"Phoebe Delancey has requested a traditional Himalayan menu."

Ned felt like he had whiplash. A low throb began at his temples, and he pressed his index finger there. "And what comprises a traditional Himalayan menu?"

"I had to do some research." Mossimo handed him a piece of paper.

Ned put on his reading glasses and read aloud: "Yak, goat, and mutton."

Mossimo said nothing.

Ned put the list down. "I see." He was all for themes and culture, but this was beyond. At their last coastal New England–

themed meeting where American flags and lobster napkins reigned supreme, there was no mention of Shangri-la. It was unclear if Phoebe Delancey had ever traveled to Tibet, if she had ever eaten yak, and where on earth the club would source that, goat, or mutton in coastal Massachusetts. "Does Miss Delancey expect these specific meats?"

Mossimo shook his head. "I doubt God knows what Miss Delancey expects. But since I have no experience with these dishes, I propose outsourcing to a catering company."

"That won't be necessary!" Ned hopped to his feet. Catering was the biggest ticket item in any private event. If the catering were outsourced, the club would lose all revenue for food and drink. Ned understood this required yet another meeting with the Delancey women—an *emergency* meeting. "I will call Phoebe right now. Before you go, do you have head count for the new member dinner tomorrow?" he asked hopefully.

"Sixty-five," Mossimo replied.

"I'm guessing we need to order more liquor?"

"Unless you'd like me to serve the champagne reserved for the Delancey wedding."

Ned grimaced. "I like your humor, Chef."

Mossimo did not smile.

Neither could Ned.

As he googled *yak farms near me*, Ned dialed Phoebe Delancey. It went straight to voicemail. The clock was ticking. He'd have to find a way to lure her out of Tibet and back to New England.

His internal line rang again. "Good news," Jane said. "The board has scheduled a meeting to hear your concerns about Adam. It's next Friday."

Ned glanced at the calendar. Friday was not soon enough. "Thank you, Jane." Ned jotted it on the calendar and said a silent prayer.

To take his mind off of things, he wandered down the hall to the pro shop. It always cheered him. Vince was behind the counter, signing in Neiman Shrive. "Good morning, Neiman," Ned said.

Neiman grunted. "Well, it's morning. Don't know if I'd call it a good one."

Ned wondered if word was traveling through the membership about the missing kayaks and liquor; he hoped not. "Hopefully a round of golf will cure that."

"My knee tells me it's going to rain, but I'm not getting it replaced, no matter what the doc says," Neiman went on.

Apparently they were still talking about his morning. And his knee. "Let's hope the weather and your knee cooperate so you play well today!"

Neiman scowled. "I always play well. If you got out of that fancy office, you'd see for yourself."

The pro shop was not proving to be cheering.

As soon as Neiman left, Vince waved him over. "Hey, boss. A new member reserved a tee time for a foursome this morning." He tipped the sign-in sheet toward Ned so he could read it. "Is this okay?"

Stan Crenshaw & three guests, 10:00 am. Ned groaned. New members were not invited to play the course until after their membership was formalized. That meant after dues were paid, and traditionally, after the new member dinner.

Vince could tell Ned wasn't happy. "Normally, I would've reminded Mr. Crenshaw of the rules, but he said he's bringing his brothers as well as a friend, who are interested in joining. And I got to thinking—that could be three more memberships for you."

Ned needed all the members he could get. "Do we know if he's paid his dues yet?" If Adam were still working in the office, he'd be able to tell his father from memory.

Vince had done his homework. "I called upstairs. Jane said no, not yet."

Ned let his gaze travel to the window where the greenery outside called. How tired he was of being stuck inside, of the problems cluttering his desk and his mind. The board had outvoted Ned and greenlighted Stan Crenshaw as a new member. And now here was Stan, already breaking rules and barging in, powering up the hill to the club—probably behind the wheel of his garish RV—and dragging along relatives just as wonderful to boot.

It would be so easy to say no to Stan Crenshaw. It would be so satisfying.

But if what Stan represented was true, if Ned could secure more members, that would make the board happy. And if they were happy, they might be more sympathetic to Adam at the upcoming meeting. And maybe, just maybe, peace could be restored to Ned's house.

Ned closed his eyes. "Let Mr. Crenshaw play."

On his way back to his office he grabbed the Pilgrim Box from the hallway. His day couldn't get much worse.

The club needs a signature cocktail. Gin and tonics are classic. We can name it Bitsy's Flask.

Marcy is still hogging the courts. When is someone going to deal with her?

Since when is it okay to drive your convertible up the golf paths? Was there a cardiac emergency on the fifth hole? I'm looking at you black Mercedes, FIBRIL8.

The woke agenda is taking over. I hear our club pilgrim logo is at stake. That some bra-burners want a female pilgrim? That some snowflakes want to cancel our pilgrim? What's next, a turkey?

Ned took off his glasses and rubbed his eyes just imagining the board discussion these comments would ignite. He read through a few more, but there was only one that caught his attention. *People should feel safe here. The women are counting on you.*

Ned froze. He pulled open his desk drawer and found the one he'd saved. Yes—it was written in the same block print. Ned read it again, a feeling of dread settling within.

This was different than wedding menu themes. It was different than pushy blowhards barging in to play golf before dues were paid. Someone did not feel safe at Mayhaven.

He took this, along with the former comment, and clipped them to his notes for the next board meeting.

At the end of the day, there was some hope. Phoebe Delancey finally returned his urgent calls; no she did not want mutton or goat or yak on her menu—wherever did he get *that* idea? She'd meant Himalayan spices. After being asked which spices she meant, there was a long pause and the menu returned swiftly to New England clambake. But there would be Tibetan flags around the new fishpond for photos—Shangri-La was still at the heart of her vision.

The koi hatchery had also called. The main highways were still shut down from the hurricane, so it would be a few more days until they could update the delivery. The Delanceys might have to let that go. Honestly, there were worse things than a fishless pond at a wedding.

Several times, Ned interrupted these calls and duties to trot down the hall to the pro shop. On none of those trips did he spy Stan Crenshaw or his guests. He wasn't sure what he expected to see, but it was an itch that needed scratching. On the third visit, Vince asked, "Would you like me to call you when they come off the course?"

"Just taking in the beautiful day as much as one can from the inside." He headed back to his office feeling sheepish. What was wrong with him?

At the end of the day, he was on his way out when he heard a commotion coming from upstairs. The noise level coming from the bar and restaurant was akin to a sports bar on Super Bowl night. He needed to see what was going on.

At the top of the stairs, Ned wished he hadn't. Every seat at the bar was taken. The TV was on, the music cranked, and jocular voices rose up over the top of it. Ned surveyed the crowd. Neiman Shrive sat at one end of the bar with his usual old-fashioned. Was that a smile on his face? Beside him was Bill Fryer, and his wife, Elizabeth, their cheeks flushed and their wine glasses empty. They dined at the club regularly, but Ned had never seen them in the bar before. Then there was Dick Delancey. His mouth was hanging open like he was catching flies, a look of wild delight in his eyes as he hung on to every word of the guy seated next to him. Ned couldn't see the face, but one look at his hulking backside and he knew: Stan Crenshaw. Two other men seated to Stan's left were of similar build; the twin brothers, and beside them, the friend. Only one of the four wore collared shirts, and two wore baseball hats: dress code violations, all.

As Ned approached, Stan said something apparently so hilarious that everyone, including staid Elizabeth Fryer, threw their heads back in laughter. Dick Delancey actually slapped the bar.

Dick saw Ned first. "Have you met Stan, our new member? What a hoot!"

"Stan is my new neighbor," Ned said. He offered his hand and Stan shook it. "How'd you enjoy your round?"

"Not bad," Stan said. Up close Ned could see just how big and red-faced Stan really was. As were his brothers, who regarded him with the same vacant looks.

"My brothers, Mikey and Joey." Stan nodded toward the twins, identical right down to their tattooed biceps and grunted greetings. "And that's our friend, Tony." At least Tony stood up to shake hands. Ned stared at his feet: He'd worn flip-flops to golf in?

"Stan is taking us bowhunting." Dick Delancey informed Ned of this like he'd been invited to foxhunt at Balmoral by King Charles. "He's going to teach us how. Did you know Stan hunts?"

"Why yes, I did hear something about that," Ned said softly. "Scarecrows, I believe?"

"What?" Dick looked confused but moved on. "We'll have to rent a cabin somewhere. Make it a real men's weekend."

"No cabin needed," Stan said. "I just bought an RV. Customized."

Ned needed to get out of there.

"Whatcha drinking?" It was Stan asking.

"Oh." Ned paused. He had not come up here for a drink. Still, Stan didn't know that. "Another time, thanks! Just wanted to say hello and welcome."

Stan regarded him for a beat and then clapped him on the back, roughly. "I owe ya one, Birch." He looked around until he was sure he had everyone's attention. "We didn't exactly hit it off when I moved here, me and Ned. There was a matter of the wrong side of a door in someone's face." Stan relayed this with delight then turned back to Ned. "The wife says I owe you a drink."

Was he really sharing this embarrassing incident with a group he'd just met? Yes, he was, because everyone looked uncomfortable until Stan laughed raucously, and they were all freed to join in. *Sheep*, Ned thought.

"You don't owe me anything," Ned said. He almost meant it.

• • • • •

At home, the kids were in their usual funks. Both he and Ingrid had worked late; in fact, Ingrid wasn't even home yet. There was nothing for dinner.

"If we don't eat soon I'm going to die," Adam huffed, pacing around the kitchen.

"No one's going to die. Let's see what I can find."

"Hurry," Adam said, plopping into a kitchen chair dramatically.

As much as he loathed how much the kids were on their

phones, he was relieved when Adam distracted himself with a game. He was still staring into the fridge when Ingrid burst through the front door.

"They're throwing me a party!" she announced, tossing her purse on the counter and planting a kiss on Adam's head.

"Why would someone throw you a party?" Adam asked, not looking up from his game. "It isn't your birthday."

"No, it's not. It's better!" Ingrid looked between her husband and son excitedly. "It's a party for the Tree House. Where's Darcy?"

Ned had to shout upstairs for her three times. Darcy came down with a look like she'd been yanked away from some very important business.

"Hi, honey," Ingrid said, looking happy to have a larger audience.

But Darcy walked right past and pulled the fridge open. "What's for dinner?"

"Have a seat, I have news," Ingrid said excitedly, sitting down at the table. Ned followed. Darcy halted by her chair, sizing up her family like she'd been seated at the worst lunch table in the school cafeteria.

Only Adam seemed to be interested in his mother's party. "What's the Tree House again?"

"Seriously?" Ingrid stared back at them with an air of defeat, which was the emotion she expressed right before she slipped down the waxed slide of anger. "It's the big mansion on the hill overlooking Mayhaven Lake. The one that no Realtor could sell?"

Darcy yawned. "Did it finally sell?"

"Yes!" Ingrid said, looking hopeful.

"Cool. Who sold it?"

Ingrid's excitement turned to outrage. "Your mother!"

"That's incredible," Ned said, hopping up. "We have to celebrate!" As he bent to hug his wife, Ned glared over his shoulder at the kids in an attempt to rope them into some kind of adulation, but no one took the bait. "This was the *unsellable* house. And your mother went and sold it!"

"It's the biggest sale in the office in five years," Ingrid mumbled. "Full ask. Cash offer. That's why they're throwing me a party next week."

"And we will be there!" Again, Ned looked pointedly at the kids. "Right?"

Darcy and Adam looked less than enthused. "Right," Darcy said flatly.

"What *is* for dinner?" Adam asked.

FLICK

How many times did he have to explain to his mother that guys did not wear suits to the club? "Mom, it's not a funeral home. It's a golf and tennis club. People don't dress like that."

She was standing in his room holding up a fancy garment bag between them. "It's a new suit. And you'll look sharp."

She didn't get it. "How I'll look is like I don't belong."

As soon as he saw her expression falter, Flick felt like an ass. Who was he kidding? He hadn't had any clue how people dressed at Mayhaven, either, until after he worked there. Just look how he'd dressed for his interview that first day.

"I only want us to look nice," Josie said, shoving the garment bag in his closet with a huff. "Maybe you'll find a funeral to wear this to. Maybe it'll be mine!"

"I'm sorry," he called after her, but she was already stalking down the hall. To be fair, he was already worried enough about what *she* was wearing, but he knew better than to ask.

Flick really did not want to go. It had already been a long day in the kitchen, and he'd spent it preparing food for the very thing he was attending tonight: the new member dinner.

Outside of the menu (prime rib, lemon-basil buttermilk chicken, heirloom tomato burrata salad), he had no idea what to expect.

Mossimo had teased him, telling Ricky and Wendy and the others, “Make it your best, people. Mr. Flick is going to be dining with us this evening!”

In front of them Flick laughed it off, but it was not lost on him how awkward it already was. He’d finally felt like one of them in the kitchen: he knew where the spices were, which knife to use for chopping vegetables and which for slicing meat. He knew when to give Wendy a wide berth and just how much ribbing Ricky would take, depending on how the dining room was running. Just by looking at Mossimo he knew when he could make a joke and when to keep his head down and his mouth shut.

Being on the other side of the kitchen door with the members was terrifying. He hoped Spencer and Blaine and those guys wouldn’t be there. He wasn’t sure what to hope for when it came to Darcy. The last he’d seen her was yesterday afternoon when she ran out of the pro shop like she’d seen a ghost. Right before she snapped his head off. Honestly, he could not figure that girl out.

Now, as he dressed for the club dinner, he studied himself in the mirror. Did he look different since leaving Queens? The same brown eyes with long eyelashes looked back at him now. Flick understood he was a good-looking kid, not because of arrogance, but by the silent messages from those around him, especially the girls. Still, today he looked different. One glaring detail was the blue button-down shirt his mother had bought along with the suit. She hadn’t totally messed that up. He’d tucked it into a pair of khaki pants and shoved his feet into loafers he still had from a cousin's wedding. But they were too burnished, not weathered in that leisure-boat-shoe way the guys at the club all seemed to wear, where the leather looked like it came from their little sister's pony's saddle. Whatever. Flick wouldn't be caught dead in boat shoes. These would have to do.

To his relief, Stan had not entirely dressed like a mobster. Maybe he'd taken notes when he played at the club yesterday, because he'd toned it down with a charcoal jacket and slacks. To be sure, it read a little like a limo driver, but better than the purple TV-ad attire of his dry-cleaning past. Josie, however, was true to Josie. Flick had to give her props for that at least. Her dress was short and tight, her lips painted in her signature Going-Out Red. At least her dress was patterned with flowers and not a safari animal. When Flick kissed her cheek and told her she looked pretty, he meant it.

He had to admit it, Mayhaven was right out of the movies that night. His mom and Stan went ahead in the Lambo, since it seated only two, which was fine with him because he was pretty sure Josie would've shrieked the roof off when they pulled in. The sun was low over the hills, casting the clubhouse in dizzying pink and peach hues. Flickering topiaries lined the walkway and ropes of twinkle lights draped the upper decks. Music rippled softly through the French doors.

"It's like a fairy tale," Josie breathed. When they walked through the double doors together, he paused beneath the chandelier recalling the afternoon he'd first set foot in here looking for a job. How things had changed.

They followed the music upstairs. The dining room was already crowded with cocktail-swillers, as Mossimo called them, everyone decked out in their summer whites and navy. Fresh-cut bouquets adorned each table, and Flick flashed back to Wendy complaining loudly as she'd tried to make room in the walk-in fridge for the flower arrangements. Until that day, Flick hadn't known how temperamental hydrangeas could be. The things he was learning here.

His mother and Stan headed straight for the bar. There was no sign of the Birch family.

Flick tried to smile as his mother introduced him again and again. Some of the members frowned, trying to place him. Each time Flick rescued them.

"Hi, Mrs. Standish, I work in the restaurant."

"Hello, Mr. Goldman, we met on the course. I drive the beverage cart?"

Always the confusion gave way to relief, and Josie would glow with pride. "This is Flick. He's my son!"

Eventually he escaped out to the deck. He was leaning over the railing when he felt someone sweep up from behind. "Imposter!"

It was Wendy, dressed in black and white, for evening service. She held a tray of champagne and laughed at his expression. "Look at you. All grown up and fancy, now."

It was hard to tell if she was teasing or being mean; it often was with Wendy. He reached for a flute of champagne. "No way, junior. Not on my watch."

"Sorry," he said. How many times had Spencer and Blaine done the same to him?

"Oh, grow a pair. I was joking." She waited while he took a flute and drank it. The champagne was sweet and dry and he liked the way the bubbles rushed down his throat. "Want another?"

"Really?"

"Hurry up."

He held his empty glass uncertainly.

"Oh, just give it to me."

When he swapped it for another she winked. "Be sure and tip the servers, junior."

"Thanks, Wendy."

It was then he saw Darcy, framed by the French doors. Flick sucked in his breath. In all the times he'd seen her that summer, it was mostly in her work uniform or denim shorts. Tonight, she wore her hair long and a short white dress, really not much more than a slip. It was lovely and sexy at the same time, and it made him think of moonlight spilling. "You're here."

Darcy did a shy twirl, looking absolutely adorable doing it. "I'm here. Look at you, Creevy."

"Look at you." He raised his champagne glass, then thought better of it.

"No way. How'd you get that?" She closed the distance between them and grabbed his arm. "You're the liquor thief, aren't you?"

It was a joke, but he glanced about, nervous. "Easy. Not something a new member wants to be accused of on their debut night."

But she thought it was hilarious. "Oh, come on. Can I have a sip?"

Another risk, he thought, as she tipped back his flute. What if Mr. Birch saw? Maybe he shouldn't have taken Wendy up on her offer.

It must have been the booze, because a crazy thought suddenly occurred to him: Josie would love Darcy. He was about to ask her if she wanted to meet his parents, but someone else had also noticed Darcy.

"Birch."

Spencer Delancey stood on the opposite side of the deck with a handful of kids Flick didn't recognize.

His heart sank as Darcy bubbled like the champagne they'd just thrown back. "Hey, Spencer!"

"Who's he with?" Flick asked her glumly. Already he could feel her slipping away in their direction.

"That's Shelly Cravitz, she's back from college for the summer. And her sister, Teagan. I used to golf with Teagan."

"Oh."

Sure enough Teagan noticed her at the same moment, and waved her over.

"Do you mind?" Darcy asked.

"Go on," he said, trying to sound like he meant it. He looked away when Spencer raised his glass in Flick's direction.

Dinner was like molasses. Flick didn't know anyone at their table, but at least his mother seemed to be having a grand time. She must've had a few glasses of something herself, because her cheeks were flushed pink and she laughed easily. But she held her own, telling everyone where they lived ("Oh, Maple! What a nice neighborhood!") and where Flick would go to school ("A junior! What colleges are you applying to?") and how excited she was to learn to play tennis ("Molly is good, but you will love the other pro, Dennis. He's *amazing!*"). All the while, Flick wondered what was going on in the kitchen without him. He pictured Ricky plating salads as quickly as Wendy could take them out. It was where he should be.

During the long welcome speech, he couldn't help but

sneak glances to where Darcy and her family sat. Like a kick in the balls, the Delanceys were seated with them. Another kick, Spencer had taken the seat right next to Darcy and kept turning to talk to her. Flick tried not to stare at the way their heads bowed in each other's direction, faces close. He told himself it was to hear better over the noisy crowd, but he knew at that proximity Spencer could smell her perfume. Flick was painfully aware of how good it smelled.

Once or twice she caught him staring, but she didn't wave or come over. At one point she laughed so loud at something Spencer had said, her voice carried all the way over to his table. By dessert, Flick had had enough. "Can we go soon?" he whispered to his mother.

"What? Aren't you having fun?" Her eyes had the glassy look of happiness mixed with wine, and she looked especially young in the candlelight. He didn't want to ruin this for her. "I've got a headache," he lied. "I've got my own car, remember?"

She studied his face. "Thank you for coming tonight, baby. I know it's not your thing."

What Flick wanted to tell her was that he'd tried, that it turned out the pretty girl wanted the pretty boy. That, besides the girl, he had nothing to say to anyone else in this room. He had dressed up and shown up, but it was much easier on the other side of the swinging kitchen doors for a guy like him. Maybe that was how it would always be.

"Try to make it through dessert," Josie said.

When dessert trays came out, Flick tried to make eye contact with Wendy. She was hustling, carrying a platter loaded with cakes and tiramisu and tiny crystal cups of sorbet. It must've weighed a ton. He was half tempted to stand up and offer to hold it for her when she arrived at his elbow. "Cake or sorbet?" she asked, straight-faced.

He shook his head. "I'm good, thanks. Everything else was delicious, by the way."

"Good." Wendy was a pro; she gave no indication they knew each other, let alone did this very job together. Flick felt a little bad as she moved on to Mrs. Evans, seated next to him.

"What flavor sorbet do you have?" Mrs. Evans asked.

"Raspberry," Wendy said.

"You don't have lemon?"

"No, ma'am, I'm sorry."

"You usually have lemon."

Wendy smiled tightly and shifted the heavy tray. "Not tonight, I'm afraid."

"How unfortunate."

Irritation rippled through Flick. He wanted to tell Mrs. Evans to pick a dessert or shut up. He wanted to relieve Wendy of the tray, but he knew she'd kill him.

"I guess I'll have to settle for raspberry." Mrs. Evans sighed and looked around the table like she was taking one for the team.

Wendy was about to set the disappointing dish of raspberry sorbet in front of her when another member, who looked like he'd had a few too many, staggered past their table. Flick watched in alarm as he bumped into Wendy and kept going. Both Wendy and the tray lurched forward. By some miracle neither capsized, but the dish of sorbet slipped from her other hand and right onto Mrs. Evans's lap.

"Oh!" Mrs. Evans cried, hopping up like it was molten lava. "Oh, my pants!"

There was a rush of napkins offered and apologies uttered. "I'm so sorry," Wendy cried, scooping up the cup with her free hand.

"They're ruined!"

Wasting no time, Josie leaned across the table. "Wendy, do you have club soda?"

Wendy disappeared into the kitchen and returned with the soda and a fresh towel.

Mrs. Evans was not interested. "This is linen. From Italy."

Flick had no idea what that had to do with anything other than making Wendy feel worse. Luckily his mother pressed on. "Trust me, it works," Josie assured her. "Flush it with the soda, then blot it with the towel."

Flick couldn't believe the entire table was left gaping at a woman flushing and blotting her pants. His eyes stayed on Wendy, who suddenly looked very small.

"It's working," Mrs. Evans proclaimed.

"Can I get you anything else?" Wendy asked her, timidly.

"I think you've done enough," Mrs. Evans snipped. As soon as Wendy left, she turned to the table. "The help here is just awful this summer."

Flick was about to stand up when his mother put a firm hand on his knee.

The woman next to Mrs. Evans, whose name Flick had already forgotten, turned to Josie. "You saved the night and the pants!"

Josie beamed. "An old hotel industry trick, from my years in New York."

"Ah!" the woman said. "So you worked in the hotel industry?"

Josie nodded. "Domestic."

"Domestic! My father owns a chain of Hiltons, mostly international." She looked between Stan and Josie expectantly. "Where are your properties?"

Flick sucked in his breath.

"Oh no, nothing like that!" Josie corrected her. To her credit, she even laughed. "I worked in housekeeping. That's what I meant by domestic."

"Housekeeping?"

"Yes, at the Wyndham Garden. By LaGuardia."

"How interesting." The woman looked ready to dive into her sorbet.

That's when Stan spoke up, "Nothing like working hard and raising a kid all on your own. She's an independent woman, this one." He put a meaty arm around Josie and for the first time Flick wanted to hug the man.

He looked about for Wendy, hoping she wasn't too upset. That's when he noticed Darcy and Spencer's seats were both empty.

"You can go," his mother said, leaning in. "Thanks for making it through dessert."

Flick glanced around the dining room one more time.

"Yeah, I think I will." He pecked Josie's cheek.

On his way out, Stan caught his arm. "Hey, kid. You did good tonight. Made your mom happy." Flick had enjoyed absolutely nothing about the night, but Stan was alright.

Outside, the night was a cool balm to how hot and uncomfortable he felt. His shoes hurt and the neck of his collared shirt was choking him. He was unbuttoning it when he heard someone crying. Flick followed the sound to the side of the clubhouse.

Underneath the upper decks, he saw a woman standing in the shadows. Wendy.

"Hey," he said, stepping toward her. "You okay?"

"Oh, not you, too." She sniffed and straightened. "I'm fine, Flick."

"That wasn't your fault up there." He noticed a bottle of wine in her hand.

"Yeah, tell that to Mrs. *These-pants-are-from-Italy*. She didn't have to be so nasty to me." Wendy took a swig of the wine and looked at him. "How can you stand these people?"

He felt bad for Wendy, but that wasn't fair. "They're not my people."

But his or not, people were coming. Flick heard the voices before Wendy.

"Hide that," he said, nodding toward the bottle of wine.

She stashed the bottle on the ground behind a rock just as Darcy, her friend Teagan, Blaine, and Spencer rounded the corner of the clubhouse, laughing. At first, they didn't even notice Wendy and Flick under the deck.

But as they passed, Darcy turned. "Flick?" She started to come over but hesitated as soon as she saw Wendy. "Oh, sorry."

Flick's heart sank with the realization: she thought she was interrupting them.

"All good," Wendy said, flatly. She'd never liked the teenage members.

Darcy paused, hanging back from the others. "I was looking for you," she told Flick.

"Oh yeah?" No matter how much he wanted to, Flick couldn't let himself believe her. The way she'd acted around Spencer all night spoke louder.

"We're going down to the lake. Want to come?"

Flick stared back at her and for a heartbeat he thought he would say yes. But she'd blown him off all evening. "No thanks," he willed himself to say.

"Okay." She looked almost disappointed. Flick watched her gaze dart between him and Wendy before she veered back to her friends. "Guess I'll see ya."

"Yeah. See ya." Flick stared after her until she disappeared into the darkness of the pines, bound for the lake. He wondered if he should go after her; he wondered if he just should go home. But there was no time to do either. Someone else walked around the corner of the clubhouse. Wendy stepped back and Flick heard the bottle of wine clatter.

"Who's there?"

Flick recognized Mr. Welter, one of the board members. He realized this looked bad.

"Hi," he said stepping out into the light from under the deck. But Mr. Welter's eyes were on the ground, on the tipped-over wine bottle.

"Is that yours?" he asked Wendy.

Flick could almost feel Wendy's sharp intake of breath. They were screwed. "Oh, that? I came out for some fresh air and saw it—"

"Don't you work here?" he asked, walking closer. "What's your name again?"

She cleared her throat nervously. "Wendy. I work in the kitchen."

"I thought so." He looked at Flick, then back at Wendy. "You're not supposed to drink on the job," he said. Then, "We've had a lot of alcohol go missing from the bar lately. I think perhaps we should go inside."

Wendy began to sputter, and Flick could sense her panic. This was her only job, and all she talked about was her new apartment and her bills and before he could think of his mother and their new membership or his own job, he sputtered: "It's mine."

"Excuse me?" Mr. Welter said, looking at him for the first time.

Wendy spun around to face him. "Flick. Don't."

But he stepped forward into the light where Mr. Welter could better see him. "I'm Flick Creevy. I work here, too. I took the wine."

DARCY

He was the first thing she noticed. When she considered the crowd of members in their predictable summer outfits having their predictable conversations, Flick Creevy stole her gaze. He was outside on the deck, a straight drive from where she stood in the dining room. Darcy found herself moving toward him before she even realized it. But he wasn't alone—he was talking with one of the servers, Wendy. Wendy was in her early twenties with curves as pronounced as her attitude. Darcy knew they worked together, but seeing them now made her wonder how closely. She paused in the doorway, waiting for him to notice her. When their eyes met, there was no mistake—he was glad to see her. They shared champagne and a few laughs, and Darcy couldn't help but notice there was something different about the way he was looking at her that night. Different in a way that made her feel like she belonged in that slinky dress she'd almost been too afraid to wear, just as she belonged next to him under a sky glowing as pink as her cheeks felt. It wasn't the champagne.

But then, Teagan, her old teammate from the golf team, showed up. Along with her sister, and with them, Spencer. Spencer, who had promised to talk to his father. When she crossed the deck to say hello to them, she realized too late that Flick hadn't followed. Then her mother called her in for dinner, and Flick's table was nowhere near hers. But Spencer—well, he was seated right next to her.

Darcy stole peeks at Flick's table. He looked so handsome all dressed up. His mother and stepfather looked a little like fishes out of water, and she felt a pang of sympathy for them. Maybe she would go introduce herself. But then Spencer leaned in and started talking. To her disbelief, they talked all evening. Spencer told her he'd gone to bat for Adam, mentioning to his dad that he was a good kid. Maybe that claim seemed a little overstated, since to her knowledge Spencer barely knew Adam. But he seemed so genuine, and even more surprising, so interested in keeping the conversation going. All before telling her that her dress was unreal. *Unreal.* When she heard that, the rush was better than any champagne buzz.

Later, when a few of them ditched dessert and headed out to the course with a bottle of Tito's that Spencer magically produced, Darcy couldn't miss out. She tried to get Flick's attention, but he was busy talking to his mother.

And then she found him: alone outside with Wendy. Wendy was crying, and there was a bottle of wine between the two of them, and Darcy didn't know what to make of it. But she knew what it looked like. "I was looking for you," she told him.

"Oh yeah?" he'd looked past her, at Spencer and Teagan and Blaine, who were already leaving her behind, and the look on his face made her feel like a door had been closed. Flick wasn't coming with them. He was busy doing whatever he was doing with Wendy, and Darcy felt like an idiot for standing there. So she'd taken off with the others and they'd hung out down on the dock, dangling their feet in the water and passing the Tito's up and down the line. Spencer sat right next to her. Eventually, Blaine had to leave. Then Teagan and her sister did, too, leaving her alone under the dark sky with Spencer. It was everything she'd wanted since the start of summer, and now she had no idea what to do with it.

Buzzed and overwhelmed, when Spencer leaned over and pressed his lips to hers Darcy didn't just let him. She kissed him back. It was everything she'd dreamed of—happening right there on a starry summer night with the best-looking senior at school who had never even noticed her until that summer at Mayhaven. Lily would die. Two weeks ago, Darcy would have, too. But as Spencer Delancey slipped his tongue in her mouth, it was Flick she thought of. When Spencer ran his hand across the front of her chest, brushing one breast and then the other, Darcy's breath caught. When he tried to lower her onto the dock, she went with it. As Spencer moved over her, Darcy looked up. The sky swirled and blurred, each point of light fading in and out of focus. *You wanted this*, she told herself. But when Spencer slipped his hand up the skirt of her dress and the length of her leg, she sat up. "I'm sorry," she said, heart pounding. "I can't."

Spencer sat back on his haunches. "Can't or won't?"

Darcy slipped her spaghetti strap back over her shoulder, feeling the heat between them instantly chill. "What's the difference?"

He didn't say anything, just shook his head. "Whatever."

Darcy felt like a fool. Like the *little girl* Ashley Riley had called her at the party.

"I've got to go," he said, standing.

She rearranged her dress, wishing she could rearrange the

last few minutes as easily. "Hey," she said, trying to salvage some small thing from the night, "thanks again for talking to your father about Adam."

"Who?"

As they trudged back up the hill to the clubhouse, the scent of pine sharp in her nostrils, Darcy trailed a few paces behind. Spencer didn't wait for her.

• • • • •

There was no text from Spencer the next morning. Or from Flick. It was everything she'd expected, but still it stung. It was Sunday, which meant no camp and no organic opportunity to run into either of them and nothing to distract herself with. She weighed herself and saw she was up a pound. Her head throbbed from the Tito's and her stomach roiled, but she couldn't let herself eat breakfast. Two diet pills later she went for a run. It was scorching outside, and her body ached with effort as she ran down Maple and onto Woodside Drive. By the second mile she barely had the energy to turn back and walk home. Throughout the afternoon, she checked her phone, and after a lunch of iceberg lettuce and a handful of tomatoes (she was starving by then), the scale again. When there was no change on either, Darcy threw her phone across her room. It hit the far wall with a deadening *thud*. She was almost disappointed when she picked it up and realized there wasn't a single scratch or dent. It was just kissing and touching, she told herself, recounting the details of the night before for the hundredth time. But then why did she feel so tired and used up?

Sometime that afternoon, her mother banged on the door and poked her head in. God, Darcy wanted a lock. "Are you feeling okay?" Ingrid asked, her face clouded with the usual surplus of concern and suspicion. "You didn't come down for breakfast or lunch."

"I ate lunch," Darcy insisted.

"That tiny salad? Is that all you've eaten today?" The woman was a criminal investigator; she hadn't even been in the kitchen when Darcy had made it.

"Fine," Darcy said, hopping out of bed and whisking past her. "I'll eat." In the kitchen, she feigned making a turkey sandwich while Ingrid watched and tried to make small talk. She knew what her mother was doing. Well, Darcy could play that game, too. She took a big bite of the sandwich, and then another. The texture was like sand and the weight of it lead, sitting in the pouch of her cheek. When her mother was finally satisfied and left her alone, Darcy spit the mouthful into the trash bin and handed the rest to Fritzy. She waited until the dog consumed every crumb. "Good boy," Darcy whispered, pointing out a piece he'd dropped on the tile floor. Evidence was everything.

Back in her room, she fell into a fitful sleep. She awoke to her phone buzzing. It was just Lily. Tired of evading her, Darcy answered, but she didn't mention the vodka or Spencer or the dock. She'd been made a fool and her life was a joke. What else was there to tell?

• • • • •

Monday morning it took everything to drag herself to work. God knew what people would be saying about her. Blaine had a big mouth and even though it was clear she was dead to Spencer, people would talk. Darcy wasn't stupid; as the girl, it would all reflect badly on her. Spencer was just being a guy;

blameless and untouchable. As for Flick, he'd made his choice. So when she trudged into the clubhouse steeling herself for the onslaught of whispers and looks, she was jolted by a different frenzied buzz among the counselors. *Someone had been caught stealing from the bar. A new member. A kitchen worker. That new kid, what's his name?*

Flick Creevy.

"There's no way," she told Lily, in hushed tones as they waited outside for their campers to arrive. "He likes his job, and his parents just joined. He wouldn't upset his mom like that."

Lily eyed her suspiciously. "Do you have a thing for him you haven't told me about?"

Darcy scoffed. "What? No!" She'd barely mentioned Flick to Lily, not the texts or the long talk in the golf cart or their night in the RV—none of it. There were a few times she'd started to, and even more times she wanted to, but something always stopped her. Like the diet pills. Like the weight loss. That summer, Darcy needed to keep certain details to herself. It had become a mason jar full of summer insects, like the fireflies she used to collect on the clubhouse beach at night, with her brother when they were little. Only these weren't fat, perky fireflies who jazzed up a dark night. These insects were different, fast and dangerous, with razor-sharp stingers. Even though it took all her concentration, she had to keep the lid on tight; if she let even just one go, they'd hurt everyone she cared about.

But it was getting harder to keep things from her best friend. Lily was starting to look at her the same way her parents did, like she was holding something back from them that they needed. And now Lily was asking about Flick, which bothered her more than what happened with Spencer, somehow. Darcy couldn't withstand much more, so maybe it wouldn't be the worst thing if she threw Lily a morsel. A tidbit. Just to get her off her back.

"Spencer and I fooled around the other night," she blurted out.

Lily's face fell. "And you're just telling me now?" She grabbed Darcy's hand and tugged her under the deck, out of earshot, the exact spot where Flick and Wendy had stood the other night.

"I'm sorry," Darcy said. "I wanted to tell you, but I'm still trying to make sense of it."

"I don't even know where to start. What happened exactly? Are you guys a thing?"

Darcy laughed bitterly. "No chance. He hasn't even looked at me today."

Spencer was over by the picnic tables, talking with the other lifeguards without a care in the world. Ashley Riley was with them. When she looked over at them, Darcy shuddered.

"Tell me everything," Lily insisted.

"Our families sat together at the party. At first I thought he was just being polite in front of the adults, but he kept talking to me: about Adam, about camp." Darcy paused. "I know it sounds crazy, but he seemed really interested. In me.

"Later, a bunch of us went down to the beach. Spencer and Blaine had a bottle of Tito's, and we shared it. I got pretty buzzed. Eventually it was just the two of us left."

"And . . . ?"

"And we kissed. It felt nice, at first. Really nice."

"Then what?"

This was the part that embarrassed her the most, even in

front of her best friend. “It went from kissing to groping fast. It became clear he wasn’t interested in me as much as he was *that.*” Darcy glanced around warily. Campers were starting to trickle in. This was not the time.

Lily was still staring at her in disbelief. “C’mere.” She gave Darcy a long, hard hug. “Boys suck,” she said, into her hair. “Tell me the rest later, but don’t let him get in your head today. It’s prime real estate. He can’t afford the rent.”

Darcy hugged Lily back. It was a relief to share some of it, even if it was ugly. Even if it was just the tip of the iceberg.

As they collected their campers and headed to the courts, Darcy’s worries turned to Flick. People would be quick to blame all the liquor thefts on him, which was so unfair, especially when she’d been with Teagan, Blaine, and Spencer who *had* stolen a bottle of vodka. If Flick was even drinking that bottle of wine she’d seen that night, she was pretty sure it had more to do with Wendy.

Mondays were Flick’s day off, but she found herself looking for him anyway. Unable to stand not knowing, she texted him: You okay? I heard about what happened Saturday night.

There was no reply. She tried to focus on the kids through tennis lessons and a messy clay project at the craft barn. Finally, she and Spencer were thrown into one another’s path. Darcy was helping her campers wash the clay off their hands at the outdoor spigot, when he walked by with another guard. He looked right at her. “Hey.” No meaningful look. Not even a smile. It was about as personal as the weekly grocery-store fliers that the postal lady shoved in their mailbox—addressed to *current resident.*

“Hey,” she said back. She wouldn’t give him the silent treatment, but she also wouldn't say his name. Spencer Delancey had stung her.

By the time she checked her phone again, she had three texts, all from Flick.

I'm fine.

How about you?

Looks like you had fun Saturday.

Had fun? They were talking about him, not her. And no, she had not had fun. But reading his texts buoyed her. Flick cared.

She left Lily with the campers and went to find her dad, not even stopping to knock on his office door. "Dad, I heard about Flick."

Her father looked as unhappy as she did. "Honey, you know I can't discuss employee issues with family."

"Dad." She sat on the couch. "It's me. And Flick is . . . a friend. Besides, I know you like him, too. Just tell me—is he going to lose his job?" Suddenly she couldn't bear the thought of Mayhaven without Flick.

Her father sighed and pushed his chair away from his desk. "Honey, Flick admitted to it."

"To all of it—the kayaks, the silver, the missing alcohol? I don't believe that."

"To the wine, at least. But I really can't discuss this, you know that."

She had to tell him the truth. "Dad, I was with a bunch of members Saturday night, and they stole alcohol, too."

"What?" Her father looked so disappointed. But he needed to know, even if it got her in trouble, too. "You were involved?"

"Dad, I'm almost seventeen. Kids drink. But no, I didn't steal anything. And I didn't realize they had until we were down at the beach."

"Did you drink, too?"

Darcy stared at her sneakers. "Yeah." Then, "I'm sorry. I would never do anything to jeopardize your job. We were all the way down at the lake and it was a big group and . . ."

When she looked up she was shocked to see his expression had softened. "Is that the first thing you think I worry about when you mention drinking—my job? It's *you* I worry about."

"I'm sorry," she said, again. "I just wanted you to have all the facts."

He didn't answer, but instead stared out the window at the golf course. Before, whenever they had to talk about something difficult, they would save it for out there. Out there they could walk side by side, eyes on the fairway, and talk about anything. Somehow it was easier. Their hands were occupied with their clubs, their minds with the intricacies of the swing. Words would find their way around the edges of all that. And whatever was said they would play through it—so that by the ninth hole, when they made the turn, feelings had been aired.

"It used to be easier when you and Adam were little," her dad said, a wistful look in his eyes. "I thought the late nights and the feedings and the physicality of it all was hard, but the truth is those were the easy days."

Darcy didn't know about all that, but being a teenager was hard, too. "What about Flick? We both know he didn't steal all that stuff."

"I don't know what I know anymore." Her father's expression shifted from reminiscent to pained. It was how he looked a lot, lately. "All I know for sure is that Flick said he took the wine. And that's going to make people ask questions."

What people didn't know was what kind of kid Flick was. Her whole summer Darcy had been watching Spencer and Ashley and their crowd, wanting to be like them, wanting to be around them. Flick was different from them, and different from her, too. Darcy would never have admitted to taking the bottle of wine. Not because of her father's job—but because she was too cowardly. Flick was not a coward.

"I hope he gets to keep his job."

Her father nodded. "I know you do." Then, "I'll do what I can."

There were no guarantees, but what was left was hope. Before she left, she went and kissed her father on the cheek. "Thanks, Daddy."

His face lit up. "You haven't called me that in ages."

It was true. Maybe she'd try to do that more often.

She was halfway to the door when he called her back. "Hang on. With all the chaos, I almost forgot. Tomorrow is the golf clinic for your group of campers, but Danny is out sick. Think you can help Vince teach it?"

She froze. Danny usually handled the younger golfers. "Vince is teaching the little kids?"

"You know how great he is. I'm sure he can adjust his teaching for little ones, too. It's just for one day, okay?"

It was not okay. But her overwhelmed father was asking. And he'd promised to look out for Flick. "I'll try," she said, and she hurried out the door before he could get a good look at her.

NED

He hated the look on Flick Creevy's face when he came in. On the rare occasion there were employee problems, they were minor and removed from Ned's personal life. Not so with Flick Creevy. Even Darcy was now wrapped up in this, which made Ned wonder what exactly was going on with the two of them; but that was another problem. Now, as he looked at the boy's solemn expression as he sat across from him, Ned was reminded of just how much had happened since he'd hired him at the start of the season.

"Would you like to tell me what happened Saturday night?"

Flick looked about ready to throw up. "Alright, sir."

Ned listened carefully as Flick recounted the evening. He had been at the member dinner. He saw his coworker Wendy, who was upset over spilling dessert on one of the members, and he felt bad. So, he snagged a bottle of wine from a table and brought it outside to where she was crying, as a means to comfort her.

"Surely you realize the transgressions with this one decision. For starters, you're underage, Flick. That's against the law. You not only took a bottle, but you then offered alcohol to another employee who was on the clock at the time, which is also against the rules."

Flick did not argue any of this.

"I'm very sorry, Mr. Birch. I really am. I was trying to help a friend and I went about it all wrong."

Ned felt for the kid. "I'm sure you'll understand, this is something we need to address." As predicted, Ned had had calls from not only Dan Welter, the member who'd discovered Flick that night, but also from members of the board, and of course, Dick Delancey.

"He was your hire, but I do like his stepfather," Dick had said that morning. There was Dick, inserting his own interests into what should have been a clean procedural response by the chairman. "That said, a lot of people think the kid is responsible for the other thefts around here. It makes sense—it all started after he was hired. Plus, there's just something cagey about him, don't you think? I don't know, every time I look at him, I just get a feeling."

No, Ned did not think any of those things about Flick. And just what *feeling* was Dick referring to, Ned wanted to ask.

"What does your family think about this?" Ned asked Flick, now. Ned had wondered about this detail a good bit. Here was yet another thorn with the new neighbors. Stan had shown no evidence of being a reasonable person; Ned could easily imagine him blowing up and coming to his stepson's defense in ways that worsened things at home and at work.

"They're not happy. They're new here, and I've embarrassed them." His face clouded. "Especially my mom."

To Ned's dismay, the boy started to cry. It wasn't crocodile tears, either—Flick kept his head down and swiped at his cheeks and then pulled himself together and looked Ned in the eye.

Ned leaned back in his chair. The board had enough to do. He didn't need to involve them in this, too. "It's unfortunate, the choice you made the other night. But for the rest of this summer, you've proven yourself. I'm going to put you on disciplinary action.

"First, your next paycheck will reflect the cost of the bottle of wine you took. Second, you are not allowed to work the floor or drive the cart this week. You will be solely on kitchen duty. If there are no further incidents, you may return to the rest next week."

The kid looked so relieved, Ned was afraid he might stand up and hug him.

"Lastly, you will write a letter of apology that I can share with the board. As I've told you before, I like to think of Mayhaven as a little family. As a new member, you're part of that now. People make mistakes sometimes—what's important is that you own them and learn from them. Sound fair?"

"Very fair. Thank you." Flick exhaled a huge sigh of relief. "I really am sorry."

"Enough apologizing, I've already accepted. We'll see you tomorrow."

Later that afternoon, Jane appeared in his doorway.

"Please tell me this isn't about fish or weddings."

"No, I think you're going to like this," she said, holding up a handful of papers. She lay them ceremoniously on his desk. "Three more membership applications."

"Well, that was fast!" Ned flicked through. Sure enough, Stan's brothers and their friend Tony had all applied.

"The board will be thrilled," Jane said, summing up Ned's exact thoughts.

"Though the timing is a little suspect," he added. "After what happened with his stepson this weekend. I just put Flick on probation."

"You think they pushed these out, just to keep Flick here?"

"Perhaps." To be fair, Stan had said, well before any of this happened, that he wanted his family and friend to join. It was the reason Ned had let them golf before their membership was official. "Speaking of, have they paid their dues yet?" The other two new families who'd recently joined had. Living next door to Stan, Ned could tell that money wasn't the problem.

Jane made a face. "Strangely, no. And between us, the restaurant billing shows a rather large bar tab for last Friday. Apparently Mr. Crenshaw and his guests enjoyed themselves and treated everyone to quite a few rounds of drinks and food. Shall I put in a call?" It was standard office policy. Nothing personal.

"Please do," Ned said, decidedly.

"Since you brought it up, where do things stand with the koi delivery?"

Dick Delancey had asked the same thing, earlier. "It's the one-week wedding countdown!" he'd said. "I've got three hundred guests, but still no damn fish?"

"I called this morning, and the roads around the hatchery are finally clear. They're starting their drive tomorrow."

Dick's mouth worked like he had eaten something bad. "Cutting it pretty close."

"The koi will be here," Ned had assured him.

Now, with Jane, he could be more frank. "What, really, is all the fuss? The bridge over the pond is done, and it looks great. So, unless Phoebe has switched her theme to snorkeling, I don't see the urgency for a bunch of fish to be swimming under it."

"You didn't hear about the underwater photographer?" Jane smiled wickedly. "Kidding. But you'll be pleased to know I've confirmed everything else."

"Thanks. I'll be relieved when this wedding is over." Still, there was the nagging feeling he'd forgotten something. "Jane, do I have any more appointments scheduled today?"

"No, there's nothing else on the calendar."

"I feel like I'm supposed to be somewhere."

Jane shook her head. "Your afternoon is wide open."

Instead of leaving Ned went through the wedding details one last time: the Maine seafood distributor would depart Portland with an entire truckload of fresh lobster, oysters, clams, and mussels in the predawn hours Friday morning. The pantry housed ten cases of Krug (since padlocked, upon Dick Delancey's insistence). The florists, band, photographers (there were three!), extra bar and serving staff would arrive the day of. They would get this done, right down to the last silver candlestick. Ned's contract was up for renewal. Dick was chairman. He stayed late making sure everything was in order.

On the way home, Ned realized that he had two missed calls from Ingrid. When he tried her back, it went straight to voicemail. Whatever it was must not have been important.

Ingrid's car was not at home. Inside, Adam was pacing about the kitchen. "Where have you been?" he cried before Ned could even set his bag down. "I'm starving. Mom's gone and there's no food."

"Huh." Ned couldn't recall Ingrid mentioning a house

showing that afternoon. She must have gotten a last-minute client call. "Don't worry, Adam, I'm sure there's something we can throw together."

But, there was not. The fridge was unusually bare. "Let's order pizza."

Adam, Darcy, and Ned ate their pizza without Ingrid. No one seemed to know where she was, but they saved two pepperoni slices for her.

"Mom doesn't like pepperoni," Adam said, reaching for one of the remaining slices in the box.

"Easy buddy, you've already had four," Ned said, pushing the box away. "And sure she does. Doesn't she?" For the life of him, Ned suddenly could not recall his wife's favorite pizza topping.

Darcy shrugged. "I think she likes mushroom?"

"Mushroom?" That couldn't be right.

As if in reply, the front door swung open with a bang, and the three of them startled. "Mom!" Adam said. "Can I eat your pizza?"

Ingrid trudged into the kitchen, holding a big gold cellophane balloon. She was all dressed up, but she did not look celebratory.

"Where'd you get that?" Darcy asked, eyeing the balloon.

Ned sensed something was off. "Hi, honey. We were wondering where you were."

"Yeah, where were you?" Adam repeated, snagging a slice of pizza.

"Where was I?" Ingrid dumped her bag on the floor. She started to laugh, but it came out more like a cackle. "Where were *all of you*?"

Ned felt the need to stand, but he was afraid to move. "We were just having dinner. Want some?"

"Mom, you don't like pepperoni, right?" Adam asked.

Ingrid didn't answer. She pointed her finger at them accusingly, the cellophane balloon trembling violently at the end of its string. "I was at the party."

"Party?" they echoed in unison.

It was the wrong thing to say. The very worst thing.

"You all missed my party!" Ingrid cried.

No, no, no. They'd forgotten the party that her office was throwing her for selling the Tree House, the house that no one could sell. It was Ingrid's shining moment. And they'd missed it. Ned hopped up from his chair. "Oh, honey I am so sorry! We forgot your party was today." He went to hug her.

Ingrid held out her hand like a crossing guard halting traffic. Ned stopped. His wife was shaking-mad but she also looked about to burst into tears. "For *all* the things I do for *all* of you people every stinking day, the one thing I have asked for this summer—*the one damn thing*—was to come to my office party and support me for a change." She glared at them. "And none of you came!"

A blanket of silence fell across the kitchen.

Ned cleared his throat, arms still open. "Honey, we will make this up to you—"

"Save it!" Ingrid stalked past him, straight to the knife set on the kitchen counter. The family watched in horror as she withdrew a steak knife like a sword from its sheath and stabbed the gold balloon.

"Mom!" Adam cried.

There was an earsplitting *pop* and the balloon wheezed to

the floor in a cellophane puddle. "That is how this family made me feel today." Then before anyone could say anything else (but what was there to say, really?) she stormed out of the kitchen and up the stairs.

Ned remained frozen in place.

Darcy huffed. "Well, *that* was crazy."

Adam lifted the lid of the pizza box and peered inside. "Does she like pepperoni or not?"

There was a small *thud* and a wail from the top of the stairs. *"I like mushroom!"*

Darcy rolled her eyes. "Told you."

FLICK

There were four words that a parent could say that were worse than being grounded. Worse than having your car taken away. Worse than any punishment. Josie's brown eyes shone as she spoke them to Flick: "I'm disappointed in you."

The words were tiny but mighty, just like his mother. And Flick felt each one hit him dead center in the gut. His whole life, Flick had relied on Josie, and Josie alone. Since the father they never spoke of did not come back, having left to pick up a six-pack of beer one winter day when Flick was just a baby, he had only ever had Josie.

His mother worked so hard just keeping a roof over their heads and the bills paid that there had always been a silent agreement between them. Go to school. Do your work. Don't mess up. That Saturday night when Mr. Welter led him back inside the twinkling clubhouse dining room, Josie only had to look up at her son's face through the candlelight to know he'd messed up. Badly.

Because it was a club event, and it was as acceptable to make a scene as it was to douse white pants in red sorbet, Mr. Welters let him go tell his mother, first, in private. There was some mercy.

What followed was an admission to something he didn't do and a hasty departure home. As Flick followed the taillights of Stan's Lamborghini down the dark winding road home he was tempted to veer off. In just five hours he could be back in Queens, crashing at Mateo's house, sleeping on his bedroom floor like they used to when his life made sense. At the last intersection before his posh new neighborhood, Flick thought about turning toward the highway. But he couldn't do that to his mother.

The worst part was that Josie did not flip out when they got home. She closed her car door, clicked across the garage floor in her high heels, and let herself calmly inside. There was no yelling. There were no questions. In the kitchen, she poured herself a glass of water at the marble island and sipped it slowly before she finally looked at him. It felt like an eternity. And then she said those four words. Flick was still reeling from their impact when she excused herself and went upstairs.

Stan's reaction was the next shock. He ambled in after them, closed the garage doors, and went about the house locking up like he did every night. Then he went to the fridge and took out two cans of beer. Flick watched as Stan slid one down the island counter in his direction. It stopped in front of him, right out of a movie.

"You know what you did," he said, cracking his can open. "Let your mom cool off, and maybe she'll talk to you in the morning."

Flick's stomach was sour, but the gesture couldn't be refused. He cracked open his can and took a nervous sip. "I'm sorry."

"Save it for her," Stan said, not unkindly. He held his beer aloft and it took Flick a second to realize he wanted to offer a cheers. Now? But he held his can up. "To a mother's love," Stan said. "There ain't nothing fiercer."

• • • • •

Josie ignored him all day Sunday. She refused to utter a single word, which she'd never before accomplished, and when she finally did, there was very little talking. Mostly there was yelling. Flick was encouraged: his mother was back.

"What the hell were you thinking?" she cried. She stood in his doorway, hands on her hips, her face as fiery as her fuchsia workout clothes. The Peloton had done little to help her pedal off her rage.

"Mom, I'm sorry." Flick wanted to tell her the truth, that he hadn't stolen the wine, but then she'd force him to tell the club and Wendy would go down. Or worse, she'd tell the club, herself, which was more Josie's style. Instead, he told her what he would tell Mr. Birch later: "I was trying to comfort Wendy. I screwed up."

"Boy, did you! We're new up there," Josie said, coming to sit on the bed beside him. "That was our one shot at a first impression. What will people think?"

Flick dared to meet her gaze. "Is that what you're most upset about? What other people think?" It was his turn to be mad. "What about what I think? You moved us here to a place where I have no friends and nothing to do, except work at that club. Nobody here is anything like me. But you can't wait to be like them." He threw his arms open as if trying to scoop up everything that was wrong. "I hate this place, Mom. I hate it. So, I don't care what anyone around here thinks."

Josie's hand flew at him and he flinched. She'd never hit him before. Instead, she wiped the tears streaming down his cheeks. He hadn't even realized he was crying. And then she pulled him against her, hugging him so hard he could barely breathe. He remembered Stan's words from the night before.

"Baby, I moved us up here for you," she whispered in his ear. "I thought it would be good for you. The schools. The fresh air. The nice neighborhood."

Flick buried his face in his mother's hair and inhaled. She smelled like her favorite lavender shampoo, and it made him feel like a child again. "I don't recognize anything anymore, Mom. Including us."

Josie pulled away and looked at him. Her eyes were soft now, but she didn't give in. "I'm sorry it's so hard, but it's early yet. You've got to give it a chance. Please, go see Mr. Birch and give it a chance."

"You're going back to the club after what happened?"

Josie nodded. "We're going back. After you make this right."

That night, he got two texts. Neither were from Darcy.

Why'd you do it? It was Wendy. He'd wondered when he was going to hear from her.

It's done. Don't worry about it. Flick still didn't fully understand himself. The only thing he could come up with was that by the time he'd run into Wendy on his way home, he'd felt like he'd already lost any chance of anything good that night. Wendy had been cut down by a member. Darcy had run off with Spencer. When Mr. Welter showed up moments later, what more did he have to lose?

I'm going to tell Mossimo she texted.

Don't he replied. You've got too much at stake. He and Wendy were not close, in fact she'd been toughest on him in the kitchen, but he respected how hard she worked in spite of how hard she seemed to have it. The job was her meal ticket in the purest sense.

I don't need any favors.

He knew her pride was at risk, but pride cost less than her apartment.

Sometimes we all do.

Let me think about it. Thanks junior.

Monday, he met with Mr. Birch. It was a shock to hear that he could keep his job, but it would still be hard to show his face. The news was probably lighting the grapevine ablaze. That night he texted Mateo.

Almost came to see you the other night.

Yeah? Why didn't you?

Mom. Life. Stupid job. Flick told him everything. Mateo thought he was crazy to take the fall for the wine, but he also knew his best friend better than anyone.

At least they didn't fire you.

Not sure I'm the guy for the job anymore.

Don't sell yourself short. What about the girl?

Not the guy for her either.

Bullshit. Stay open man.

Mateo said things like that. *Stay open.* Flick was pretty sure his best friend missed him as much as he did Mateo, but they'd never admit it to one another. *Stay open* was the next best thing, maybe better.

• • • • •

When he walked through the clubhouse doors on Tuesday morning, he reminded himself to stay open. There were looks and whispers among the counselors, but he didn't see Darcy. Mossimo was waiting for him in the kitchen.

"I heard what you did," Mossimo said. He strode up to Flick and placed his hands roughly on either side of Flick's face, his dark eyes intense. Flick's instinct was to recoil, but, before he could, the chef kissed him on one cheek, then the other. "I know loyalty when I see it."

When Mossimo let go, Flick turned to the sink already full of dirty pots and got to work scrubbing. He didn't want the chef to see him cry.

He managed to hide out in the kitchen for most of his shift, but near the end Mossimo asked him to run down to the pro shop and deliver a lunch order to Vince.

Flick was relieved not to bump into anyone in the dining room or hallway. But his luck ran out when he ran into Bitsy Babcock, just as she was exiting the women's locker room.

She set her bag down and wagged a finger at him. "You listen to me—I heard about that booze swipe on Saturday night, and I don't blame you one bit. I don't!" She shook her head for emphasis. "Those affairs are dreadful. If you needed a sip to get you through, so be it. Besides, those fat cats can afford to share. They drink plenty as it is." She winked.

"Thank you, Mrs. Babcock," Flick stammered. "It was a mistake. Won't happen again."

Bitsy's eyes twinkled. "Next time, come find me. I share!"

Man, he loved this lady. "Here, let me help you with your bag." He bent to retrieve her gym bag.

"Don't be silly!" She whisked it off the ground so quickly, it tipped. Some of its contents spilled onto the carpet. Flick stared.

In the spillage was a hairbrush, a bottle of sunscreen, and two silver forks. The forks were the same dark patina as the club's fancy Blackstone silverware he set tables with for special occasions. The same silverware that had been going missing.

"Oh dear." Quickly Bitsy scooped them up and into her bag. She righted herself and hoisted it over her shoulder. Before he could think of what on earth to say, she looked right at him and shrugged sadly. "I like nice things."

"Mrs. Babcock—" He paused. Mrs. Babcock wore many hats at the club: legacy member, board member, and now thief.

Mossimo would want to know. Mr. Birch would want to know. But what would that mean for Mrs. Babcock? Flick knew it would not be good.

"You have to turn me in," she said, looking down at her hands. They were manicured and bejeweled and roped with aging veins. Mrs. Babcock was tiny and elegant, but now she looked small and sad. She drove a Jag. Why would she be stealing from the club?

Flick swallowed hard. "No, I don't," he said.

"No?" Her penciled eyebrows shot up. When he shook his head, she stood on tiptoe and pecked him on the cheek. "You're a dear. Tell you what, I'll save a set for you!"

"Please don't do that," Flick said. "You have a good day." He had a sandwich to deliver. He was not the police. And he was in enough trouble already.

The pro shop was empty. "Hello?" he called, looking around for Vince. But the back office was vacant, too.

It was then he saw a group outside. Vince stood waving goodbye to a cluster of campers that Flick recognized as Darcy's. When he went to the window he spied Darcy on the putting green, collecting golf balls. His heart flip-flopped against his ribs.

Flick hadn't seen Darcy since Saturday night, when she'd gone off with Spencer and the others. Yesterday she'd shot him a text asking him if he was okay. But this time he wasn't going to let her get back in his head. It was clear on Saturday night that she'd made a choice.

Outside, there was no sign of either of them. Flick walked along the clubhouse hoping he'd find Vince so he could hand off his lunch order and avoid Darcy altogether. Just his luck, he spotted Darcy first, carrying a bucket of golf balls. He waited until she disappeared into the sports storage shed. Someone else rounded the corner of the shed right behind her. It was Vince, with a bag of kiddie clubs on each shoulder. Flick held back as he, too, disappeared into the shed. Now he'd have to wait.

He was leaning against the clubhouse with the lunch delivery, when he heard a scuffle from inside the shed. "Oh, come on." It was a man's voice, and he sounded annoyed. Flick looked up just as Darcy burst through the shed doorway. Her face was flushed. She glanced over her shoulder as she broke into a run. She was going so fast Flick barely had time to brace himself before she slammed right into him.

"Whoa!" he cried.

Darcy fell backward onto the grass before springing to her feet again. But it was long enough for Flick to get a good look at her.

Her eyes were wild. Alarm bells clanged in his head. "Darcy." He reached for her hand. "What just happened?"

She was out of breath, her entire focus on the shed behind her. "Nothing, let me go."

Vince appeared in the shed doorway. He, too, looked ruffled. Something had happened. And Flick needed to know what it was.

"Can I help you?" Vince barked. He adjusted his baseball cap on his head, then spied the bag in Flick's hand. "Is that my lunch?"

Darcy yanked her hand from Flick's and hurried for the clubhouse door.

"What's going on here?" Flick bellowed. The voice that came from his mouth was not his own.

Vince stared back at him, eyes narrowed. "Excuse me?"

"You heard me." Flick moved toward him, and Vince stepped back. Yes, he had read the situation right. The guy had guilt all over him. Suddenly it all made sense: Darcy had been dropping hints all summer, but Flick hadn't pieced them together, until now. *Did you ever try to forget something bad from the past?* "What just happened in there?"

"Flick, don't! Please."

He spun around. It was Darcy. Her hand was still on the door handle, but she hadn't gone inside. Despite a level of fear that caused her to slam right into him, she was still there, watching and waiting. Begging him not to do anything. There was a reason for that. And Flick finally understood what it was.

Without warning, a wave of protectiveness crested inside him. Flick charged at Vince. He struck him with both hands right in the chest, sending him flying backward through the shed doorway.

"What the fuck?" Vince caught himself, and as soon as he did Flick shoved him again.

"Flick!" Someone was screaming his name. Vince pulled his fist back to swing, and in reply Flick grabbed him by the collar of his shirt and rammed him up against the wall. Tennis rackets toppled from the overhead shelf onto their heads. A bucket clattered to its side and golf balls spun about their feet, but Flick did not let go.

"Get off me!" Vince screamed.

There were other voices now, too. And then there were hands—hands on Flick's shoulders and arms, hands pulling him off of Vince, who had fallen on his ass and now skittered backward across the ground like a crab.

A golf cart roared up. People were firing questions. Flick sank to the grass, cradling his head in his hands.

"He lost his mind!" Vince shouted, as someone helped him up to his feet. "Get that kid out of here. He's fucking crazy."

Someone hauled Flick up, grabbed him by the back of his neck and steered him to the clubhouse doors.

When he sat across from Ned Birch, blood streaming from his nose, there was nothing he could say. Mr. Birch handed him an ice pack and stared. "What the hell happened?"

Flick could feel his left eye swelling shut already. "Where's Darcy?"

"What? Flick, you've got to tell me what went on out there. Vince is saying you attacked him and members say they saw it." Ned's expression was pleading, and Flick almost felt sorry for him.

"Please, I need to talk to Darcy."

"Why?" The darkness that clouded Ned's face shut Flick up. "What does any of this have to do with my daughter?"

Flick knew right then and there his fate was sealed. "Nothing," he said quickly. "She's my friend. I just want to see her."

Ned slammed his fist on the desk. "You can't see Darcy, Flick! And you can't stay here, either. You'd better hope I don't have to call the cops!"

DARCY

As soon as the golfers dragged Flick off of Vince, she knew she could go because Flick was safe.

She plowed through the clubhouse doors so fast she didn't see her brother standing at the window. "Adam!" She halted, swiping at her tears. The last thing she needed was for him to get upset, too. "Sorry, I didn't see you." He started to say something, but she pushed past him. "Not now, Adam. I'm in a rush."

"Darcy!" he called after her, his voice strained with worry. "Darcy, wait."

But she could not wait. She ran into the women's locker room. Thank God, no one else was in there. In the shower stall Darcy pulled the curtain closed behind her, and sank onto the cold tiles.

Her body heaved with each memory; every instance Vince had made her feel helpless and dirty rolled over her like a tidal wave. In the beginning, it was a word or a look, things offered with a flippancy that left her wondering if *she* had been the one to misread the situation—if she had said or done something wrong. Today any doubt had been silenced. Now it wasn't just about her; now Flick had been dragged into it, too. She'd tried to stop him—she'd screamed his name, but he wouldn't listen. The moment she picked herself up off the ground and saw the look on his face she realized Flick knew. There was no more pretending.

All year she'd listened to the voice that urged her to keep it quiet—keep it secret—don't tell. But it was too late for that now. Now, there were other eyes. As soon as the golfers had raced over in their cart, it was out of her hands. It was out, in the full sun, for all to see. So she'd run. Like the very coward who'd kept her mouth shut all this time, she did the only thing she knew, and she ran to hide.

When she couldn't shed another tear, she stood at the sink until the water ran ice cold. She splashed her face, smoothed her hair, and took a deep breath. There was no telling what was happening on the other side of the locker room doors, but she couldn't hide anymore. All that mattered was finding Flick.

Outside, the hallway was quiet—too quiet. She stole a peek out the nearest window, and saw campers coming up the hill. The golfers were gone, as was their cart. So, too, were Flick and Vince. The sun was still shining.

Softly, Darcy tiptoed down the hall toward her father's office. Before she reached the door a sound came from the base of the stairwell, and Jane stood up. She'd been sitting guard, Darcy realized. "Your dad's a bit tied up right now, honey." Jane made a face. "You can't go in there, I'm afraid."

Darcy studied Jane's face for clues. "Tied up?"

"It seems there was some kind of altercation. He's talking to the person involved."

"Person?" Until today there were two people involved, now there were three. Darcy forced herself to ask. "What happened?"

"It seems one of the kitchen staff had a disagreement with poor Vince. He got pushed around a bit, but he'll be fine. Your dad sent him home to recover."

Her father had sent Vince home. Which meant Flick was the person. Not her. Not the grown man who'd made her feel strange and sick and ugly in her own skin. Darcy felt like she might throw up. "I need to see my dad."

"You'll have to wait, honey," Jane said, steering her gently away, down the hall, to the doors. With each step, Darcy felt her bravery falter. Each step closer to the exit door was like a step toward safety. Sweet, gentle Jane was unknowingly ushering her away from doing what she needed to do, and yet Darcy did not turn around. She didn't even try. In her ear, Jane's words sounded like they were coming from underwater. "I'm sure everything will be okay, don't you worry."

The campers were leaving, and Darcy would, too. "Where are you going?" Lily called after her. "I've been looking for you!"

Darcy could barely get the words out. "I don't feel well," she said, brushing by her best friend. She forgot all about Adam. All she could do was picture her bed, which she would crawl into, and the thick curtains, which she would pull closed.

Later, she heard her mother's voice coming up the stairs. "Darcy?" Then a knock at her door.

"I'm sick," Darcy managed.

Her door opened. "You left Adam at work. I had to drive up and get him." When Darcy offered nothing in return, her mother sighed. "Do you want some tea? Ibuprofen?"

Darcy pulled the pillow over her head. "What I want is to be left alone."

Not long after Adam knocked. "Go away," she hollered. But he would not. She could hear him pacing out in the hallway. What was he so worked up about? Well, she had her own problems. Finally, he gave up and left.

In the darkness beneath her covers, Darcy replayed the afternoon again and again.

Hours later, there were more knocks at her door. It was Adam, again. "Please come out, Darcy. I need to tell you something. It's important."

"Just go!" Darcy screamed. She didn't even have the energy to feel bad when he finally did.

She stayed in bed until she heard the front door slam. Finally. It was the cue she'd been waiting for, and she got up and slipped down the hall. Her father stood in the foyer, unlacing his sneakers. Even from the top of the stairs she could see how wrecked he was. Had Flick told him the truth? Had Vince been called back in?

Her father veered into the kitchen where she heard her parents talking, the rise and fall of urgency, the timbre of their voices grave. When she couldn't stand it a second longer, she tiptoed downstairs. From the doorway she heard her father say, "I fired him. I had no choice."

"Vince?"

They looked up and saw her in the door. "No, honey. Flick." Her father blinked in confusion. "Why would I fire Vince?"

Darcy stepped into the kitchen. "I quit." She hadn't planned to say this, she hadn't even thought it. But there it was. "I will never go back to that place. Ever."

Despite his exhaustion, this roused her father. "Darcy, it's been a rough day, what're you talking about?"

She looked between them; her father looking wrung out, her mother like she was trying to decode the message. "Is this about Flick?" her mother asked.

Darcy coughed out a laugh; it was a strange, strangled sound. They still didn't know. Her parents harbored no suspicions, no gut instincts. There would be no spotlight on her, no interrogation or examination of the ugliness that had coursed beneath the surface of her skin for so long now. Their intense conversation did not concern her, and they were blind to her brokenness, standing right there in front of them, in their very own kitchen.

She swallowed her anger. "I said I quit." Before they could say anything else, she ran back up to her room and slammed the door.

No one called her for dinner. No one tried to coax her out. Everyone retreated to their corner, wrapped in their own disappointments.

Later that evening, she heard her parents come upstairs. There was the sound of more footsteps. Adam said something. His voice was shrill with frustration, but all Darcy heard was, "Not now, Adam." Her parents' bedroom door banged closed and then so did his.

When the sky grew dark a note was shoved under her door. It was from Adam: Talk to me Darcy.

Poor Adam didn't understand what was going on.

But she was too raw to pretend everything was normal and listen to him go on about his Xbox game or his car videos or whatever he was doing. She was afraid if she opened her mouth ugly truths would come out. It was better to pretend to be sick.

Tomorrow, Adam would have forgotten all about it. Tomorrow she'd sit down and watch YouTube car videos with him.

Midnight was too far off, so she didn't wait for it. Neither had Flick. He was already sitting in the grass at the base of the RV steps, head in his hands. He got to her before she got to him.

"I'm sorry," she cried, falling against him.

"Don't say that," Flick said, burying his face in her hair. "Don't you ever apologize for any of it."

And yet there was so much to be sorry about.

When they separated, she ran her hand down his cheek. "Are you hurt?"

He put a finger to his nose. "Nah. Just got a bloody nose."

"And him?"

Flick's jaw flexed. "I wanted to kill him. But he's fine."

But Flick was not. "You got fired." All because he'd defended her. And kept her secret, too. "What did your parents say? They must be so upset."

"They're not happy. But I'll tell them the truth at some point."

Flick couldn't even tell his own parents the whole story, because it was hers to tell. "My parents have zero clue," she told him. "They look right at me and can't even see what's wrong."

Flick sat back down in the grass, and she lowered herself next to him. He took her hand. "Are you going to tell them?"

It was the last thing she wanted to do, but now Flick was involved. "I can't let you take the blame."

"That's not the reason. You should tell them because they're your parents. Darcy, they would want to know. If they know, they can help."

Help. It meant blowing a whistle. Sending up a flare. Showing her distress to the world. "That's what I'm afraid of." She didn't want help. There was too much shame, too much uncertainty about her role in all of it.

Flick lay back in the damp grass and she let herself, too. It was like a cool compress to the hot ache within her. "I feel like you started to tell me all summer," he said, his voice rich with regret. Darcy rolled over and lay her head on Flick's chest. She pressed her ear to his heartbeat, its steady rhythm the only thing certain.

"You know, I wasn't sure it was really happening, until today. There were always little things, things that made me doubt myself—maybe I had misunderstood him, maybe I had sent the wrong signal. There were times I actually wondered if I was crazy." She thought back—to Vince's hand brushing her backside when he instructed her to adjust her setup. To the way he sometimes winked at her, which could've been nothing more than a high five between coach and athlete. But then the comments started, comments that made her want to crawl out of her own skin at a time she was already uncomfortable and unsure of herself. Like the day she showed up at her last tournament in a new golf top that her mom had surprised her with for good luck. Vince had stared at the shirt a moment too long: "Wow, you're really blossoming. Going to make a lot of boys squirm." After shoving her trophy to the back of her closet, she'd peeled the top off and bypassed the laundry bin for the trash. "I started to hate the game I loved. I started to hate myself."

Flick squeezed her, his arms warm and strong and safe. When the tears came, there was no shame in front of him.

Before dawn, she snuck back in the house and slid between her bedsheets. For the first time that summer Darcy finally felt like she could sleep. She was on the verge of a dream when she thought she heard the rumble of a car engine, outside. Then there was a screech, like tires. But her eyelids were so heavy. In the morning she assumed she'd dreamed it.

NED

Before any of his family had risen, Ned got up and escaped to work early. He had a final meeting with the father of the bride that he could not have cared less about, but he was eager to get through. But it was hard to think about anything other than the assault on Vince. Ned still could not make sense of it.

The Crenshaw-Creevys were truly lucky: Vince had graciously decided not to press charges. When Ned offered to call the police, Vince had even insisted he not. "No, no," he'd said, emphatically. "The kid is clearly going through something and needs help. Let's not make it worse for him."

"Are you sure you're okay? No injuries? You have every right to get checked out by a doctor." Ned was genuinely concerned, but he also knew this could turn into a worker's comp issue in a heartbeat.

Vince just waved him away. "He's just a kid, I'm fine. Besides, you don't want the cops crawling around up here, do you? The optics would not be good for Mayhaven."

Ned was surprised. After all, no matter how great a guy Vince was, he'd been assaulted at work. The man deserved a bonus. Ned gave him the rest of the week off.

As he turned his car into the club driveway, Ned glanced up at the sign: *Mayhaven*. The solemn-looking pilgrim stared into the distant hills. Usually when Ned looked at the sign he felt a calmness come over him, but that morning it dissipated at the sight of a golf cart racing across the lot in his direction.

His head groundskeeper, Ben, screeched to a halt alongside his car.

"We've got a problem."

Overnight someone had driven their car across the golf course and torn it to shreds. Ned bounced wordlessly along beside Ben in the cart as they traced the tire tracks through the dug up turf.

"The worst is up ahead," Ben warned. At the crest, they stopped to look: tire tracks streaked angrily across the first fairway and across the next. "Over there." Ben pointed to the fourth hole, adjacent. There in the center of the fourth fairway were wide sweeping circles of torn up earth and ripped up grass. It looked like a scene out of a monster truck rally. "Take me back to the clubhouse," Ned said. "I need to call the police."

The police came in two separate cruisers. They walked the course and surveyed the damage with Ned. Meanwhile, golfers trickled in, examining the crime scene in awe. Some cursed their lost tee time in such fine weather. Some shook their heads in solidarity. A few trekked across the damaged fairways to gawk for themselves before heading home in dismay: the course was closed indefinitely.

The investigating officer found Ned in the parking lot. "Any thoughts on who may be responsible?"

Sandwiched between the shock of the course damage and

the impending nuptials he needed to make happen, Ned hadn't allowed his brain to go there yet. It was still spinning between images of the shredded fairways and calculations of lost revenue. The question begged a clear head, and Ned's phone was blowing up in his pocket just as golfers were blowing up upon arrival at the scene. "No, nothing like this has ever happened here," he said. It was true. But even as he spoke the words, a sinking feeling began to overtake him. Quickly, Ned pushed it away. He wasn't ready to face it just yet.

"We need to take photos and measurements," the officer said, making a quick note. "I'll find you when I'm done."

"I'll be in the clubhouse," Ned told him. He couldn't bear to watch any longer.

"In the interim, you may want to call your insurance company."

Jane made the call and reported back right away. "The insurance company is sending someone out, but they don't have anyone in this region. It won't be until next week."

It was the worst possible scenario. This was high season; the club couldn't be closed for long without reimbursing membership. Ned needed to get the damage assessed and repairs started as soon as possible. He called an emergency board meeting for eleven o'clock. He hadn't even had a cup of coffee that morning, he realized, when Jane buzzed in again.

"I'm afraid I have more bad news," she said, warily. "You may wish to check your email when you have a moment."

Ned put on his reading glasses and opened the first forwarded email.

From: Stanley Crenshaw

To: MayhavenCC/office

I am writing to cancel our membership application. We are no longer interested in belonging to Mayhaven.

From,

Stan Crenshaw

After it were three more, two from Stan's brothers and the last from their mutual friend.

He closed the emails and dialed Jane's extension.

"Yes, Mr. Birch?" She sounded worried.

"Jane, did the Crenshaws pay their dues yet?" If they had, Mayhaven reserved the right to hang on to seventy-five percent of the dues. The member requesting cancellation could either roll their membership into the next year or walk away less seventy-five percent. It was common practice, and it would be a boon for Ned—Stan's membership dues without Stan. The very thought of it made him nearly giddy.

"Hang on a sec, I'll have to check."

When Jane came back on, her voice was even more glum. "No, Mr. Birch. I'm sorry, they never paid."

The loss of the four new memberships would be a big hit to his job and the budget. The board had just congratulated him on securing them.

Sure enough, Dick Delancey showed up early and outraged. He'd gotten the email about the course and the emergency board meeting. "What in the hell happened out there?" he shouted as he walked in.

"Dick, I'm treading water in a sea of shit," Ned said. "Let's tackle your wedding walk-through and let the police do their part." For once, Dick shut his mouth.

Together they inspected the tent setup and the dining room layout, and happily neither one could find a problem. They reviewed the orders for specialty chairs, table coverings, and napkins. Ned was relieved Phoebe was otherwise occupied at the spa with her bridesmaids. The linens were not cream, but ivory, but neither Dick nor Ned could tell the difference and they agreed it was not worth mentioning. Mossimo ran through the menu and timetable for dinner.

Dick's only question: *Can someone bring me a Manhattan before the ceremony? Neat.*

The last stop was the koi pond, something Ned had been dreading, but after the course damage it hardly seemed a blip on the radar of hell. They were halfway to the pond when Ned broke the news.

"About the fish," he began.

Dick jerked to a stop. "Don't even tell me they're not here yet."

Ned said nothing. He knew it was not his place to question member requests—no matter how utterly stupid or insane. But really, what did it matter? The fish would not be attending. They would not be in the photos. For Christ's sake, they were not ring bearers or toast makers. Look at what was there: The newly constructed bridge over the water! The sparkling pond, the bubbling fountain! Ned would bet his life no one would even notice the pond was empty. Except for one person. And that person was looking at him like he'd just canceled the whole affair.

Dick threw up his hands. "Son of a bitch! This goddamn day is supposed to be Shangri-La, whatever the fuck that means."

Well, Ned wasn't alone in that question, apparently.

Dick's face contorted with fresh red outrage. "My daughter wants flowers and fish. This is her third engagement, and the first time she's made it anywhere near the aisle. I told her I would make this happen!" Dick was screaming mad at Ned, but he looked like he might cry rather than take a swing.

Suddenly Ned got it. Dick Delancey was a father doing this for his daughter. He didn't give a rat's ass about koi or water features or photos. It was about making his daughter, Phoebe, happy on the day he was giving her away. And the realization made Dick an almost-human-being that Ned felt sorry for. "Dick, they are on their way. I'll keep calling and I'll stay late if I have to. Let's not give up yet."

They were heading back to the clubhouse when the investigating officer waved Ned over. Dick followed.

"We've finished our work on-site," he told them. "I have one question."

Ned really wished Dick would go inside. He would fill him in with the others at the board meeting. "I'm the club chairman," Dick said, instead. "Speak freely."

"Is there anyone you can think of who might have done this?" the officer asked. "Anyone who might be angry enough with you or the club that they did this for revenge?"

Dick and Ned exchanged a look. Try as he might, Ned couldn't deny the feeling that had shadowed him all morning. "There is one person."

At eleven o'clock just as the emergency board meeting he'd called was getting started, Ned pulled out of the club driveway. He'd left Dick in charge. Ned had to get home.

The police were on their way to Flick Creevy's house. As

awful as he felt about naming Flick, Ned had his own kids to take care of. Darcy and Adam were home alone, and the last thing he wanted was for them to be upset or involved.

He was a few minutes behind the officers, so he called the house. No one answered. Ingrid was out with a client, so he tried Darcy's cell but it went straight to voicemail. Ned had a bad feeling that went beyond the lousy evening at home last night. Darcy had been so emotional about the fight that happened, and Flick being fired, that she'd quit her job. The more he thought about it, for some reason Adam had also been pretty upset last night. He kept banging on Darcy's door until she yelled and Ingrid asked him to please leave his sister alone. All night he'd thought the stress he was feeling was about the incident with Vince and Flick, but he realized now that his entire house had been on edge, too. Ned wasn't sure why, but it suddenly felt extremely urgent that he get home.

As he whipped along the rural roads between Mayhaven and Maple Drive, Ned's thoughts spun: to Ingrid, who'd asked him to make time for a family meeting, saying she was worried about Darcy. He thought of Adam, who had paced much of the night before in the hallway. Adam had been complaining about Darcy, saying that he needed to talk to her. Ned was struck by the realization that that was exactly what Flick had said to him yesterday afternoon when he was hauled into Ned's office after he attacked Vince.

Everyone had wanted to talk to Darcy. A dark feeling overtook him, and Ned accelerated. At the next intersection he ran the stop sign.

When he spun into his driveway, he noticed two police cruisers parked next door. An officer stood outside, leaning up against one of the cars. Ned assumed the others were inside with Flick's family. Ned nodded at the officer and the officer nodded back.

He was about to go inside, when he noticed Flick's car. It was parked at an odd angle, partially blocked by one of the police cars. Something was off. Ned walked to the edge of his yard for a better look and sucked in his breath. The tire treads were so thick with turf that they'd left a muddy set of tire prints all the way from the driveway up to where it was parked. Dried grass was sprayed across the driver's door. Good God—Flick had done it.

As he stood there staring, a third police car swung up the street and into the neighbor's driveway, lights flashing. The Crenshaws' front door opened and the noise within filled the quiet morning outside: it sounded like a woman crying. Two officers exited the house, and behind them came Flick, escorted by a third. His hands were handcuffed behind his back. He was wearing a white T-shirt and shorts and he looked like a scared kid. Behind him Josie Crenshaw filled the doorway with her voice: "Please, you have to believe me. My son would never do this," she was crying. Stan was holding on to her.

"Ma'am, I've asked you to stay in the house until we go. You can follow us to the station," one of the officers told her. He spied Ned standing at the far edge of the yard. "Sir! I need you to stand back. Police business."

Quickly Ned retreated. He should give the family privacy. He should go inside. But when he got to his driveway, he couldn't tear himself away.

As Flick was put into the back seat of the police car, Josie began to howl on the front step. It was all too much. Ned was about to turn away when there came a similar sound, from his own house.

Ned spun around to see Darcy standing there in her pajamas, eyes wide. "What's happening?" She ran down the driveway and he reached out to stop her.

"Everyone, stand back!" the officer shouted. "Sir, take your kid back inside now."

"Honey, we have to get back in the house," Ned urged.

"You're having him arrested? Because of Vince? You can't let them do this!"

Everything was spiraling out of control; Ned had to get his daughter safely back inside. "Now!" he shouted, and Darcy blanched but obeyed. He was about to follow when out of the corner of his eye he became aware of something large and fast-moving. Before Ned realized what was happening, Stan was upon him.

"You called the cops on my kid?" Stan towered over him, and Ned stumbled backward on his own front steps.

Stan halted at the bottom of the steps, but he looked ready to come up and kill Ned. "How could you do this?" he shouted. "He's innocent, you son of a bitch!"

Two of the officers were right behind him. "I'm going," Stan told them, holding out his arms and stepping back. "I'm sorry, I'm going." He walked with them back to his own yard.

Ned collapsed on the front step. This was so much worse than he'd imagined.

One officer remained by the RV, standing patrol between the Crenshaws' yard and the Birches', ensuring everyone stayed on their own side. Meanwhile, neighbors stood at the edges of their yards; some huddled down the street talking and pointing. All of Maple Street was watching. It was time to go inside.

Ned had pulled himself to his feet when he heard the sound of metal on metal. The sound was grisly, like something being struck repeatedly. It was coming from down his own driveway. Ned hurried back down the steps. There, in front of the garage, was Darcy. She stood over a pile of glittering metal with his sledgehammer in her grip. Ned took a step toward her as she swung it skyward. It wasn't easy—the hammer was heavy and Darcy was slight—but her strength was as impressive as it was gruesome. Frozen, Ned stared as his daughter hauled the hammer up and brought it down. The object that was its target exploded with the blow, gold and silver fragments spiraling in all directions. Ned started to run. He ran toward his daughter as she lifted the handle again. He ran through the shards of plastic and metal skittering across the pavement and crunching beneath his feet. And then he stopped. What once were Darcy's golf trophies lay in a heap at her feet, a dazzling display of metallic fragments. And then it hit him.

The truth hit Ned Birch like a cannonball in the middle of his driveway: Darcy's abandoned love of the game. Her distant disposition. Her ambivalence and anger that summer. The look on her face the other day when he asked her to help Vince teach the campers a golf lesson. The look on Vince's face later that same day, when he convinced Ned not to call the police, that he'd be happy to just let it go. And lastly, the anonymous comments in the Pilgrim Box: *People should feel safe here.* A flame conflagrated in Ned's brain as he stared at his daughter standing in the glittering pile of wreckage.

Darcy let go of the sledgehammer. The handle clattered to the pavement.

"Darcy," he whispered. He had missed all of it, right there in his own house and at his own place of work and with his own child. He had failed. Ned Birch had failed them all.

Distraught, he did the only thing he could: he opened his arms.

"Stop!" It was Adam.

Adam appeared at the back gate, struggling with the latch. "Open the gate!" he cried. "I have to stop them." Ned realized he meant the police car that had just backed out of the Crenshaws' driveway. His gaze swung hard to the cruiser, pulling away slowly, Flick Creevy's head bowed in the back seat.

The gate latch popped and Adam burst through, racing toward the street. In the middle of his driveway, Ned Birch felt his heart split in half; which child did he reach for first?

"Adam!" Darcy screamed after her brother. But he was too fast and he slipped past them both. Ned took off after him. By then, Adam had run into the street blocking the path of the car.

The cruiser screeched to a stop. Heart in his throat, Ned shouted to his son to stand still. The siren whooped. Adam froze. He threw his hands up in the air.

"Take me!" he shouted.

And then he did the saddest thing Ned would ever witness in his whole life.

His fifteen-year-old son kneeled down in the road in front of their house, hands on his head. "Flick didn't do it," he cried. "Take me."

• • • • •

All summer, Adam had been watching. He'd wondered why his big sister had suddenly quit golf, the thing she loved that had consumed just about every warm, sunny day as long as Adam could remember. When he thought of Darcy he pictured her in a visor, her nose dotted with sunscreen, heading out to the course with their father. He'd watched Darcy win all those trophies, and then take them all down. He saw where she hid them, first in the back of her closet, and later down in a box in the dusty garage. It wasn't just the trophies. There were times Darcy was agitated in the car on the drive home from the club, when Adam sat beside her in the passenger seat and her leg jigged the whole way, always after a lesson with Vince. It made him worry about his big sister. He worried so much that he started watching her closer, sometimes following her, trying to see what was really the matter.

Adam saw what happened in the shed that day: how Darcy had been hanging up golf bags on the rack when Vince came up behind her. How Vince reached around his sister. And pressed his hips against her. Adam knew that was not right. From the window he watched his sister spin around and away. He saw her mouth moving but could not make out the words: he hoped they were swears. When she raced out of the shed crying, Adam felt something inside him snap.

All that day, he tried. He tried to ask Darcy about it; he tried to talk to his parents. But no one listened. Vince and the club were hurting his sister, and nobody would listen to him. So Adam did something louder, something no one could ignore.

He knew Flick kept his keys in his car. Adam had admired that car all summer. The rest was easy—because no one was paying attention.

Friday Evening

The Delancey wedding rehearsal dinner started at five-thirty. Thirty minutes before the official start time, the big red fishery truck delivering two hundred Hikarimono koi finally pulled into the clubhouse parking lot. As pitchers of blue and white hydrangea were placed on linen-covered tables on the upper deck, the fishery driver ran a long hose from the tank of the truck across the first fairway and down to the pond. Beeswax taper candles were placed in sparkling silver candlesticks as the truck pump suctioned water across the greens and into the tanks. Guests in summer whites and gauzy dresses trickled in as a funny-looking orange chute was hooked up to the truck and unraveled across the clubhouse yard, and down the hill to the pond. The guests were intrigued: What was this funny looking tube? What was happening here? High up, above it all on the upper deck, a father posed for a picture with his beautiful bride-to-be daughter, while a slew of fish slapped their tails against their holding tanks. It was time.

Just before the chute was opened, one last car pulled into the Mayhaven parking lot. Ned Birch was not dressed for a rehearsal dinner, nor was he invited. But he joined the sea of guests traversing the lawn, adjacent to the strange orange tube and headed for the clubhouse.

When the fishery truck operator opened the chute, there was a primitive gurgle followed by a deafening rush of water. Newly sprung, the fish surged down the chute that ran alongside the heels and loafers of guests, who marveled at the noise. "We should walk down to the pond to see!" someone said.

Among them, Ned Birch kept his eyes trained ahead. Despite the fact he'd waited all summer for this, he was oblivious to the chute and the fish. Ned was looking for someone.

Suddenly, without warning, there came a strange geyser-like sound. The chute that snaked across the clubhouse lawns shuddered and burst open. As guests covered their faces and leapt away from the spray, Ned Birch made a beeline for the man he'd been looking for. Down on the lawns, the orange chute twisted and rolled like a mythological snake, spitting fish and water in equal measure across the grass. As the driver shouted for help, Ned Birch ran at the golf pro. Vince, having just raised his chin to empty his flute of champagne, lowered it just in time for Ned Birch to sock him square in the face. Someone screamed. Vince toppled backward into a champagne tower, glass and bubbles erupting everywhere. In the background, a sea of fish flipped and floundered across the flooded greens as grounds-keeping scrambled for buckets. When Vince staggered to his feet, Ned punched him again for good measure. By then, staff and a few brave guests were scooping fish into wheelbarrows. A quick thinker secured the hose. Someone else brought snow shovels.

Clutching his bloodied knuckles, Ned Birch strode across the soaked lawns of Mayhaven. Steering around the disarray of guests and groundskeepers, careful not to tread upon flailing fish, he got in his car. For the first time all summer he turned on the radio and sang the whole way home.

EPILOGUE

DARCY

Secrets, she has learned, are sharp objects to hold. Still, there are reasons people try. Sometimes it is to protect yourself. Sometimes it is to protect the ones you love. And sometimes, it is out of shame. When she looks back on the summer, Darcy understands that she was guilty of all three. She also understands, now, that she was guilty of nothing other than trying to keep that secret. What happened to her—rather, what someone did to her—was not her fault. And she wishes she had believed that back then. Finally, now, she does.

Darcy will never forget the awfulness of that day when the police came to the neighbors'. It is engraved on her heart. After Flick was cleared, and after Adam came home from being questioned at the police station with her parents, her father went out. He did not tell anyone where he was going. And he was not gone very long.

They were all sitting at the kitchen table, her mother, Adam, and her. When the front door banged open, no one startled. They'd already had enough scares for the day. As her father stood in the doorway, blanched and sweaty, Darcy suddenly understood where he'd been.

When he walked into the kitchen, eyes only for her, Darcy felt the chair fly out from underneath her. She doesn't remember running to him or falling into his arms. What she does remember when she thinks back on that moment, was that it was finally over.

"Please forgive me," he cried, clutching her to his chest. "I'm so sorry, Darcy. I'm so sorry."

That's the sharpest part of a secret you try to hold back: the sorrow, because it's the sorrow that draws blood. Darcy hadn't wanted her parents to hurt like she did. What she has come to learn is that sharing your burdens with others is like wind on a mountain, and water on stone. Little by little, that sorrow is eroded by all the hands that touch it. With every passing between hands, it is molded; so that, by the time you lift it to the light, you realize all the jagged edges have been worn down. And then—finally—you can let go.

Darcy did not have to share her secret with Flick Creevy. Eventually Flick understood it for himself, and in trying to be a good friend, he kept her secret. But only for a little while, he later told her. Because good friends won't let you hold on to hurt for too long, even when you ask them. Good friends will tell your secret, if they love you enough. When they talk now, Flick doesn't ask her how she feels. These days, he sees so much of Darcy that he knows the answer to that, too.

High school has started. It's a new year, and when they hold hands in the hallways people look at them. Darcy tells him it's because they both look happy. Flick tells her it's because they can't believe what a lucky guy he is.

There is one trophy left that did not get smashed that fateful day in the driveway. Somehow it toppled to the side and escaped her rage. For now she keeps it in the garage; she will probably never put it back in her room again. But her mother has convinced her to hang on to it. It's a sign of what she's accomplished, and when she looks at it now Darcy doesn't just think of the wins.

FLICK

This school is nicer than his old one, he tells Mateo. Josie was right about that, at least. His classes are hard, but he's working harder. It's time to adjust to life in Rockwood, so he may as well commit. He's made a few new friends, though no one like Mateo. Mateo is coming to visit him, next weekend. His mother and Stan are taking them to the country club for dinner; their *new* country club, Fox Run.

Hope that country club is ready for me Mateo texts him one night after school. Same for Lambo.

Over Stan's dead body

How is the King?

Not so bad

How's the girl?

Even better

Two things happened after the police showed up that day. First, Stan went to bat for him like no one ever did, besides his mother. Stan pulled out of Mayhaven, got Flick a lawyer (which he thankfully didn't need), and stuck up for him in front of the police and Mr. Birch.

Flick feels bad for Mr. Birch. That summer he got a lot of bad news about the people and the place he loved. Flick has come to realize some people only see the good around them because that's what they need to see. Rockwood isn't exactly the place his mother hoped it would be. But Darcy makes him want to give it a chance.

The second thing that happened, which he still can't quite believe, was that the Birches finally came over. Stan threw a big Labor Day party in the backyard with a DJ and caterers and the whole bit. Flick didn't blame Mr. Birch for not liking Stan: Stan had been a bully. But when Ned Birch rang the doorbell holding a box of cookies, just like he did that first day, Flick was floored. The Birches didn't stay late, and Ned didn't dance (Ingrid did). But a couple days later Stan moved the RV. It's stored in a lot across town. Gestures matter, Flick realizes. He thinks about this as he picks a bunch of wildflowers on the walk over to Darcy's house. He's taking her out to dinner. After he takes Adam for a ride in his car.

NED

His father was not a good father, Ned knows. He was not a kind or pleasant man to be around, especially to those who had the misfortune of sharing a roof with him. As far as Ned is concerned, the only worthwhile lesson his father taught him was this: there is grace in golf.

Ned had long thought that the sport he loved and devoted his career to, and later shared with his daughter, was where the grace could be found. But he is finding grace off the course, too.

Ned is not sure what he will do next, but he knows his family will manage until he figures it out, thanks to Ingrid and her determination and the magic of the Tree House sale. Ned used to see himself as the head of Mayhaven, a place once dear to him and one he'd thought dear to his family. His blind spots have been wide. When he thinks of Ingrid he sees her at the helm of their family, unwavering despite the roughness of the sea or the strength of the storm. Their family is his haven, and there is no association or club on earth he'd rather be a member of.

Adam has a new job at Ingrid's realty office where he works designing online listings. He has not been allowed to watch YouTube car videos since the golf course incident, but he did clean Flick's car top to bottom and make apologies. Mayhaven has agreed to forgo the repayment of damages for the Birches agreeing not to sue the club. At first Ned could not bring himself to accept those terms: he wanted to see Vince suffer. But after legal and financial counsel, he has made peace with the idea and found a happy workaround. Still a respected man in the industry, Ned has shared their story with those who need to know; Vince will have a hard time finding work or playing any course in the area again. Just as Ned will have a hard time ever forgiving himself.

As Darcy always said, Adam sees and hears everything. Ned will try to be more like Adam.

Ned was relieved when Darcy agreed to therapy, at his and Ingrid's urging: another small grace. But his greatest relief was a few weeks ago, when she pulled her dusty bag of clubs out of the hallway closet.

Now, once a week, on Saturday mornings, Ned knocks on the back door at Fox Run country club. He is old friends with the new manager there; this time around he has permission. Before the club opens, just as the sun begins its slow climb over the hills, the manager waves them in. Together, Ned and Darcy walk the course in the gauzy hour just after dawn. They are both a little rusty, but the game comes back quickly if the words don't. Sometimes they talk about school or family. Sometimes they don't talk at all. But they walk shoulder to shoulder, for the love of it, and there is grace in that.

ACKNOWLEDGMENTS

First, I want to thank you, the reader, for choosing to spend some of your time at *The Summer Club*. Writing a novel begins and ends with one: from the first word on the page there is only the author, writing in isolation (or in my case with two dogs at my feet). Later, an entire team moves in, from agent to editor to publisher to art director to marketing, and beyond. So many hands touch these pages, the notion humbles me every time. Finally, it ends, again, with just one: you, the reader. Publishing is an endeavor that involves so many, but at the heart of every step is our reader. And for you, I am eternally grateful.

To my agent, Susan Ginsburg, with every book I am reminded what a lucky girl I am to have you in my corner. You have been a tremendous partner since we teamed up, and I am ever indebted to your industry savvy, your humor, and your encouragement. Emily Bestler, of EBB, has been my steadfast editor and collaborator since book number one. Where there is a blank spot on the page, Emily has an idea! This time around, I struck gold with the additional editorial expertise of Lara Jones. Between you both, *The Summer Club* has been brought to life. The hands I mentioned above are many, and I need to recognize them all. Tremendous thanks must be given to publisher Libby McGuire and associate Dana Trocker, both publishers extraordinaire. Also to senior managing editor Paige Lytle and managing editorial assistant Shelby Pumphrey for all their support. To senior production editor Sonja Singleton, and Lara Robbins, copy editor and timeline wizard. Huge shout-out to art director Jimmy Iacobelli and art designer Claire Sullivan, for this gorgeous cover; you keep outdoing yourselves! Thank you also to director of marketing and social media Morgan Pager, publicist Sierra Swanson, and marketer Zakiya Jamal, who is always a joy to work with! Finally, a special high five to Hydia Riley, who bravely dove in to merge two iterations of our final edit on a time crunch. I'm ever grateful to all of you, from first readings and brainstorm sessions to adjusting production schedules to accommodate editorial efforts. Indeed, it takes a village.

Away from the offices of New York sits my little writing room, nestled in the western corner of Connecticut. I have my own hometown team, here, to thank as well. Thank you to my Sherman readers and supporters, and especially the Sherman Library, where I took out my first book as a child and now share my books as an author. As I wrote this novel, I was reminded of my fourth grade teacher, Mrs. Dawn Beucler, who wrote the kindest (and lengthiest!) notes in the margins of my classroom journals, and my high school English teacher Mr. Ron Olson, who insisted writing was something I not only could do, but must. To Professor Stephen Riley from Skidmore College, whose reactions to my early efforts as a student in his creative writing seminar forever changed the way I thought about myself. Teachers really are some of the greatest people on earth.

My own family was plush with teachers. To my parents, Marlene and Barry Roberts, who read aloud to us early and often. And were the most enthusiastic reviewers of my earliest work, a hamster-western, *Rodent on the Ranch*. In memory of my brother Joshua and to my brother Jesse, to whom this book is dedicated: there were a lot of long vacation car rides where the seeds of family drama plots were first sowed. Thank you for enduring! To my own little family: to John, who listens earnestly, and encourages heartily—and, good sport that he is, never asks me to edit. This chapter is so much sweeter because of you. To Grace Mae, who is venturing out into the world this year, away at college. (For once) I haven't the words to express my love of the vibrant young woman you are becoming. Never stop. To Finley Kate, whose heart is tender and whose ideas about the world she's growing up in are passionate, let your voice be heard. I was never as brave as either of you, and I count my lucky stars nightly that I get to be your mom.